Perfectly oblivious

ROBIN DANIELS

BLUEFIELDS

For Alan - Because you kept telling me I should write a book...until I did.

prologue

BIANCA

Beginning of Freshman Year

A NEW FAMILY WAS MOVING IN ACROSS THE STREET. THE house next door to the Perkins's had been vacant for over six months. The couple that lived there before had had no kids, were hardly ever home, and kept to themselves. So, when the house went up for sale, my heart wasn't exactly broken. I sat in my bedroom window, watching the movers unload box after box, when a shiny black SUV pulled up in the driveway.

A woman jumped out of the passenger seat and ran across the lawn. The movers were hauling an expensive-looking grandfather clock into the house. It was well wrapped, but she hovered behind the men anyway, as if her presence alone could lift the clock if they were clumsy enough to drop it. A man quickly climbed out of the driver's seat and scolded the woman, telling her to let the movers do their job.

"Great." I sighed out loud. "Another lame yuppie couple." I popped open a can of Diet Coke and wondered what the universe had against me. Was it too much to ask that someone with kids, preferably cool ones, moves in? We lived on a picture-perfect street in a middle-class neighborhood just outside of Orlando, Florida. I should have had loads of friends close by to hang out with. But sadly, my street was filled with yuppies and old people. Mr. and Mrs. Perkins had three kids, but their youngest had gone off to college last year, leaving my sister Beth and me the only youngsters on the block.

Resigned to defeat, I stood to shut my blinds when the back door of the SUV opened. *Well, well, well, what have we here?* Out stepped a boy with headphones in his ears and a phone in his hand. He was tall, and it was hard to see what he looked like because he had a baseball cap pulled low over his face. If I had to guess, he seemed about my age, but I was too far away to tell.

Since I'm nosy, I needed a closer look. I wasn't going to get it peeping at him like a stalker from my bedroom window. I needed to stalk him from a more convenient location. The Perkinses had a basketball hoop hung over the garage, and Mrs. Perkins said I could use it anytime I wanted. So I grabbed my basketball, slipped on my flip-flops, and headed downstairs.

I'd hoped to catch the new kid's attention by shooting some hoops on the driveway next to his. But after five minutes of flawless shots, his face was still hiding under his hat and his eyes hadn't left that stupid phone. I wasn't desperate enough to go talk to him (Ok, I almost was) so I devised a plan to get his attention in a more *subtle* way.

On my next shot, I intentionally hit the backboard so the ball would bounce off and roll toward him. If he'd seen that shot, I'd have been super embarrassed. I'd never want anyone to think I sucked that bad. But, as luck would have it, embarrassment was not in my cards. *Mortification* was a better word for what had happened. The missed shot that was supposed to bounce somewhere in his general vicinity was alarmingly accurate. It beaned him in the side of the head, knocking his cap off.

"What the hell?" he grumbled as he rubbed his head and shot a dirty glance in my direction. Oops. Not quite the first impression I was hoping to make. So much for subtle.

"Sorry." I offered a quick apology, then ran to fetch my ball from the street. I made it back to the driveway, and he strolled over. Now that his baseball cap was off, I could see that he was pretty stinking cute. He had light-brown hair that was long enough to be messed up from wearing his hat but short enough not to stick out under the sides. His blue eyes sparkled (yes, I know how cheesy that sounds, but there is no other way to describe them), and he had a cute button nose. I must have admired him a little too long because he cleared his throat and smirked, revealing the most adorable dimples.

Crap, crap, crappity-crap. He totally realized I was checking him out. Play it cool, Bianca, play it cool...

"Hey," was all I could manage. I gave him a head nod. Great; in my attempt not to look desperate, I managed to look like a loser instead.

"You play ball?" he asked, a cocky smirk plastered to his face.

"It would seem so. Seeing as I'm standing here, under a basketball hoop, holding a ball of the basket variety." *That's good, Bianca; go for snarky. Maybe he'll forget the moony eyes he caught you making at him.*

The new kid snorted. His cocky smirk morphed into a cocky smile. "Well then, I propose a deal. I challenge you to a game of PIG. If you can beat me, I promise to pretend that I *don't* know you purposely tanked that shot as an excuse to talk to me."

My eyes bugged and my jaw dropped for a moment before I was able to regain my composure. So that's how he was going to play it?

"Hmmm..." I pretended to think as I brought my finger to my lips. "Then I guess if you win, I promise to forget that you're a conceited ass."

No way I'd let him think he had the upper hand in this conversation. I was congratulating myself mentally on my awesome comeback when he swiped the ball out of my hands and dribbled it to the hoop, making a layup. He rebounded his ball and passed it to me. *Well, Mr. Show Off, two can play that game.* I duplicated his layup with ease and passed the ball back to him.

He made his next basket from where the free throw line would have been. Again, I matched his shot. He looked at me, eyebrow raised, and took the ball to the far end of the driveway. He launched a three pointer, which he made with no problem. Judging by his expression, he figured this would be a tough shot for me. He didn't know that I'd been playing point guard on both club and school basketball teams for the last three years. He passed me the ball and I strutted to the back end of the driveway. I sent off a perfect three-pointer. It cleared the rim as the net swished.

I was enjoying his shock when the hovering woman from earlier stuck her head out of his front door. "Cam, honey. Time to come in and start hauling some of these boxes up to your room."

"Be right there!" he yelled back, never taking his eyes off me. "Guess we'll have to finish this another time."

"Guess so," I challenged.

"I'm Cameron Bates, but most people just call me Cam."

"Bianca Barnes, but most people just call me Bea."

"Bee? As in Bumble Bee?"

"Yes, you moron. My parents named me Bumble Bee." I rolled my eyes. So he obviously wasn't much older than me, or he wouldn't have responded like a stupid middle-school boy.

I corrected him. "*B*, as in the first letter of my name."

"What kind of a nickname is *B*? Sounds like something you'd call a crabby old lady." The smirk was back. As adorable as it was, I wanted to smack it off his cute little face.

"Well, since my name is Bianca, I'm guessing it was

either call me Bea or call me Anca. Only a horrible parent would call their child Anca. I guess Bea was the better option."

Cam contemplated for a moment before responding. "I can't play ball with a chick who's named after an old lady. Guess I'll have to come up with something else. I'm thinking Bebe..."

"Bebe? What do I look like, a show poodle?"

He grinned, knowing he'd ruffled my feathers. "I was actually thinking it sounded kind of *hot cheerleader*."

"Which isn't much better than a show poodle."

"No, dork. *Bebe*, as in the first letter of your first name and the first letter of your last name." He laughed, his smile turning wicked. "But, if you want to go with the show poodle theme, I could always call you Cece or Fifi?"

"Sounds to me like you're sticking with the hot cheerleader idea," I grumbled.

"Bebe it is, then." Pleased with himself, he turned and walked toward his front door. "See you around, Bebe," he mocked, closing the door before I could respond.

I stood there for a moment, wondering how a simple snooping mission could have gone so wrong. Cam was cute and clever but definitely a pain in the ass. Of course, I was a pain in the ass, too, so I shouldn't fault him for that. However, he *was* into basketball, which I could totally work with. I walked back across the street and plopped down on my front porch. Cameron Bates was my new neighbor. Maybe the universe didn't hate me after all.

BIANCA

Beginning of Junior Year

"Bea, time to get up."

"Go away, you wretched beast of a morning person," I grumbled, pulling the covers up over my head as I heard my door fly open.

"Get your cute butt up, and get ready for school. You don't want to look like a slob on the first day. People will have the wrong impression about you for the rest of the year." Beth looked around at the tornado of clothing and dozens of Diet Coke cans littering my bedroom floor.

"Ok, maybe they'd be getting the right impression, but that isn't the impression we want them to have." She crinkled her nose. "I'm leaving for school in an hour, with or without you." Her singsong voice made my eardrums hurt. How anyone could be so perky at six o'clock in the freaking morning was beyond me. But Beth was perky all the time, so I should have been used to it by now.

Bethany was my twin, so to speak, my *Irish Twin*. But we looked nothing alike. Beth was tall, five-nine to my five-five. She had long legs and feminine curves, while I was petite and looked more like a twelve-year-old boy. Her full C cup made my barely B's look pathetic. She had long, straight blonde hair and sun-tanned skin that glowed as if it'd been kissed by the gods. The only physical trait we shared was the same huge green eyes and long, dark eyelashes we inherited from our mother. Even her name was more beautiful. Bethany… It sounded like an angel or a mermaid or a mystical unicorn princess. Definitely something magical. The name *Bianca* just sounded like a cranky old lady, as Cameron so politely pointed out.

I trudged over to my door and shut it, then locked it, so I wouldn't be discovered participating in my morning ritual. I hurried over to my window and cracked the blinds ever so slightly. *Damn, I missed him.* I'd been spying on Cam (my neighbor across the street) daily since he moved in two years ago. Now that we were going to be juniors, he'd morphed from super-duper cute to amazingly hot.

Both of our bedrooms were on the second story and faced the street. He lived kitty corner to me, but I still had a direct view into his bedroom. Normally I'd spy on him while he sat at his desk doing homework or playing video games.

This summer, though, he started working out in his garage every morning. He wanted to be more ripped when basketball season started. Since he worked out shirtless most days, I religiously spent my summer perfecting my Peeping Tom skills. I guess even Cam wanted to look good on the first day of school, because he was nowhere to be found. Instead of getting my daily fix of shirtless Cam, I got in the shower, imagining shirtless Cam while I washed the sleep out of my eyes.

Forty-five minutes later, I strolled into the kitchen, hoping I passed as acceptable by Beth's standards. I'd tamed my long brown wavy hair, put on my cutest low-rise boot cut jeans (none of that skinny jeans crap for me) and a tight gray V-neck T-shirt. I'd even taken the time to apply light makeup, highlighting my faint smattering of freckles. Beth gave me the once-over, nodding with approval until she reached my feet. She stared at my well-worn red flip-flops and sighed but didn't say anything. I learned long ago that if I kept my toenails painted she wouldn't say anything about the flip-flops. Today, each big toe even had a shiny gem in the middle of a white flower. *Sorry, Beth; that's the best you'll get from me.*

"Hurry and grab something if you want to eat; Cam will be here any second. I don't want to be late on the first day," Beth instructed.

"Yes, Mother," was my standard reply.

Beth scowled at me and went back to eating her toast. She hated it when I called her *Mother*, because our mother died shortly after giving birth to me. Neither of us remembered her. It was sad but didn't usually bring me to tears. Beth was different. She felt cheated. Our mother was the only topic that could sour her perpetually happy mood.

My parents had tried for years to have children but couldn't. The doctors weren't sure why. Mom and Dad had given up hope when she got pregnant with Beth. After so many childless years, they'd been blessed with a beautiful baby girl. Imagine their surprise when they learned Mom was pregnant with me. Beth was only four months old at the time. I wasn't planned, but my parents were ecstatic.

During the second half of the pregnancy, my mom developed preeclampsia. At thirty-two weeks, her condition got worse and she went into organ failure. Dad rushed her to the hospital, where doctors delivered me eight weeks early. They couldn't stop Mom's kidneys and liver from shutting down, though, and she died the same day I was born.

My dad always called me his miracle. That God had taken my mom but spared me was extremely unfair in my eyes. But my father had never counted it anything less than a blessing. Beth must have gotten her continual optimism from Dad. I think that gene skipped me.

Being born at thirty-two weeks made Bethany and I just over eleven months apart, hence the *Irish Twins*. The school start cutoff is August 31. Since Beth's birthday is September 15 and mine is August 20, we ended up in the same grade. When people who don't know us see that we're both juniors, they assume that we're twins. It's easier not to correct them.

Beth is definitely the older sister, though, and it shows when she gets all motherly. I pretend to be annoyed by it, because that's what any good little sister would do. Dad never remarried, so with no mother in the home, my sister is the closest thing I have. She loves to play the part, and most of the time, I don't mind letting her.

"Good morning to the most lovely non-twins I know." Cam's words startled me, and I dropped the toast I'd been buttering.

Beth questioned his greeting. "I don't know if that's much of a compliment, considering we're probably the *only* non-twins you know." He wrapped her in a bear hug, lifting her in the air, and she giggled in response. *Gag me.*

"My, aren't we in a good mood this morning?" Beth asked him. "What could possibly have you all smiles and sunshine at this hour?"

"Can't a guy just be happy to be in the same room as two beautiful women?"

I rolled my eyes. Cam was such a goober. He was a smartass extraordinaire when talking to me but sweet as syrup when he was around Bethany. I called him out on it once, and he told me that Beth was too angelic for him to be anything less than a gentleman around her. That response earned him a punch in the arm, to which he replied something about me being the evil twin.

Cam walked around the island and grabbed my toast off the counter, inhaling half of it before I could stop him. "Hey, you jerk! I was going to eat that."

I slapped him on the shoulder as he walked by. He leaned toward me, speaking in a low voice. "Thanks for the breakfast, Bebe." Then Cam poked me in the side, waggled his eyebrows, and headed out the side door to the car.

I grabbed my other piece of toast and darted out past him, screaming, "Shotgun!" Just as I reached the passenger door, Cam hot on my heels, he picked me up and slung me over his shoulder like a caveman. I kicked and swore under my breath, secretly loving every minute of his closeness. Instead of putting me down on the ground, he sat me on the roof of the car.

"Sorry, Bebe, you know the rules." He slipped into the passenger seat, leaving me to find my own way down. I hopped off the car and took my usual seat in the back.

"Stupid rules. I don't know how these rules became official, considering I didn't have a say in creating them," I complained.

Grumbling, I buckled my seat belt and slouched low. My knees were pressing hard into the back of Cam's seat, which he'd conveniently pushed all the way back. He shot me a wicked grin in the rearview mirror but didn't say anything. I stuck out my tongue at him, and he made a kissy face.

Bethany opened the driver's door and gingerly slid in behind the steering wheel. Even if she hadn't been wearing a skirt, she would've never been rude enough to shove her knees into someone's back. But Beth wasn't as fun as I was, and Cam never tortured her the way he did me.

"Bea, you know the rules," Beth reminded me. "The person with the longest legs gets the front seat because it has the most room." She lectured me on this regularly.

"Well, I'd like to contest that rule," I argued. "This is my car, too. I shouldn't have to ride in the back all year because Jolly Green Giant up there doesn't have one."

"And I think you lost the right to contest the rule when you got a speeding ticket only a week after you got your license," Beth replied.

Dad had grounded me from driving for a month after that. When the month was up, Bethany kept driving everywhere, and I kept letting her. I think I made her nervous. She's a super cautious driver. I don't mind letting her drive as long as I get to sit up front. But it seems I'll be relegated to the backseat for the rest of the year. Lame.

"Whatever you say, Mother." I stuck my earbuds in, turned up some music, and ignored Beth's disapproving look. I added a little extra punch behind each knee jab I sent into Cam's seat when we went over speed bumps. He only chuckled and shook his head, but I took great pleasure in the fact that he couldn't retaliate from the front seat. Guess I'm ok with being the evil twin.

We walked into school with plenty of time to find our new lockers. Home, stinky, dirty home for the next year. At least we were upper classmen now. All the lockers were assigned alphabetically by grade. The junior and senior wings were closer to the main hall of the school, so I wouldn't have to break a sweat running from my locker to my classes this year.

Our school wasn't that small, but I wouldn't consider it big, either. There were about four hundred kids in the junior class. Because Beth and I share a last name and our first names both start with *B*, her locker had always been on my left. Unless someone new moved in this year, with a last name that fell between Barnes and Bates, Cam's locker would be on my right again. One big, happy Bianca sandwich.

For all the grief I give her, Beth is my best friend. I know that's weird, because usually sisters have that sibling rivalry thing going on. I guess not having a mom brought us together in a way that a lot of siblings might not experience. It doesn't hurt that my sister is the nicest person on the planet. That's not an exaggeration, either. She's so sweet it's almost sick. People think she's fake until they get to know her, because nobody's that nice and good.

Beth's always happy and optimistic. She's obedient, gets along with teachers, never swears, befriends new people, stands up to bullies, and says yes to almost every guy that asks her out. Even if she isn't interested. Bethany Barnes is one of the most popular girls in school, and not just because she's a beautiful cheerleader. It's mostly, well, because she's Beth. I, on the other hand, am only *kind of* popular. That's probably due to the fact that I'm Beth's sister and we're always together.

"Looks like we get to be locker lovers again this year, Bebe." Cam gave me his sexy smolder. I was turning into a puddle of mush on the inside, but on the outside I plastered on a cheesy smile.

"Lucky me." I batted my long lashes about a hundred blinks a minute. He laughed, then shoved my head into my open locker. Cam and I had always had a pretty normal friendship. You know, girl likes boy, boy treats girl like one of the guys. We had similar interests and senses of humor. Of course, we shared an undying love of basketball. He teased me like any other immature boy would, and I responded with wit or sarcasm because I didn't want him to know I had a huge crush on him. Lately, though, Cameron Bates was a big heap of confusing perfection. One minute he'd speak to me in a way that most girls would consider flirting. Then, seconds later, he'd stick my head in his armpit or make some other brotherly display of affection. Who does that? He'd never stick Beth's head in his armpit—or any other girl's, for that matter. I probably shouldn't read too much into the flirting, because Cam is a notoriously big flirt.

I started unloading all my crap into my locker when a gaggle of giggling cheerleaders walked up behind us. "Hi, Beth. Heeeey, Caaameron," Angelica Valdez purred. She has the most grating voice in existence. I think people ignored how annoying it was because she looks like a Latina goddess. Long, dark hair, big brown eyes, perfectly creamy caramel skin. Boobs the size of softballs. *No way those are real. What parent gets their teenager a boob job?*

The way Angelica drew out Cameron's name, like she was intimate with him, made me want to punch her in her perfectly painted face. She wore a lot of makeup. It made girls like me look lazy. She sidled up to Cam and ran her fingers up his arm.

"You coming to our first game on Friday?" Angelica whispered close to Cam's ear.

"Of course I am. I wouldn't miss it." He slid his arm around Beth's shoulder, obviously hoping to make Angelica back off. The move wasn't unnoticed; she glanced at Beth and then back at Cam with predatory eyes.

Being the lady charmer he was, Cam's follow up was quick. "Beth has been talking non-stop about how good you guys are this year. She says you're the best tumbler on the squad."

I seriously doubt Beth said that. I happen to know for a fact that she's not particularly fond of Angelica Valdez. They were friends by force, not choice. But Cam's not an idiot, and he's extremely good at keeping the peace.

Angelica was all smiles, pleased with his compliment. "Well, make sure you sit close on Friday, and I'll throw in a back flip *just for you*," she crooned.

Sure, you will. Any excuse you can get to show him your cheer spankies. I don't know why I was so annoyed. Cam would never actually hook up with a girl like Angelica. He had taste. At least, I think he did. He dated plenty but had never had a girlfriend, even though he could've had his pick of girls at our school. Sometimes I wondered if he had a thing for Beth. He was always so nice to her and spent a lot of time at our house. He'd never asked her out, though. Never made a move or even asked me about her. Despite our mocking banter, Cam was one of my closest friends. If he liked Beth, I'm sure he would have said something…maybe…

I was über annoyed by the fake love fest going on around me. Instead of throwing up in my locker, which is what I wanted to do, I turned around and slammed it shut. That startled Angelica from her bedroom stare.

"Oh, hi, Bianca, I didn't see you there." Her voice was tinted with disdain. She most certainly did see me there, and her greeting was about as disingenuous as they get. It's no secret that I'm not Angelica's favorite person because I spend so much time with her would-be boy toy. But I love my sister, and she has to get along with Angelica, so I always play nice.

"Sorry if I startled you, Angelica." *No, I wasn't.* "My locker doesn't shut all the way unless I slam it." *Yes, it does.* "It was good to see you. Hope your first day of school is super neat-o. Better get going before I'm late to class. Toodaloo." I wiggled my spirit fingers at her.

"What was that all about?" Angelica asked Beth quietly as I walked away. "Your sister is such a weirdo. I don't know why you spend so much time with her."

I left the pom-pom brigade behind and made my way toward English. About thirty seconds later, I felt a tug on my backpack. "Hold up there, tiger." Cam slid his arm around my shoulder.

I had to concentrate to maintain my composure. You'd think as often as he touched me I'd be better at that. But Cam always scrambled my brain and set my pulse racing when he got close. We had first period English together this semester. He kept his arm comfortably draped across me as we continued to class.

"What the heck was that back there? Neat-o? Toodaloo?" he asked. I snickered at the thought of how ridiculous I must have sounded.

"Did you just step off the set of *Leave it to Beaver?*" Cam teased.

"Hey, now. *Leave it to Beaver* is some quality television

programming," I argued. "I just didn't want to give Angelica the satisfaction of responding the way she wanted me to. So, I went with something confusing." I stopped for a moment and then thoughtfully added, "Of course, just about any response probably would've confused that itty-bitty brain."

Cam laughed loudly. "Well, I think you were successful. She looked at you like you'd sprouted a second head."

That sent me into a nice daydream. One where Angelica was backed into a corner by a two-headed me, slobbering and spitting as I spoke. I was saying things like *gee whiz* or *peachy keen* while she screamed in fear that my un-coolness might be contagious.

"Earth to Bebe. Anyone home?" Cam waved his hand in front of me.

A pair of gorgeous blue eyes snapped me back to reality, bent down to my level and mere inches from my face. We'd reached our destination. Cam pulled me from my pleasant, vindictive thoughts and straight into even more pleasant but much more inappropriate ones. Heat crept up my neck and into my flushing cheeks. *Get a grip, Bianca, or soon you'll be no better than the Angelica Valdezes of the world. Quick, find a stinging response...*

"Yes, I'm home, but I'm not sure you always are." I tapped my finger against his temple.

"Ouch, Bebe. That really hurts my feelings." Cam pouted and placed one hand dramatically over his heart, obviously not hurt in the least.

"I think you need to kiss them better," he continued. "And you know where my feelings are, don't you?" He slowly removed the hand over his heart and brought it up so his index finger was pointing at his puckered lips. *Oh, for the love of everything holy. Cam was suggesting I kiss him. On the lips!* I quickly drew back and faked a disgusted look.

"Oh, come on, Bebe. You know you want a piece of this." He started flexing his biceps and asking me which way to the beach and if I wanted tickets to the gun show. *Yes, Cameron Bates, I definitely want tickets to your gun show. Especially if it's on the beach. Mmmmm…shirtless Cam.* Luckily, the warning bell disrupted his display of teenage testosterone.

"Get inside, you big ape," I ribbed, scooting into the classroom. "Before Ms. Cutter actually does ask for tickets to your gun show." Ms. Cutter was a very cranky and very lonely middle-aged woman. For some reason, she was always extra nice to Cam, and I frequently teased him about it.

I kept taunting him as I walked to my seat. "If you want, I'll donate a picture of you for Ms. Cutter's desk. She can keep it next to the one of her cat." Cameron cringed, but my taunt had the desired effect. He needed to stop being adorable so I could get my hormones under control.

BIANCA

BY THE TIME FRIDAY ROLLED AROUND, I PRETTY MUCH KNEW
what to expect for this semester. I had an easy load, academi-
cally speaking. Beth was an overachiever, but I chose to work
as little as possible. This meant that Beth would be in honors
classes and I'd be with all the average students in the regular
ones. I was bummed that I didn't have a ton of classes with
my BFF. We did manage to get third period government
together (along with Cam) as well as fifth period PE. Of
course, Angelica was in PE with us. That basically canceled
out the advantage of having gym with Beth.

I had three classes with Cam. Besides English and government, we had chemistry together during sixth period.
Cam and I had chosen to be lab partners for the semester,
which earned us a disapproving look from Mr. Gardner.

We'd shared every science class since freshman year and started every semester as lab partners. We'd also failed to *finish* every semester as lab partners because we screwed around too much, eventually getting separated.

When Mr. Gardner had pointed between the two of us and asked if "this" was going to be a problem, Cam said "No, sir" at the exact time I answered "Probably." That earned me an elbow to the gut from Cam and an eye roll from Mr. Gardner. But our teacher left us alone and walked back to his desk. I think he secretly loves us.

Lunch was the only time I intentionally didn't spend with Beth or Cam. Strange, I know, since all juniors and seniors had the same lunch. I *could* have eaten with them, but it was kind of an unspoken agreement we had. The three of us spent so much time together that it would've been easy to overlook our other friends. At lunch Beth ate with the cheer squad, Cam ate with the boys basketball team, and I ate with the girls basketball team.

I made varsity as a freshman even with my height handicap. Our team wasn't quite as good as the boys team, so Cam didn't make varsity until his sophomore year, something I gleefully held over his head. Hey, the guy's ego was large enough; someone needed to deflate it every now and then.

It was awkward eating lunch with the team that first year. People were nice enough, but I always felt like an outsider. The freshman wonder freak. Now that everyone on the team was closer to my age, I actually enjoyed the bonding time.

"Look at those idiots acting like middle schoolers,"

Madison said. She glared across the cafeteria to where the boys team sat. They were busily engaged in a chocolate-milk chugging contest. It involved lots of chanting and cheering.

"At least they don't *look* like middle schoolers," Missy replied wistfully. "Some of the guys got pretty ripped over the summer." She turned to me. "Did Cam spend his entire summer break working out or what?"

"How should I know?" I scoffed. *Of course I know, because I'm his super pervy secret stalker.* "He has a pretty good gym setup in his garage. I'm sure he was hitting the weights at least a little."

"Or a lot," Missy countered. "I wonder how much he can bench?" *235.* "Or if he can make his pecs dance?" *Probably.* "I bet his abs are amazing." *Pretty much.*

I snap out of my trance before anyone notices. *Fan-freaking-tastic. My inner peanut gallery needs to put a lid on it, or I'm going to slip and say something out loud.*

"Well, Missy, you'll get your chance to peruse the merchandise soon enough," Emma guaranteed. "The coach who decided to hold girls and boys pre-season conditioning together this year deserves a pay raise."

That comment earned a table full of "Mmmhmms" and "Amens." My face contorted as my lips pursed and my eyebrows bunched together. I didn't want anyone perusing Cam's merchandise but me. But of course, I couldn't say that.

The thing is, I've had a crush on Cameron Bates since the day we met, when he gave me that ridiculous nickname that only he's allowed to use: Bebe. I still think it sounds like something you'd call your pet poodle. But my crush is something I'll take to the grave. Not because there's anything wrong with liking Cam. As far as high school crushes go, he's definitely a worthy selection. The problem is the damn universe. It's out to get me.

"What about Brady Jones?" Emma asked, eyes darting around the boys' table. "He's looking way hotter this year. I swear he grew six inches over the summer."

"It's amazing how a little height and well-placed weight makes a boy look more like a man. Brady is definitely looking manlier this year. So is Cam." Missy giggled at her own comment. She was the most boy crazy person on the team, hands down. Her hyper-focused fawning over Cam was driving me nuts. I wanted to say something, but I needed to keep my mouth shut. The Fates might hear.

You see, every time I like a boy and I express my interest in any way, he ends up asking Beth out. It's happened so many times that I think I'm cursed. In sixth grade, there was Billy Norton. We played basketball together during lunch. I told my friend Connie that I liked him, and the next morning he passed Beth a note, asking if she'd go out with him.

In seventh grade, Jesse Thomas volunteered to write a history report with me. He was so cute and funny. I wrote in my diary, all about how I had a major crush on him. As soon as we turned in our report, he called me up to ask about Beth, what kind of stuff she liked, and if she had a boyfriend. The next Friday was Valentine's Day, and he sent her a candy gram with a pink carnation.

Eighth grade was the worst. Sam Waterford sat behind me in homeroom. We were constantly talking and goofing around. I *honestly* thought he was into me. The spring dance was coming up, and I told Beth that I wanted to ask him, but I was too scared. She spent all night giving me pep talks and making the perfect plan to woo him. The next day at lunch, Sam marched right up to our table and asked Beth if she'd go to the dance with him. Beth started to panic and looked at me, not knowing what to do. Then she politely declined him. She told him that our dad wouldn't let us go to dances with a date because he thought we were too young. That didn't stop Sam from asking her to dance that night, three times.

Beth felt horrible. She hadn't done anything to encourage Sam. She barely even knew him. But that was Bethany Barnes for you; boys flocked to her. She made it up to me, of course, and I couldn't be mad at her. We pulled Sam's picture out of the yearbook and taped it to the wall. Then we stole some of the darts from dad's dartboard and spent the evening eating rocky road ice cream and seeing who could get closest to hitting his picture right between the eyes. Plus, the following Monday someone wrote "Sam Waterford kisses like a fish" on the outside of the handicap stall in the girls' bathroom. When I questioned her, Beth said she'd never do something to vandalize school property. The glint in her eyes told me she was lying.

These were only a few of the times when boys chose Beth over me. I can't really blame them; she's perfect and I'm average. After Sam, I swore that I'd never openly admit whom I liked. Not to another person, not to my diary, not even to myself when I was alone. If the universe didn't know who I liked, then it couldn't steer him toward Beth.

She'd never purposely pursue a guy I was into, but I had no control over who pursued her. It's not like I *never* dated. I just waited for boys to ask me out instead of me asking them. It did happen on the rare occasion. I figured if they chose to ask me out, they must like me at least a little. That, or they thought Beth was out of their league.

"Do you guys think Cam would go out with me? Or at least make out with me?" Missy asked, and I cringed. I better put a stop to that train of thought.

"I don't know if you're his type, Missy," I replied. Then, for good measure I added, "But I bet Mike would be happy to make out with you." Missy looked horrified as everyone busted up in laughter. Mike McGinnes was by far the least desirable guy on the team.

"I'd have to be pretty desperate to make out with Mike." Missy pouted. "Are you suggesting I'm desperate, Bea?"

"Of course not," I defended. "I'm suggesting that you're a little loose lipped." The table erupted in giggles again, and I had to dodge the empty juice bottle Missy threw at me.

"I'm just playing." I laughed at her, even though I wasn't playing.

Apparently, I had two problems. First, was that Missy seemed determined to snag my man. Second, and more importantly, the boys who asked me out weren't the ones I was interested in, and the boys I was interested in were destined to like Beth. Which is why *nobody* could ever know how I felt about Cam. I'd be devastated if I admitted my feelings for him only to find out he's always been in love with my sister.

Plus, let's face it: as far as leagues go, he was way out of mine. I basically had two options. Either I could forget about Cam and focus on more attainable goals or start praying that the universe would be kind. That Cam would wake up tomorrow realizing he preferred moderately cute, sassy, basketball players to beautiful, curvy cheerleaders. I think my Magic 8 Ball might tell me my outlook was not so good.

I've told Beth my theory, and she thinks I'm nuts. She says I'm being insecure for no good reason. That's because Beth has never had a sister like Beth. She's always pumping me for information on who I like, but my lips are sealed tighter than Fort Knox. Sometimes I wish I could tell her, and I know it frustrates her to no end. Maybe even hurts her feelings a little. But, so far the strategy has worked for me. Cam has never asked Beth out, and I haven't had my heart broken by him yet. It *is* making my plan to become Mrs. Cameron Bates and have beautiful basketball-playing babies slightly more difficult. I'll figure out how to get around that one eventually.

The conversation at the lunch table had digressed to whose butt was the cutest and who was most likely the best kisser. None of us actually dated guys from the basketball team. Not since Madison and Caleb broke up last year. In Madison's mind, Caleb being a jerk translated to the whole boys team being jerks. If we dated any of them, we were siding against Madison. Since she was team captain and she was also kind of a witch, we felt it best to stay on her good side. Not that any of the boys team were beating down our doors looking for dates. The no-dating rule didn't stop us from ogling and gossiping about them, though.

Madison spoke up, sounding highly agitated. "Am I the only one who thinks that the boys team is a bunch of immature meatheads?" Nine heads whipped in her direction and simultaneously nodded yes. Poor Madison. Spending ten weeks of conditioning on the court and in the weight room with the boys was going to be torture for her. That would probably make her torture us. On the bright side, I could watch shirtless Cam flex his muscles the whole time I was being tortured. That'd definitely make it more bearable.

CAMERON

I SAT AT THE LUNCH TABLE, TRYING TO SPLIT MY ATTENTION between the milk chugging contest and the girls basketball team. At least half of those girls wanted to go out with me, and if I got caught staring, I'd have given them all the wrong impression. There was only one girl I wanted to stare at: Bianca Barnes. I'd been hung up on her since the day we met. It was love at first shot.

I was sitting on my new front lawn when she wandered out of her house and into the driveway of my next-door neighbor. I kept my head down because I didn't want her to notice I was checking her out. She looked about my age and was smoking hot. Not to mention, she was carrying a basketball. I'd made a mental note to thank my parents for buying this particular house.

I kept my earbuds in so I'd look busy but turned the music all the way down so I could hear if she decided to talk to me. No way was I going to approach her. Only idiots talked to girls first. The biggest question on my mind was, could she actually shoot the basketball? Lots of girls pretended to be into the sport so they had a reason to talk to me. But *this* girl didn't know I played. Either she actually *liked* basketball or she thought it'd be a good excuse to check me out.

Bebe didn't just like to play, she was *good*. In five minutes of shooting, she'd only missed one shot. She kept sneaking peeks at me but never stopped to strike up a conversation. I was worried I'd have to break guy code and go talk to her. Then it happened.

I watched her glance at me and then launch the ball really hard at the backboard. Her placement guaranteed that she'd miss the shot and the ball came flying at me. I only had about a second to decide if I was going to duck or let it hit me. If I ducked, I'd be admitting that I'd seen the ball coming, and she'd know that I was watching her. If I didn't duck, I was going to get hit, probably in the head. I decided to brace myself for impact, and the rest is history. Ever since that day, I've vowed to make Bebe my girlfriend.

Unfortunately, that's proven harder than I thought it would be. We've become really good friends. It's cool, except I think I've been friend zoned. That's *never* happened to me before. I can't figure out what's wrong. I'm a good-looking guy: six-two, muscular, athletic. I've got dimples, which usually drives girls crazy. But, no matter what I do, Bianca seems to be immune to my good looks.

I've tried everything: teasing her, picking on her, poking her, pulling her ponytail, trash talking when we play basketball. She just keeps her cool and dishes my crap right back at me. Last year I started flirting with tons of other girls when she was around. I figured if she wasn't persuaded by my shenanigans, maybe I could make her jealous. If she cares that I flirt with anything that walks, she doesn't show it.

"Hey, Cam. Who you starin' at? Someone on the girls team catch your eye?" Caleb asked, and I shook my head. I'd zoned out for a minute.

"Yeah, man, all of them," I lied. "Just trying to figure out which lucky lady should get my attention this year."

Brady piped up. "Bianca's looking pretty hot today. There's nothing sexier than a girl who could probably beat my ass on the court."

"She's got nice legs, but her boobs are too small," Mike said. I reached over and slapped him across the back of the head. Mike was a dumbass.

"Watch it," I warned.

"What the hell, Cam. I wasn't hatin'. I'd still tap that." Mike was freaking clueless. What part of *watch it* was unclear? I leveled him with a hard stare.

"That's my best friend you're talking about. If you want the use of your legs, you'll think twice before talking about her boobs again. Same thing goes for the rest of you losers." My eyes scanned the table. If anyone else admitted to thinking about Bebe's body parts, there'd be hell to pay.

I turned my eyes back to Bebe. I was getting desperate. I could probably get 90 percent of the girls in school, and I was fixated on the one who didn't want me. All summer long, I'd wondered how I could switch up my game and get out of the friend zone. My new plan had two parts. First, get in good with Bethany. Bianca and her sister were best friends. If I didn't have Beth's approval, I'd never win Bebe over. So I started spending a little more time with Beth, being super sweet. It wasn't a difficult task; Beth was beautiful and popular. I genuinely liked being her friend. But a girl like Bethany could never be enough for me. I needed someone who challenged me. I needed Bianca.

The second part of my plan was a little riskier. Up until this year, all of my tactics had been covert. That way I didn't look like a desperate douche if she wasn't into me. But maybe I'd been sending the wrong signals or being too subtle. It's not like Bebe was naive or prudish. She went out with guys. I know for a fact that she's kissed at least a couple.

The day Ben Rogers came into the locker room bragging that he got to second base with her was almost the last day of Ben's pathetic life. I was fuming mad. Luckily, I knew that Ben was a lying sack of crap. After school, I confronted Bebe and she laughed, saying he was lucky he got a goodnight kiss. I still wasn't thrilled, but the info kept Ben's face intact and kept me out of juvie.

Like I said, Bebe isn't naive or prudish; she's just not like other girls. This meant one of two things. Either she wasn't into me, which would completely suck, *or* she's totally oblivious and has no clue how I feel. I'm hoping for the latter, hence part two of my Make Bebe Fall Madly in Love with Me Plan.

I needed to be more obvious; flirt with her the way I flirt with all the other girls. I'd tested the waters this week. She didn't slap my face or throw up on my shoes, but she wasn't exactly eating out of my hand, either. On Monday, I got right up in her face, inches from those perfectly kissable lips. For a second, I thought I'd broken through her shell. But it only lasted a moment and she was back to regular old Bebe, sucking the life out of my ego.

The table of girls was watching us. Giggling and whispering, they were probably trying to decide who had the cutest butt. Bianca was staring, dreamy-eyed. Who the hell could she be looking at? I waved to catch her attention but failed. I guess I'm not the one on her mind. Which means... Hold up. Was she daydreaming about one of the knob heads on the basketball team?

No way she could be interested in one of these losers. What the freak? I was trying to figure out who she was staring at, when Bebe caught me watching her and stuck her tongue out at me. I was momentarily stunned, reality sinking in. Bianca Barnes, *my* Bebe, liked someone on my team. And it wasn't me.

I didn't know how much longer I could handle being *just* friends. I kept telling myself that I wasn't acting on my obsession because of my stupid guy code. But in reality, I was worried that I might be rejected. And for the first time in my life it actually mattered if I was. Bebe was one of my best friends. I'd be destroyed if I told her how I felt but she didn't feel the same. Our friendship would be destroyed, too. I might even lose my friendship with Beth. She wasn't shallow enough to cut me out of her life completely, but things probably wouldn't be the same.

It was time for Cameron Bates to bring his A game. It might have been too soon to tell Bebe I loved her, but maybe I could take her on a date. Of course, I couldn't call it a date. That'd freak her out. Besides, I wasn't sure she was even interested in being more than friends. But if I could get her alone and do something *date like*, it'd be a good practice run. Flirt up a storm and see how she responded. Maybe, if things went well, my test date would lead to a real one.

BIANCA

Sixth period chemistry, my least favorite subject but
still my favorite class of the day. The class where I got Cam
all to myself. Well, not *all* to myself. Brady Jones and Mike
McGinnes, two of Cam's basketball buddies, were partnered
at the table next to us. But amazingly, we were free from any
of Cam's usual groupies. A whole fifty minutes without some
ditzy bubblehead pushing her bum or thrusting her bosom
his direction. For the next semester, in sixth period, it was
just us.

"Yo, Bea baby, what's up? You're looking *extra fly* today."
Mike was leaning on the table, head resting in his hand,
licking his lips at me. All he needed was a wife beater and
he could've doubled in an Eminem video. The guy had
dumbbells for brains. I guess I shouldn't be surprised that

he missed the memo saying it was no longer cool for skinny white kids to pretend like they were thugs.

I rolled my eyes. "You know, Mike, you should be less worried about how fly I look and more worried about looking at your fly." I nodded my chin up but pointed my lips down toward his pants. His zipper was fine, but the momentary look of panic on his face was priceless. I laughed, then winked at Brady, who was stifling his laughter behind a fake cough. Cam was roaring and practically rolling on the floor. Boys were so easy to amuse.

When Brady was done "not laughing," he looked at me and smiled. "Thanks, Bea; that was the best part of my day."

"Glad I could entertain you."

"Keep 'em coming and maybe I'll stay awake in class this semester." Brady patted me on the back, then headed over to his seat. Mike followed, licking his wounds as he went.

Mike might not have been the sharpest tool in the shed, but Brady was pretty cool. He was funny, nice, cute, and, unlike Mike, Brady had actual brains for brains. He was tall and lean and had an amazing complexion. He had to have been at least half something nonwhite, because his complexion was darker than just tan. More of a creamy coffee color, with big chocolate eyes. It was hard to guess his heritage with a last name like Jones. I'd ask him, but I was always worried about offending someone with a question like that.

Whatever his ethnicity, it made his amazing smile really stand out. He had the whitest, straightest teeth I'd ever seen. He could've been a toothpaste model. I bet his parents paid a fortune for his mouth. I didn't know him very well, but maybe it was time to start branching out. I couldn't live in Cameron fantasyland for the rest of my high school career. Especially if I wanted to have a social life.

Homecoming was early this year, toward the end of September. Less than a month away. Beth would have at least a few guys who asked her to the dance, and Cam would get multiple invites. Unless I wanted to play third wheel to my sister—or worse, third wheel to the guy I liked—I better start making myself more available.

I'd never asked a boy out, though I'd had a few that were brave enough to ask me. I'd even made out with a few guys. I'd never been serious with anyone, though, because I was too busy pining for Cam. I'm pretty sure Cam wasn't saving himself for me, because he went on lots of dates and kissed lots of girls. He never asked anyone out, either, and when I questioned why, he spouted off some misogynist bull crap about a guy code. How chasing a girl would make him look desperate and let the girl think she was in charge.

I told him he was an idiot, but that just made me a big, fat hypocrite. I had a code of my own. One that prevented me from asking any boy out, much less Cam. Asking a boy out would be admitting to the universe who I liked. And, in turn, the universe would send Cupid's arrow, stamped with Beth's name, straight through that boy's heart.

Nope, no way. I couldn't ask anyone to the homecoming dance, so I needed to catch someone's attention long enough for him to ask me. It could be any guy, as long as he was cute and cool. I didn't need a boyfriend. Just someone to keep me from joining all the losers in stagville.

"What's going on in there?" Cam was snapping his fingers in front of my face. "You've been spacing out a lot this week."

"Sorry, just thinking."

"Thinking about what? Your devilishly handsome lab partner?"

As if I would admit that. "OMG!" I squealed, doing my best groupie impression. "Do you have ESPN? How did you know? Are you like, psychic or something?"

"Well, you did have a dreamy look on your face. I'm pretty sure if you looked up my name in the dictionary, *dreamy* would be the definition. It's only natural that I assumed you were thinking about me."

Cam reached up and tapped the tip of my nose with his finger. He looked me in the eyes, forcing me to hold his gaze. His finger slid slowly off my nose and down to my lips. He tapped those, too, then left his finger pressed against them. I opened my mouth to deliver a witty retort, but he shushed me. "Shhhhhh, it's ok, Bebe. I leave most girls speechless. Give in to the power of my charms."

Ok, I'll give in...swoon. No. Bebe, stop being weak. You can do this.

"I don't think so, Romeo." I managed to pull his hand from my face even though my brain was protesting. "You know your Don Juan routine doesn't work on me." *Liar, liar, pants on fire.* "And I hope you washed your hands recently, since you decided to rub your finger all over my face." *I was never washing my face again.*

Somewhere in the room, our teacher cleared his throat. "Ahem… Do I have to separate you two already? It's only been a week. I think that'd be a new record."

"Sorry, Mr. Gardner." Cam was quick to apologize. "I can't find my pen, so I was asking Bianca if I could borrow one of hers." Cam reached across me to grab the pen I was holding. His hand lingered on mine a bit longer than necessary before snatching the pen away. Then he grabbed the pen out of my ponytail and reached all the way around my back to put it in my right hand. What was that all about? He could've just taken the pen from my hair and avoided the extra touching. Not that I minded the touching. I probably *didn't* mind it a little too much.

Mr. Gardner dimmed the lights and started clicking through his PowerPoint presentation on the periodic table of elements. This was a very good thing since I was blushing again. It was also a bad thing, because I needed to pay attention, but my mind was racing. I was thinking about chemistry, all right, just not the kind of chemistry that Mr. Gardner was teaching us.

Eventually, I was able to focus, even though Cam was sprawled out with his knee touching mine through most of the lecture. Right as the teacher was finishing up, Cam leaned over and whispered in my ear, "Are we still on for the football game tonight?"

I answered quietly without turning to look at him. "Absolutely; we can't miss the game. Angelica promised to show you her undies…I mean, her back flip."

Cam chuckled softly, sending tingles down my neck as

he whispered in my ear once again. "Cool, I'll be over to your place by six."

Good. That'd give me enough time to blow off some steam on the Perkinses' driveway before showering. Heaven forbid Cam continued whispering in my ear all night. I was all hot and bothered after two stupid questions. It was going to take me the rest of the afternoon to calm down enough that I could interact rationally. On second thought, maybe I should skip playing basketball and go straight to the shower. A long, cold shower.

I STOOD IN FRONT OF THE MIRROR, ASSESSING MY REFLECTION. Not too shabby. I didn't look hot, but I wasn't trying to. Girls that dressed trashy and wore tons of makeup were working too hard. I was safely in the cute zone tonight. Corduroy shorts and a cute baby-doll style shirt, the customary flip-flops on my feet. I'd gone with my normal light makeup look but switched up my usual hair style, opting for two long French braids, one down each side of my head. I was about to head out of the bathroom, when my dad called up to me.

"Bianca, sweetheart. Cam's here."

"Tell him I'll be right down; I need to grab my purse."

I hated carrying a purse. But the cheer squad had to be at the field early, so Beth had already left with some friends. Which meant that I *finally* got to drive my car. Since my pants didn't have pockets, it also meant I needed something to put my phone and keys in. Maybe I could get Cam to carry the purse around for me? He probably would if I asked him to, since he loves attention. Toting my cute pink purse around all night would guarantee he got a lot of looks. The boy had no shame. I grabbed my purse, tucked in some lip gloss, then headed down the stairs.

"What time do you think you'll be home?" my dad asked.

"I don't know?" I glanced at Cam. He looked amazing, as usual. "You think people will want to go out for pizza after the game?"

"Probably. I'm not even sure I can make it all the way through before grabbing food. I guess it depends on if we're winning or if it's a normal game." Cam snickered. Our football team was horrible last year, so chances are they'd be awful this year, too. Nobody went to the games because they were exciting or to show school spirit. They mostly went because it was something to do. I went to support Bethany. If she had to spirit finger through the suck fest that was a Franklin High School football game, I supposed I could sit through one and cheer her on.

"Don't worry, Mr. Barnes. I'll have her back by morning." My dad loved Cam. He had the parent-charming gene secured tightly in his DNA. He always told my dad he'd have Beth and me back by morning. And my dad always countered with eleven.

"How about by eleven?" Dad answered.

"That was going to be my second suggestion," Cam

reassured him.

"All right, then, you two kids have fun. Behave yourselves, and for heaven's sake, Bianca, drive slowly. I don't think your bank account *or* your social life could survive another speeding ticket."

"Yes, sir," I barked, saluting him, then pushed Cam through the front door before I got any more of my dad's lectures.

"Do you really want to stop for food first?" I asked once we were pulling out of the driveway. "I could swing you through a drive-thru real quick."

"Nah, we don't have that much time. If we don't get there pretty soon, the student section will be full and we'll get stuck behind the marching band. Last time that happened, I was singing the school fight song for a week. I took a lot of crap for that. Not even *I* can get away with something as lame as singing the fight song in public."

It was only a ten-minute drive to the school, but Cam got comfortable anyway. He pushed his seat all the way back, threw his feet up on the dash, and reached over to tug on my pigtail. After a good, long yank, he dropped his arm and settled it across the back of my shoulders. Great, here we go again. More unnecessary touching.

Sure, Cam and I had physical contact all the time. Especially when we were playing ball. I guess we hugged often enough. But *that* had always felt so normal. Good friends bumping into each other. The touching *this* week seemed more intentional, almost flirty. Cam flirted tons, but never with me. Maybe I was reading signals that weren't there. Two years of wishful thinking were starting to affect my judgment. Best not to hope or assume. You know what they say assuming does. It makes an ass out of you and me, but mostly just me.

We pulled up to the school a few minutes before kickoff. Cam paid for my ticket. A little weird, since he'd never offered before, and we'd been to lots of football games together. The crowd was thick, and he was trying to clear the way. But I'm small and he's a giant, so I was getting manhandled and falling behind.

"Come on, slowpoke." Cam reached back and grabbed my hand as he pulled me through the surge of people. I looked down at our hands. Our fingers weren't laced together, but his ginormous hand was securely wrapped around my tiny one. I blinked slowly, shook my head, then looked up at the back of Cam's.

Holy crap on a stick. Cameron Bates was holding my hand. I mean, I wouldn't say we were "holding hands" since I was behind him and he was *dragging* me through a crowd. But he was unmistakably holding my hand. On purpose. He'd *never* done that before. *Breathe, Bianca, just breathe.*

We got to the student section, and he didn't drop my hand until I pulled away to find a seat. What the crap? Was he going to *keep* holding my hand? In front of God and all our friends? I'm not sure I could handle much more of this without my head exploding. I needed a distraction. I looked down at the cheerleaders and saw one of them waving in our direction, and it wasn't Beth. Perfect.

"Look, Cam." I pointed down to the side of the field.

"Your girlfriend is trying to get your attention."

"Huh?" he asked, confused. When he finally saw Angelica waving her pom-poms and wiggling her fingers (and I'm pretty sure shaking her boobs), he chuckled and waved back at her. Angelica was far enough away that we couldn't hear her, but she mouthed something that looked like *for you* as she blew Cam a kiss. Then she did an impressive back handspring followed by a slower back walkover into the splits.

I've got to give it to her; Angelica really was a good tumbler. However, I don't think that was the message she'd been trying to send with her last move. Cam gave her a complimentary clap. She stood up and gave him a bashful-looking curtsey. *Oh, please.* Nothing about that girl was bashful. She knew what she wanted, and everything she did was calculated to get it.

I hope Cam wasn't really into that kind of girl. If that's the sort of thing he wanted, then I could kiss my chances good-bye. I wouldn't act like that. Not even for Cam. He sat on the bleachers and yanked me down next to him while I continued to glare daggers at Angelica's backside.

"What's wrong?" he asked. "Dare I say you look jealous?"

"Ha!" I scoffed. "If I wanted your attention that bad, I could just sport some of Bethany's spankies and strut around in a short skirt. I'm pretty sure it's not the back handspring you were busy admiring."

"Hmmm." Cam pretended to be deep in thought. "That sounds like a really good idea. We could leave now and go straight back to your place..."

I slapped him on the arm. "Oh, shut up, you perv." I

pretended to be angry, but I was having a hard time holding in my laughter. The thought of me in a cheer uniform was utterly ridiculous.

"No, seriously." He kept going. "Do you even own a short skirt? Because I've seen Beth in some knee-high socks, and I bet she'd let you borrow them."

"OH. MY. GOSH." I slapped my hand over his mouth. "I'm not removing my hand until you promise to control your horn dog thoughts." He raised his eyebrows and then bit my hand playfully. "Gross." I pulled it away quickly and wiped the slobber across his cheek. Then he did something shocking. It happened so fast I didn't even have time to react.

In one swift move, Cam lunged for me. He wrapped me up tight in a bear hug, pulled me onto his lap, leaned me back, and...licked my face. I squealed, wiggled, and begged for mercy. I guess this was the wrong reaction, because it only fueled the fire. He then assaulted my sides by tickling me relentlessly. I thrashed and kicked and started calling him foul names, but on the inside, I was having an emotional panic attack.

"STOP TORTURING ME!" I yelled with a laugh. *No, don't stop*, my hormones screamed. I wondered how long I could endure his closeness, but I was saved by the approach of Brady, Mike, and Caleb.

"Looks like you could use some help there." Brady grabbed my arm and tugged me away from Cam's lap.

"My knight in shining armor." I fake swooned as I laughed. I sat back down next to Cam, and Brady sat on my other side so I faced him. "Thanks for the rescue. I think

I was seconds from peeing my pants on his lap, though it would have served him right."

"I'm happy to rescue any damsel in distress. Especially if it's you." He smiled.

This was flirting I could handle. It was so easy to tease and laugh when it was Brady. If Cam did and said the exact same things, it'd be like a nuclear reactor melting my brain. Brady struck up a comfortable conversation. We talked about school and basketball and other random stuff. The next thing I knew, it was almost halftime. I looked over at Cam, and even though he was talking to Caleb and Mike, he seemed annoyed. Mike could definitely have that effect on people.

I leaned in close to Cam and whispered, "Do you need someone to get you out of your conversation?"

"Funny," he muttered. "I was just wondering the same thing about you."

"Oh, no. I'm actually having a nice time. I doubt I'd be as content if I'd had to talk to Mike for the last forty-five minutes." I smirked, but for some reason Cam didn't return the smile. He still looked annoyed.

It was dark out by now, and even though it wasn't supposed to be cold tonight, the wind had picked up. I was starting to get chilly. It was still summer in freaking Florida. I hadn't expected to need a jacket. I shivered slightly and wrapped my arms around my torso.

"Are you cold?" Brady asked me. "Because you can have my jacket if you need it."

I was about to say thanks and take the jacket from him,

when Cam jumped to his feet. "Don't worry, Bebe, I've got you covered." He climbed up a row and sat directly behind me. Then he spread his legs and pulled me back against his chest. He wrapped his arms loosely around my shoulders and rested his head on the top of mine. I froze. Alarm bells went off in my head, and my thought process slowed to a crawl. Yeah, he's got me covered. Literally.

"This should block the wind from blowing against your back. You'll be fine as long as I stay here," Cam assured me. I started to protest, but he leaned down and spoke into the back of my hair. "Just go along with it, Bebe. This'll get me out of my conversation with Mike."

Understanding finally hit me; Cam needed an excuse. To get away from what was probably an annoying feminine conquest story that was really a load of bull crap. I relaxed a little and shrugged my shoulders. The position that seemed intimate just seconds ago now felt more like a buddy keeping me warm. I admit I was a little disappointed, but I'd take it. Friend Cameron with his arms wrapped around me was better than *no* Cameron with his arms around me. I turned to Brady. "Thanks anyway. I think I'll be warm enough now."

Brady's face fell slightly. It'd be hard to continue our conversation from this position, at least without bringing Cam into it. So, I decided to lean back and watch my sister at work. Bethany was an awesome cheerleader, bubbly and full of smiles. Plus, she was as good at tumbling as Angelica was.

Cam and I sat in companionable silence until the end of the third quarter. We watched the game and cheered. We occasionally chatted with our friends, but true to his word, Cam continued to keep me wrapped up. For a while, he grabbed the end of my braid and rubbed my hair between his fingers and against the tip of his nose, almost absent-mindedly. Like he didn't realize he was doing it. At the start of the fourth quarter, Brady got up to go to the bathroom and Cam leaned in to the back of my head again. "I'm starving now. You want to grab some pizza?"

"You don't want to finish the game?" I was starting to get hungry, too, but I didn't want to leave the comfort of his arms. Who knew if I'd ever be in this position again?

"Nah, I don't care if we miss the end. The other team is leading by so much we'll never catch up. Beth's riding home with her friends, right?"

"She didn't say she needed a ride, so probably. Should we wait for Brady to get back and see if the guys want to join us?"

Cam was quick to dismiss that idea. "I think I've had my fill of Mike for the evening. We can't really invite Brady and Caleb without inviting Mike, so I think we should *quietly* slip out."

"That sounds subtle," I laughed sarcastically, "but I'm on board."

Cam stood up, and the cold air hit my back once again. I immediately regretted my decision to go for pizza. We gave a quick good-bye to Caleb and Mike without explaining where we were headed, then climbed down the bleachers. On our way to the parking lot, a gust of wind hit, and I tried unsuccessfully to subdue a shiver. Cam put his arm around my waist and pulled me in to his side as we walked.

"Guess next time I'll have to bring a jacket," I said, opening the door to my car. "Nonsense," Cam responded with a wicked grin. "You don't need a jacket; you have me." He winked as he slipped into the passenger seat.

CAMERON

So far, tonight had been a success. But the night wasn't over, and I didn't want to get too cocky. Still plenty of time to screw something up. Bianca looked freaking adorable when she came downstairs sporting two long pigtails. Pigtails, for heaven's sake. It was enough to drive any man crazy with lust. When I saw her, I had to control the urge to pull her close and plant a big, wet kiss right on her glossy pink lips. I don't think Bebe would have found that very amusing, and I'm sure her dad would have been less than thrilled, so I decided to be patient.

I'd been pretty aggressive at the football game. I paid for her ticket and found an excuse to hold her hand. She pretended to be disgusted when I bit her, but I knew better. *Nobody* is disgusted by Cameron Bates's mouth. I'm not sure what came over me; the need to kiss her was so strong I couldn't help myself. I pulled her on my lap, leaned her back…then chickened out and licked her cheek instead. Not the most romantic move.

Once she was on my lap, I needed an excuse to keep her there. I wondered what else could I touch without getting slapped? I chose tickling, and Bebe was eating it up…until Brady interrupted us. It's like his whole purpose in life was to ruin my mojo. What a tool. Couldn't he tell that *I* was here with Bianca? What kind of dude barges into an intimate tickle fight and steals the girl away? Someone who wants his ass beaten, that's who.

I was working up the energy to throw down with him when it dawned on me that Bebe had been maintaining their conversation willfully. If she'd wanted to be rescued, she would have found a way to let me know. Was *he* the knob knocker she'd been staring at the other day during lunch? Bebe *never* talked about who she was into. For all I knew, he was the guy of her freaking dreams. The thought made me panic.

I'd never been so forward about touching Bebe, but tonight I was like a caveman staking my claim. I might as well have clubbed her on the head and thrown her over my shoulder. She'd been totally focused on Brady and I got annoyed. So, I did what any self-respecting man would do. I lied; a lame excuse about needing to get away from Mike. Truthfully, Mike hadn't even been talking to me, but Bianca didn't need to know that.

Unfortunately, I wasn't sure if she let me hold her

because she wanted me to, or if she was trying to help me dodge a conversation with Mike. Heck, she could have just been cold and using my body for a source of heat. Normally I'm ok with a girl using my body for a variety of different reasons, but with Bebe, I wanted it to be more than that. I wanted her to want me back. Geez. I was starting to sound like a flippin' girl.

Now we were seated in a cozy booth at Nick's Pizzeria. I thought about sliding onto the bench next to her, but I'd already been pushing my luck tonight. "What sounds good?" I asked her as I glanced over the menu. I was hungry enough to eat a whole pizza by myself.

"Nothing with onions," she replied.

"No onions, huh? I get it. You want to keep your breath nice and fresh for when I kiss you goodnight later." Now I was really testing my limits. The way she responded to that blatant come-on would definitely give me a better idea of where I stood.

"Huh," she grunted with a smirk. "Something like that."

Well, that sucked. Her answer didn't give me jack crap to go on. Was that a yes to the kiss? I ran my finger down the menu, ready to drop another hint. "If you're in the mood for pasta, we could always split the *couple's special.*" There, that should get response.

"We *could* split the couple's special, but I've seen how you eat. I doubt there'd be enough for both of us." She bit her lip in concentration as she looked down the menu. Darn, that was a good one, and she didn't even take the bait. *Come on, Bebe, you're killing me here. You've got to give me something.*

Looks like I was going to have to bite the bullet and ask outright.

"So, Bebe, what's up with you and Brady?" I asked casually. We settled on a veggie pizza—hold the onions. She was right about the onions. Those and all the sausage and pepperoni that I normally ordered would have left my breath less than fresh.

She looked at me quizzically. "What do you mean, what's up with me and Brady?"

"Well, you two were talking for so long tonight, I was wondering if you had a thing for him?" There, that wasn't so hard.

"Would it be a problem if I did?"

Not the answer I was hoping for. I was hoping for *Oh, Cam, how could you ever think I'd love anyone but you?* I'd have been satisfied with a *nope*. I didn't know what to expect, but definitely not what she said. She kept throwing the ball back in my court. How was I supposed to respond? *Yes, it's totally a problem if you have a thing for him. It's a problem if you have a thing for anyone that isn't me.* Yeah, that wasn't going to happen. I was hinting like crazy, and I still had no idea if it was having any effect on her.

"Not necessarily..." I answered. I'd play her game.

"So you're saying there might be *some* instances when it *would* be a problem if I had a thing for Brady?"

No. Yes. Damn it, woman! This was getting me nowhere.

"I'm saying that he seems into you, so if you like Brady, I suppose you could do worse. But if you aren't sure about him, you should hold out, because you could definitely do better."

"Oh, yeah, Mr. Smarty Pants, who would you suggest is better for me than Brady?"

This is it. It's do or die, Cam, do or die. "Well, let's see here." I ticked the names off on my fingers as I listed them. "There's LeBron James, Chris Hemsworth, Principal Davis, me..." I trailed off and held my breath as I waited for her response. I can't believe I just threw out my own name. That was way too obvious.

She paused and stared at me really hard. It felt like forever. Then she opened her mouth and laughed. Not a giggle or even a hearty chuckle. A gut busting, knee slapping, roll-on-the-floor-dying kind of laugh. She doubled over for a second, and when she sat back up there were tears in her eyes. *Real. Freaking. Tears.* I'm glad the thought of me being good for her is so absurd that it makes her cry.

"Principal Davis?" She let out an incredulous squeal. "I know a lot of the girls think he's pretty foxy, but you honestly think I'd be better with Principal Davis than with Brady?" She kept laughing, then finally had to down half of her Diet Coke to get it under control.

Oh. My. Gosh. What was wrong with her? I listed the most unrealistic people I could think of to make myself the obvious front-runner, and Principal Davis is who she fixated on? It's like I was as much of an impossibility as LeBron or Chris. I couldn't have spelled it out for her any more clearly than I just did. The most perfect girl in the world was sitting in front of me. I was practically telling her how I felt, and she'd totally missed the point. Either she really had absolutely *no* romantic feelings for me and was trying to let me down gently, or she was completely oblivious.

Bebe looked at me, waiting for an answer, but I had no clue what to say. I sat there, mouth hanging open like an idiot. Is this what girls felt like when they tried to have a serious relationship talk with a dude? Was I producing estrogen? Was I growing boobs? Because, man, I felt like a chick right now. Luckily, I was saved by the waitress who came out with our pizza and a refill on our drinks.

"Oh, good. I'm starved," I said. I'd tried being direct and that didn't work, so I decided to switch to avoidance.

The waitress left, and we each piled some pizza on our plate. We ate quietly for a few minutes, the weird tension growing between us. Bebe finished her second piece before she broke the silence. "Cam? Did I do something wrong? You seem upset."

"No, Bebe," I sighed, "you didn't do anything wrong."

"Then why did you get so quiet all of a sudden?"

I needed to lighten the mood or the next twenty minutes would be more awkward than two sixth graders playing seven minutes in heaven. "Well, Bianca, I'm pouting because you didn't approve of my potential suitors for you."

"You're kidding, right? How am I supposed to approve of anyone you listed? If you want my approval, you need to suggest someone realistic. Someone attainable." She waved her hand at me as if I'd only provided her with names of mythical creatures. I chewed on her words for a second. Is that what she thought about me? That I was unattainable? She couldn't possibly think that she wasn't good enough for me. If anything, she was *too* good for me. She was too good for any of the guys at our school.

I would've never thought Bebe had a self-confidence problem. She was as sassy as they came. That kind of attitude only came with huge balls, though obviously in her case they were metaphorical balls. If she didn't think she was good enough for me, and she didn't take me seriously when I tried to tell her otherwise, I had no idea how to tackle the issue. There had to be some way to get through to her.

I sat there, contemplating, and watching her start a third piece of pizza. Cheese dripped from her lips. There was a dab of sauce smeared on her chin, and she was still beautiful. All of a sudden, my crappy mood disappeared. I couldn't stay upset with her. And I wouldn't give up on her, either.

"So..." I tried a different approach. "If you're not into Chris Hemsworth and you don't think you and Principal Davis would work out, then who *do* you have on your mind? Who makes Bianca Barnes weak in the knees? Whose last name does she doodle behind her first name on the inside of her notebooks? Hmmm?"

"Nobody, right now." Liar. She looked down when she answered, which meant she was lying to me. Bebe can't look you in the eyes if she's being less than truthful, and I was going to call her on it. But, unfortunately knowing she liked someone else meant I couldn't profess my feelings.

"*You* are a big fat liar, Bebe. I've known you long enough to tell when you're feeding me a load of crap. You *do* like someone, and since I didn't make the cut, I deserve to know who it is."

"You deserve no such thing. Even if I did like someone, I wouldn't tell you." She blushed as she said that part, which was a dead giveaway. From the deep shade of red that spotted her cheeks, I'm guessing that person was on her mind a lot. "I wouldn't even tell Beth. I wouldn't tell anyone. You know my reasons, and I'm sticking to them." She folded her arms defiantly, trying to put an end to the conversation. Yeah, that wasn't happening.

"Oh, come on. You can't seriously believe all that bologna about the universe being out to ruin your love life? There's plenty of guys who would happily pick you over Beth."

"Oh yeah? Name one?"

I thought I already did. "I didn't see Brady talking Beth's ear off tonight or offering her his jacket."

"That's because Beth wasn't anywhere near him. He may be interested in me, he may not be. But if I opened my mouth to express interest in return, she'd probably get a marriage proposal from him the next day."

I rolled my eyes. "I can see that I'm obviously not going to win this argument. So I'll give up for now. But I'd like it officially recorded that I think you're delusional."

"Opinion noted." She nodded her head in finality.

We'd finished our pizza somewhere mid-argument, and our waitress had dropped off the check. I picked it up to assess the damage and slid my card in the check folder. Bebe opened her wallet. "How much do I owe you?"

"Nothing. She didn't charge us. How kind of her. She must have been enamored with my stunningly good looks."

Bebe gave me a pointed stare that screamed *cut the crap.* "Har-de-har-har. I didn't know you were a comedian. Seriously, how much is my half?"

"Seriously, nothing." She didn't know it yet, but this was our first date, and I wasn't going to let her pay for half of the dinner. "I don't want your money. Save it for your next speeding ticket."

"And he's back, ladies and gentlemen. The Cam we all know and love. Fine," she relented, "but I get to pay next time."

Fat chance. There's no way that was happening. It was going to take some work, but if I got my way, I'd soon be taking her out to many dinners. Or games, concerts, movies, bowling, and any other date-worthy activity that sounded fun. And since she'd be my girlfriend, she wouldn't spend a cent.

BIANCA

Since we left the game early, I got home around ten. Beth wasn't home yet, so I checked in with Dad and headed to my bedroom. I shucked off my clothes and pulled on my fuzzy pajamas, then wandered over to the window. I peeked through the blinds to see if I could catch a glimpse of Cam changing into his PJs. No such luck. His bedroom light was on, but his blinds were closed. Oh well; I just spent the entire evening with him. Wasn't that enough? I guess I didn't need to see him in his half-naked glory.

I flopped back on my bed, hugging my pillow. What a weird night. I didn't know what to think about it. If I'd been with anyone besides Cam, I'd have assumed we were on a date. He paid for my game ticket and my dinner. He flirted pretty hard, even for Cam. He held my hand and even cuddled with me. Ok, so that wasn't *traditional* cuddling, but I don't know what else to call it. For a second, I even thought he was going to kiss me. Of course, that was right before he licked me. So…yeah, weird night. I don't know what'd gotten into him, but Cam was definitely not acting like himself.

I heard the front door open and shut. A minute or so later, there was a soft knock on my bedroom door. "Come in," I called.

Beth poked her head through the door. "What're you doing home so early? I assumed you'd be out until eleven."

"Cam was hungry, so we left the game after the third quarter and went to Nick's for pizza. How'd the game end? Did I miss anything exciting?"

"Well, we lost the game; big surprise there. But after you left, Angelica's shirt flew up over her face while she was doing a back handspring and her boobs flopped out of her bra. Then she fell on her butt and everyone laughed at her."

"*Shut. Up.* Are you serious?"

"No." Beth laughed at me. "But next time you shouldn't ditch out early. You never know; something exciting *might* happen Then you'll be sorry you missed it."

"Eh, if something like that actually happened, I'd probably be able to find it on YouTube the next day."

"So…" She lay down at the foot of my bed. "What was up with you and Cam tonight?"

"What do you mean?"

"I glanced up into the stands a few times, and he was basically all over you for the entire third quarter."

"I know. Weird, right? The whole night was like a scene from *The Twilight Zone*." I shivered. It probably looked like I was creeped out, but in reality I was remembering our almost kiss. I needed to be careful around Beth. She could read me *way* too easily.

"How so?" she asked. I'd piqued her interest.

"Well, for one thing, he paid for my game ticket *and* my dinner. He's never done that before. He was really snippy about all the attention I was giving to Brady. If I didn't know any better, I'd think he was jealous. And, he was super flirty and touchy all night."

"Hello? News flash. Cam is flirty and touchy all the time, with everyone." Beth gave me a look that said *duh*.

"Except that he isn't like that with everyone. He's *never* like that with me, never really has been. I used to be a little bothered by it because he literally throws himself at anything with boobs. Then I just decided that I must be too much like a little sister. Acting like his normal flirty self around me probably grosses him out."

Beth laughed again. "I seriously doubt he thinks of you like a little sister. Honestly, I've always wondered if he was into you."

"You can't be serious. What on earth would make you think that?"

"Easy. He spends most of his free time with you." She paused to think. "And, you guys have so much in common. You really are a lot alike."

"Ok," I countered, "first of all, he doesn't spend *most* of his free time with *only* me. He spends just as much time with you."

Beth cut me off. "He only spends that much time with me because you and I are always together. I'm sure it's you he really wants to be around. Cam and I never talk and banter with each other the way you do."

"Which is exactly why I've been wondering if he likes you." Beth opened her mouth to protest, but I didn't let her. "He's been extra sweet to you lately, and he never teases you. He's respectful to you. He gives you lots of hugs. Plus, you guys would look like the perfect couple. Barbie and Ken, all the way. Don't you think it makes more sense?"

"Not really." Beth completely brushed off my suggestion. "So back to this weird evening you had. I need specific details if I'm going to analyze the situation properly."

I sighed. Beth was going to read way more into my night than was really there. But she also wouldn't leave me alone until I spilled the beans. So, I started at the very beginning and left nothing out. Thirty minutes later, when I finished my retelling, Beth lay on the end of my bed, staring at the ceiling. "Sounds like a date to me," she said.

"I know, that's what I kept thinking. If it'd been anyone else, I would have thought the same thing. But this is Cam, so it wasn't a date." It wasn't a logical argument, but it was the best I could come up with.

Beth's face contorted like she was thinking extra hard. Finally, she turned to me and fired off the questions I'd been dreading all night. "Did you want it to be a date? How do you feel about him? Do you like him? Do you want him to like you?"

"Oh no. No, no, no, no. We are *not* going there. You know that even if I did like him, and I'm not saying that I do, I could never admit it out loud. I'd be doomed."

"Geez, Bianca. You're still holding on to the whole *the universe has it out for me* idea?" Beth was obviously getting frustrated, but I wasn't going to give her what she wanted. She wanted me to admit that I liked Cam. I did like Cam, and she probably knew it, but there was no way in hell I'd ever tell her that.

Beth gave me a piercing stare, pinning me in place. This was her *I'm being serious* look. The one she'll probably give her kids someday when they're in trouble. "Tell me straight, Bianca," she ordered, "do you or don't you like Cameron Bates as more than friends?"

I hated lying to my sister. I almost never did it. I never really had a reason to. But every now and then, lying was the better choice. You know, like when someone asks you what you think of their new outfit, and you think it's awful. So you lie and say you love it because you don't want to hurt them. Well, this was one of those situations.

If I tell Bethany that I like Cam, then next week he'll probably ask *her* to homecoming. She'll feel really crappy, because she'd never say yes knowing I liked him. But, she wouldn't want to say no because it'd hurt his feelings. She couldn't explain why she was saying no, either, since explaining would embarrass me. So Beth would keep her mouth shut or make up some excuse about why she wasn't planning on going to the dance.

Cam would know Beth's excuse was a lie because a) he's

not dumb, and b) everyone wants to go to the dance. Then Cam would feel stupid because he was rejected, and Beth would be disappointed because she'd have to miss the dance in order to support her excuse. Plus, they'd both feel awkward and I'd be frustrated that neither of my best friends could be in a room with me at the same time. I know I sound like a whack-a-doo, but this really is *exactly* what would happen. A lie here would benefit everyone.

"You're stalling, Bea. Just answer the question," she demanded.

"No!" I snapped. "I don't like Cameron. He's just a friend." I felt horrible as soon as the words came out of my mouth. *I really am going to hell for this one.* I couldn't look her in the eyes as I said it, which is the telltale sign that I was lying, and she knew it. But I was sticking to my story, and that was that.

Beth wasn't quite ready to drop it; she had to make sure I'd put the nail in my coffin. "So you're telling me that if Cam came over tomorrow and introduced you to a new girlfriend, you wouldn't care? You wouldn't even be a little bit jealous?"

"Of course I'd be jealous. If Cam had a girlfriend, it'd mean we couldn't hang out as much. But your scenario is highly unlikely since Cam doesn't do girlfriends. He's never been serious about anyone in all the time we've known him."

"I know it's unlikely; that's why it's a hypothetical question." She was moving past frustrated and squarely into annoyed. "I want to know what you'd do if Cam showed up with a girlfriend." She waited for my answer.

"I don't know, I guess I'd tell him I was happy for him."

No way she was buying my story, but at least she was done arguing with me. We sat quietly for a few minutes before she spoke up again. "Ok, then answer me this... If you don't like Cam, who do you like?"

"Nope. Nice try, but my lips are sealed. Just give up already."

"What do you intend to do about homecoming? It's only a few weeks away. You want to go, don't you?" she asked me.

"Of course I want to go. I'll keep my fingers crossed that someone asks me. If I don't get asked, I'll go stag or stay home." *No way I'd go stag, and Beth knew it.*

"You have to go, Bea, because I want to go, but I won't go without you. It wouldn't be any fun."

"I guess I'll have to make sure that someone asks me."

"And how, exactly, will you do that?" She sounded skeptical.

"Have you ever heard of a little thing called feminine wiles?" Beth giggled, which is what I was going for. "Well, I have them in spades. Don't worry your pretty little head about me. You just make sure you have a date for yourself." Beth sighed. She didn't have to worry about getting a date. But I didn't really have any feminine wiles, and we both knew it.

. . . . .

It was a beautiful summer evening. I was walking through the desert with Cam and he was holding my hand, swinging it back and forth. We were surrounded by all kinds of exotic flowers. It seemed like a strange place for such lush vegetation, but the desert landscape only made the bright flowering plants look even prettier. The sun was setting over the horizon in the most magnificent shades of orange, pink, and indigo. Cam stopped walking and turned me around so I was facing him. He was wearing a tuxedo, and he looked absolutely gorgeous. "You look amazing tonight, Bianca," he said softly.

I looked down at my outfit, a long, white, flowing dress made of chiffon and trimmed with lace and pearls. I had the vague impression that I was in a wedding dress. Cam tucked a strand of hair behind my ear, then brought his hand to rest on my neck, his thumb gently sweeping back and forth across my cheek.

"Tell me you love me," he said. "Tell me you feel what I feel."

I looked him in the eyes and opened my mouth to profess my feelings, but the words got stuck in my throat.

"Please, Bebe," he pleaded. "All you have to do is tell me how you feel, and we can be together forever."

I wanted to tell him I loved him. That I had since the very first day we met, but the words wouldn't come. My lips were moving, but still, no sound escaped. Cam's face fell, and he looked so sad.

"Don't you care for me, Bebe? Not even a little bit?"

I tried to nod yes, but I was paralyzed. He dropped my hand and I thought he was going to leave, but instead he brought his index finger to my forehead and started tapping.

"Bianca, just tell me how you feel..." Tap, tap, tap. I wasn't sure why he was tapping me in the middle of the forehead, but it was a little bit annoying. "Say the words I want to hear, and this can stop." Tap, tap, tap, tap. Why on earth was he being so annoying?

Suddenly, Cameron was gone and Bethany was in front of me. "Bea, you know how to make the tapping stop; just admit that you like him."

Now Beth was the one doing the tapping, and I was beyond irritated. Tap, tap, tap. "I know you're lying, Bea; just tell me the truth."

Tap, tap, tap, tap. Why does she keep tapping me? Anger was starting to bubble up inside. Bethany's head became fuzzy. I shook myself to refocus my vision, and when I stopped, it wasn't Beth's head I was looking at, but a clown's. I was now facing a super scary-looking clown head, but it was on Beth's body. She'd taken off her giant clown shoe and was whacking me with it, over and over again, right in the center of my face. What the hell?

"To make it stop, just tell the truth," the evil Bethany clown said as she laughed maniacally.

"Fine!" I screamed. "I admit it. Ok? I admit it. I like him." Tap, tap, tap, tap... "I like him." Tap, tap, tap. "You can stop now, I told you..."

My eyes flew open, and I was face-to-face with a laughing Cam. He was tapping me repeatedly in the center of my forehead. Confusion morphed into relief. That only lasted a few seconds before I realized what was going on. I slapped

Cam's hand away from my face.

"What in the heck are you doing? And why are you in my room so early in the morning?"

Cam brought his hand back toward my face, and I swatted it away again before shoving him off of my bed altogether. He was laughing hysterically.

"You stupid jerk. How long have you been in here tap-torturing me?"

He did this regularly when we were in ninth grade. If he wanted something from me and I was less than cooperative, he'd tackle me to the ground with my arms pinned under his knees and tap me in the middle of the forehead. He'd do it until I agreed to give him whatever he wanted. It was a very effective form of persuasion.

"Only a minute or so." He reached up to wipe a tear that had been pooling at the side of his eye. I'm glad this was so amusing for him. I sat up in my bed so I could scold him properly.

"Couldn't you have tried to wake me in a nicer way? Perhaps waited until it wasn't the butt crack of dawn?"

"I did try," he protested. "I knocked on your door a few times. When that didn't work, I opened it and called your name. That didn't work, either. So I walked over and shook your arm, but still nothing. I probably could have made out with you in your sleep just now and you wouldn't even have stirred. Man, Bebe, you sleep like the dead. Tap torture was my last resort."

"Fine, but that doesn't explain why you're in my room so early on a Saturday to begin with."

I stared down at his prone form, impatiently waiting for an answer. Cam sat up and faced me. His eyes went wide. It took me a second to realize what had him so shocked. I quickly whipped up the covers that'd fallen off when I shoved him from the bed. In my rush to rip him a new one, I'd forgotten how scantily clad I was. I always slept in nothing but my underwear and a tank top. A very thin, almost see-through tank top...without a bra.

Heat crept through my face. Cam had just gotten a front row seat to the half-naked Bebe show. Oh, kill me now. It was karma, coming to punish me for all the early morning voyeurism I'd practiced this summer.

Cam's wide eyes turned into a dangerous smile. "Don't feel like you have to cover up the goods because of me," he teased. "I have a deep appreciation for the female form."

I picked up my pillow and chucked it at his face. "Get out of my room, you perv!" I tried to sound outraged, but he must not have been too convinced, because he made no move to get up.

"I'll leave as soon as you tell me what you were dreaming about, or rather, *who* you were dreaming about."

"I have no idea what you mean." I tried to play dumb, but he wasn't buying it.

"Oh, I think you do. I think you know exactly who you were dreaming about. It's obviously someone you like...a lot." I narrowed my eyes and pursed my lips. He had to know this wasn't information I was going to divulge. "Come on, Bebe, admit it. You were dreaming about me, weren't you? *There's no way he could possibly know I was dreaming about him.*

"What makes you think I was dreaming about you?" I folded my arms across my chest, just in case the blanket wasn't providing enough coverage.

"Right before you woke up, you were murmuring something about admitting you like him. Does that ring any bells?" *Crap. I'm so screwed. Please tell me I didn't say his name out loud.*

"What's that got to do with the price of tea in China?"

"I'm just saying that I *am* the coolest, hottest most amazing man in your life. It's only natural that you have those kind of dreams about me. My assumption is based purely on logic."

"Fine, you cocky little..." I stopped myself before uttering something that wasn't very ladylike. "If you must know, I was dreaming about Mike."

"MIKE?!" Cam screeched like a tweenage girl.

"Yeah, Mike. What's wrong with Mike?" I tried my hardest to look sincere. "I mean, he is *way* cute and he obviously thinks that I'm *super fly.* He's got impeccable fashion sense, and every time we talk, our conversations are *so deep.* It's like he really gets me, you know?" I laid it on so thick I almost had myself convinced.

This time, my pillow hit *me* in the face. "All right, all right." Cam surrendered. "I won't bug you about your dream. Won't stop me from believing that it was about me, but I'll drop it for now. Just promise me that you will never, ever speak about Mike that way again. I have to go home now and dump bleach in my ears so I can erase everything

I just heard."

Man, I loved winning. Cam got up and walked toward the door. "By the way," he said, "it's not early, lazy butt. It's eleven o'clock. Even I don't need that much beauty sleep. Get out of bed, get dressed, and meet me outside. I need to whoop your sorry rear end in some one-on-one. If you're not down in five minutes, I'm coming straight back up here to drag you out myself. Whether you've changed out of your itsy-bitsy jammies or not." He grinned at me and shut the door behind him.

CAMERON

Wow, I mean...just wow. I'd been in Bebe's room plenty of times, but I'd never seen her half-naked before. We weren't even allowed to close the door. I know she thinks I'm a big pervert, but I only put on a show to maintain my image. I'm really a gentleman in player's clothing. I'd never intrude on her privacy, not intentionally, anyway.

Seeing her in that tank top and her underwear was a little more than I was prepared to handle. Especially since the tank was kind of see-through and her underwear was that super hot boy short style. Oh man, I loved those. I know I embarrassed her. I wish I'd had more tact, looked away before she caught me staring. But I was too stunned to think, much less respond appropriately.

Bebe wasn't super busty, but that didn't really matter to

me. She was petite and proportioned well. It's her legs that got me. I was definitely a leg guy. Despite how short she was, she had long, lean beautiful legs. I know she complained about how she could never get a tan, but I thought her skin was perfect. She didn't look fake like all the girls who spent hours giving themselves cancer in tanning beds. Until today, I'd never really seen her legs above the knee. Basketball shorts were ok for dudes but a horrible, horrible thing for girls.

Bebe headed outside about ten minutes after I left her room, probably worried that I'd make good on my promise to drag her out in her underwear. Of course she'd put on basketball shorts and a T-shirt. I suppose after this morning I should be grateful that she didn't come out in snow pants and a parka.

We played for an hour before Bebe threw herself on the ground. "I can't go anymore," she panted.

For us, one-on-one wasn't a laid back, friendly competition. We were both very competitive, and she was good enough that I actually had to try. She never won anymore, unless I let her. When we met, she was already the same height she is now, but I was only about five-nine, so it was easier for her to get around me. Now that I was six-two, she had a hard time making it past my defense. I was ok with that. It made for more charging and a lot more contact.

"Fine," I replied. "All you have to do is admit that I'm the better player, and we can stop," I teased. She'd never admit that.

"You're the better player," she agreed without hesitation. I was shocked. "You don't mean that."

"Of course I don't," she said, still breathing hard. "I'm just ready for a frozen drink."

"You're a brat." I pouted.

"That's why you love me." Bebe gave me a toothy grin.

Her brattiness *was* one of the many reasons I loved her. I held my hand out to help her up. She stood, then ran across the street. "Meet me at the car." She called over her shoulder.

We got to 7-Eleven and I tried to pay for her drink, but she freaked out because I bought dinner the other night, and she ended up paying for my drink instead. I let her, because she's stubborn. When Bebe has her mind set on something, there's no changing it. Plus, I figured I wasn't breaking my oath. I wasn't lame enough to consider a Slurpee run a date.

"You want to hang out still?" I asked after we got home.

"Yes, but I can't." She sighed.

"Sure, you can. All you have to do is get out of the car, walk to my house, and sit on my couch. You can't be so out of shape that you need a rest before walking across the street?" I know I was supposed to be treating her like other girls, but I couldn't help it. I loved her responses to my teasing. I was rewarded for my rude comment with a kick to the shins. "Ouch. Why so violent?" I complained.

"Why so immature?" she retorted.

"I guess you bring out my youthful side."

"I think it's your idiot side."

I grabbed for her. She tried to dodge, but she wasn't quick enough. I scooped her up and threw her over my shoulder, then started for her side door. I thought about pinching her butt, grateful I was able to restrain myself. Bebe didn't show any restraint, though. She smacked me repeatedly on the ass as she yelled at me to put her down.

"You think spanking me is incentive to let you go?" I asked. "If anything, it's reinforcing my poor behavior." We reached the door, and she gave me one last swat before I put her down. "As much as I'd love for you to continue touching my butt, I assume you have a decent reason for not hanging out?"

"Yes, there is," she replied. "I have an English paper to write."

"Always the procrastinator." I laughed.

"Procrastinator? It's only Saturday. I'm starting early."

"Early, for a procrastinator."

"Whatever." She held her hand up to my face, then turned for the door.

I grabbed her hand away from my face, then held on to it. "Don't go. I'll be lonely if you leave," I begged.

"Sure, you will." She huffed, but she also blushed as she looked at our hands. That alone was enough to keep me encouraged.

"Now, get lost so I can do some work." Bebe pulled away from me, and I was instantly disappointed.

"All right, I'll go." I sighed. "At least I can watch you study from my bedroom window."

"See you later, creeper." She laughed, then went inside.

I trudged up to my bathroom and hopped in the shower. Ten minutes later, I was sitting at my computer. *What to do, what to do?* I opened Facebook to see if anyone mentioned a party or something tonight. My desk was situated in front of my bedroom window, so I pulled open my blinds. I wasn't kidding about spying on Bebe. Our houses were the exact same floor plan, and she and I had the same bedroom. We'd intentionally put our desks in front of our windows so we could make faces at each other when homework got boring. Bebe was sitting at her desk, absorbed in her computer screen.

I clicked on her Facebook page and scrolled through her pictures. One of her and Beth in front of their lockers at school. One of me and her at the conference championships last year. A selfie with the three of us from last Tuesday in government class. Bebe and I spent plenty of time together. When did I become so desperate that I had to Facebook stalk her in the few hours we spent apart?

I didn't know the best way to approach this. My quasi-date had been a bust. I wasn't any closer to knowing how Bebe felt about me. Every now and then I'd see a hint of a reaction when I flirted, but it vanished so quickly there was no way to be sure. She'd never treated me as anything more than a good friend.

As I saw just now on the driveway, even if I confessed my feelings she wouldn't believe me. Not without really proving how much I cared first. I'd have to show her how I felt before I said it. That way when I finally told her, she'd *have* to believe me. How could I do that without revealing my feelings to soon? This was so messed up. Why couldn't it be as simple as walking up to her and asking her out?

I needed help, lots of help, and not only the mental kind. I needed the help of the one person who knew Bebe better than I did. I opened up my phone and shot off a quick text message to Beth.

C: Hey. I need to talk to you.

B: Sure, what's up?

C: No, I need to talk to you in person.

B: Uh-oh. This sounds bad.

C: Not bad. Just need your help with something.

B: I'm on my way to practice. I'll be home in a few hours.

C: Actually, I wanted to talk to you when Bebe wasn't around...

B: Ok. You guys have a fight or something?

C: Or something.

B: Well, we live together, so talking when she's not around might be difficult.

C: She said something about a basketball meeting Monday after conditioning.

B: Well, then you can ride home with me after cheer, and she can catch a ride home with someone else.

C: Thanks, Beth, you're the best.

B: I know :-)

Hopefully she doesn't tell Bebe about this cryptic conversation. I don't think she will. If you can trust anyone to keep a secret, it's Beth. Now I only have two days to come up with a brilliant plan.

·   ·   ·   ·   ·

"Ok, you slackers, move faster! How're you going to defend your conference championship titles if you run like a bunch of asthmatic kids at fat camp?" Coach Lambert barked at us. The girl's coach was a beast. Bebe's theory was that her coach was mean because she batted for the other team and was sexually repressed. I disagreed. I saw the way she looked at Coach Adams; she definitely had a thing for him. He was an ex-college player with mad skills, and even though he was kind of old, he was pretty fit and looked distinguished. Dude made graying hair work. But, he was also married. So I'd bet Coach Lambert was nasty all the time because she had a case of unrequited love.

"I think I'm going to throw up." Bebe groaned as we met each other at the half court line.

"What's wrong, Bebe, feel like an asthmatic kid at fat camp?" I mocked coach Lambert, then turned around, heading for the end line. Boys and girls had been lined up across from each other and running half court suicides for the last twenty minutes. Bebe stood directly across the court from me so we could compete for best times. I had longer legs, so I won for the first fifteen minutes. Bebe had better stamina, though, and for the last five minutes she'd been hitting the half court line just before me. For all her complaining about throwing up, she was in pretty good shape.

After a greatly needed thirty-second rest, Coach Adams yelled the words we were dying to hear. "Ok, guys and gals, one more, then we're done with suicides…" Cheers erupted around the gym.

"…and on to burpees," he finished. Ok, not so much

the words we were dying to hear and more like the words that might make one of us die. "Last one finished from each team does an extra suicide. Ready, go."

Coach blew his whistle, and I took off in a sprint. Bebe was running pretty fast, and we ended up hitting the half court line at the same time. We both bent down to touch the line, but as I put my hand on the floor, she reached out and pushed it from underneath me, causing me to lose my balance. It wasn't enough of a push to make me eat the floor like an uncoordinated jackass, but it *was* enough to give her the advantage she needed. She sprinted across the finish line before I did, no doubt reveling in her dirty defeat.

I glared at Bebe, even though I wasn't mad that she won. I was annoyed that her sneaky cheater moves hadn't crossed my mind first. She might have beaten me, even without cheating. At least now I could blame my loss on something other than her being in better shape. She walked around the end of the court with her hands behind her head, face red, panting and dripping sweat. Gosh, she was hot, even like this. No, especially like this. Ten minutes of burpees and then we could head into the weight room, where she could be my spotting partner and I'd have an excuse to touch her.

When we finished, everyone headed to the water fountains. I cut Bebe off in line, and when I bent over for a drink, she pushed my head into the water. I held some in my mouth as I moved out of line. When she bent over for a swig, I leaned in and sprayed the water on the side of her face. She yelped and ran into the weight room. I'd pay for that later, I'm sure. What I wasn't sure about is why I was acting like an eighth grade moron with a stupid crush. I was usually good at playing it cool with the ladies. I don't know why, but she brought out my dorky side. I must be farther gone than I realized.

"Hey, Bebe," I called out as I entered the weight room and strode over to the bench press. "Get over here and spot me."

"Can't," she replied. "I already told Brady I'd be partners with him today."

What the hell? I thought she understood that she wasn't allowed to spend that much time with other guys. "Fine, if you don't think you can handle spotting all this," I waved my hand from head to toe, "I guess I understand."

"No, I just figured after the stunt you pulled at the drinking fountain it was best to keep my distance. Don't want to end up getting depantsed or something." She smirked at me.

"Touché." I'd never do something so immature. Of course, I did just spit water on her face. Now she's paired up with Brady for the next forty-five minutes, and it was all my fault.

"I'll spot you, bro." Mike wandered over. Since Brady was lifting with Bebe, I guess that left me with Mike. Lovely. It was bad enough that I had to watch Bebe talking to another guy the whole time, but now I had to listen to a bunch of dudes and bros. Mike's vocabulary could use some expansion.

I tried to focus on lifting. I didn't want my performance to suffer this season because I was jealous. But I couldn't concentrate. Every time I looked over at Bebe and Brady, they were talking or laughing, having a grand old time. I noticed that whenever he'd lift a barbell from her, he made sure their hands were touching. Bad call, Brady. The jerk better not think about stealing my girl.

I know it's childish, but I'd already hit my childish quota for the day, so I pulled a move straight out of Mike's playbook: "Picking Up Chicks for Tools." I took off my shirt, wiped my face with it, and tucked it in the back of my pants. I noticed right away that a few of the girls in the room were sneaking peeks. Missy wasn't even being subtle about it.

I couldn't help but hope that Bebe would be like all the other girls and look, too. I was pretty ripped after my intense weight training this summer, and Brady was kind of skinny, so I doubted he'd rip off his shirt in competition. I also knew that if he tried, there wouldn't *be* a competition, because I looked that much better. Hey, it's not cocky if it's the truth. If Bebe noticed my desperate attempt to get her attention, she didn't show it.

BIANCA

I KNOW I STARTED IT BY DUNKING CAM'S HEAD IN THE FOUNtain, but he'd cut in front of me. I couldn't let that go without some sort of retaliation. I didn't expect him to spit water in my face. That was immature, even for Cam. This was proof of his feelings for me. Guys that were into girls didn't spit water into their faces, plain and simple. So I was just a friend. It was disappointing but not anything I didn't expect. All the touching and flirting this past week must have been hormones overflowing because he hadn't hooked up with anyone in a while. Not that I knew of, at least.

I got into the weight room, assuming that Cam and I would lift together, but Brady walked up to me first. "Hey, Bianca. Want to be my partner?"

"Sure, why not?" I smiled at him. If I was never going to have a chance with Cam, it was time I started moving on. Brady was as cute as anyone else, and he was really nice. On top of that, I got the feeling he might be interested in me. "What do you want to work on today?"

He flexed his biceps as he examined them. He wasn't exactly scrawny, but he didn't have the chiseled upper body that Cam did. "I'm thinking bis, tris, shoulders, and chest," he decided.

"Sounds good to me." It didn't really matter what I lifted. I looked like a little boy, regardless of how much time I spent in the weight room. We grabbed some dumbbells and stood by the mirror doing bicep curls. "So, didn't want to partner with Mike today, huh?"

"Mike's a good guy, I swear. He's not even the idiot that he makes people believe he is."

"Riiiight…" I nodded my head. It was clear I didn't believe him. I shouldn't rag on Mike so much. I think he and Brady were pretty good friends.

"No, really. He's just insecure for some reason. It's like he never figured out how to talk to girls and it messes with his head. I'm not sure why he acts the way he does. Maybe he thinks that if he sets the bar really low, people won't be disappointed. If he'd just be himself and stop worrying about what everyone thought, people would probably like him better. Trust me, I wouldn't spend so much time with him if he were as dumb as he pretends to be. He's a totally different person when it's just us."

"That's surprisingly deep of you, Brady."

"Do I seem like the type of guy who wouldn't be deep?" He smiled. It was a nice smile. I blushed as we moved on to a shoulder press. I hadn't meant to offend him. I sat on the bench, and he stood behind me ready to spot.

"No, that's not what I meant," I corrected. "It's just that most guys I know aren't super open to talking about their feelings. I think it's cool you aren't afraid to stick up for him."

"Well, Bianca, I *am* a pretty cool guy." He winked at me in the mirror. I was getting fatigued, and it was obvious, so he put his hands lightly on my forearms and left them there as I pushed on with my last few reps.

"One more, Bea. Come on, you got this," he encouraged. My arms were shaking, and I seriously doubted my ability to finish the press. He moved his hands off my arms and put them over mine, helping me make it the last few inches. Then he kept our hands locked as he guided the weights down to my side and took them from me. "Nicely done."

We switched places, and he started his shoulder press. Hopefully he didn't need help, because my arms felt like Jell-O. If he got into trouble, I wouldn't be worth much.

Our conversation continued effortlessly through the rest of the workout. It was mostly small talk about basketball and what we expected from the season. Brady joked around about getting to have conditioning together this year because Coach Lambert and Coach Adams were secretly in love. They needed more time to spend on their forbidden romance. Talking to Brady was surprisingly fun. *I wonder if he has a date to homecoming yet? I wouldn't be totally bummed if he asked me. Should I hint around about it?*

I was in the middle of deciding how one brought up the subject of homecoming without sounding like she was fishing for a date, when I noticed Cam across the room. He'd taken off his shirt and shoved it in the back of his shorts. Nine pairs of feminine eyes were staring in his direction. Missy's were practically falling out of her head. Even Coach Lambert gave him a quick peek. *Maybe she's batting for our team, after all.* I waited until he sat down at the lat pull with his back facing me before I checked him out. Unlike all these other floozies, I had dignity. Who was I kidding? One minute I was thinking about going to homecoming with Brady, the next I was staring at Cam and wiping the drool from my face. I couldn't help it. His upper body was something you'd expect on a Greek god, not a dumb high school boy. I guess that made him my own personal Greek tragedy.

Feeling guilty, I tore my gaze away. I would *not* ruin a perfectly good conversation by staring at half-naked Cam. At that moment, Beth popped her head in the weight room door. "Hey, Bea. You guys almost done?" I looked at the clock. Time was up. It's true what they say about it flying when you're having fun.

"Yeah, I guess Ms. Lambert's torture hour is over. But I have a team meeting in fifteen minutes. I'm not sure how long it'll take. Do you mind waiting?"

"Actually, I've got a ton of homework. Is there any way you could catch a ride home with someone else?"

"Probably. Give me a few minutes to ask around before you take off."

Hmm, who could I bum a ride off of? Turns out I didn't need to ask anyone, because Brady jumped to my rescue again.

"I can give you a ride if you need one, Bea."

"Are you sure? We might be a while."

"Yep, it's no problem. I have a few things I need to research for a history assignment. I can do that over in the library while I wait." He jogged to his backpack and fished out his phone. "Give me your number, and I'll text you mine. Meet me in the library when you're done, and if you can't find me, call."

"Awesome. Thanks, Brady, I owe you one. Slurpees are on me today," I offered.

"No thanks necessary. I already told you, anything for a damsel in distress. But I'll never turn down a free Slurpee, so I accept."

"Well then, it's a date." Where was this bold, new Bianca coming from? It's a date? I better be careful, or the universe was going to pick up on my harmless flirting. I spoke to Beth, who was still standing in the doorway. "Looks like I found a ride."

"All right, then. I'll see you at home." She turned to Cam, not phased at all by his shirtless body. "Hit the showers, Cam, and make it quick. I don't want your stinky boy sweat smelling up my car."

"Yes, Mom," he told her. He occasionally stole my line when she deserved it. He winked at me with a conspiratorial grin and walked out the door.

CAMERON

She was supposed to get a ride from someone on the team, not turn it into a date with Brady. I was fuming as I turned on the shower. I hurried through my rinse so I wouldn't keep Beth waiting too long. I needed to act fast, or they'd be dating for real by the end of the week. I also needed to calm down. Panicking wasn't going to help me think any clearer. If I had to compete with Brady, I'd be in trouble. The guy was smoother than I initially gave him credit for.

I met Beth outside the locker room, and we walked to her car. Other than a quick *hey*, I didn't say anything. My mind was too busy thinking about what an after-school Slurpee run could turn into. We got in the car and buckled our seat belts as Beth turned on the engine and threw the car in reverse. Once we were on the road, she broke the long silence.

"Whatever is going on must be pretty bad, because you haven't spoken a single word since we left the locker room. Spill it," she demanded. She kept her eyes on the road, but her tone said she meant business.

"Beth, what I'm about to tell you cannot leave this car. Do you understand?" My voice was seconds from cracking, and my heart was racing. I couldn't believe what I was about to admit.

"Cameron Bates, what's wrong?" Her no-nonsense tone switched to one of concern.

Beth looked out the front window, steady as a rock. *Just do it, Cam. Stop being a sissy, or you'll never get the girl.* I took a deep breath and blurted out before I could stop myself.

"I'm in love with your sister." It came out in a rush.

Beth was silent for what seemed like an hour but was really only seconds. "That's it?" She laughed. "Geez, Cam, I thought you were going to tell me you were dying or that you're gay or something."

"What do you mean, *that's it?* My confession isn't a big enough deal for you?" I was incredulous.

"No, no, it's a big deal." She grinned. "You have no idea how much. I'm just not all that surprised." Excitement was rolling off her.

"You mean, you suspected that I like her?"

"Yes, I've always wondered if you did. You guys are too perfect for each other to not end up together." I'm sure I still looked panicked, because she quickly continued, "If you're worried that she knows you like her, then don't. I'm pretty sure she has no clue, based on our conversation Friday night."

I sagged with a deep sigh of relief. "Wait a minute. What conversation? You guys talked about me liking her?"

"Not exactly. She came home all weirded out Friday because you paid for her game ticket and dinner. She said you were super flirty and touchy."

"So she did notice? I was laying it on pretty thick."

"Cam, I think everyone in the student section noticed. Even Angelica complained about it after you guys left. If looks could kill, Brady would have made you a dead man."

"Well, he deserved it. Jackass horned in on my date. Apparently not everyone noticed my sweet moves, because Bianca seemed pretty clueless." I was never going to stop being frustrated that the night hadn't gone as planned.

"Oh, she noticed, all right," Beth corrected me. "She just didn't know what to think about it. I don't think she believes that you could ever be interested in her. I don't know why. You guys are perfect for each other. She has this belief that I'm awesome and she's average and that no boys would ever pick her over me."

"That's just ridiculous." I caught my mistake and rushed to fix it. "No offense. I mean, you're gorgeous and great and all, but you aren't her. If she weren't so oblivious, she'd be perfect."

"None taken." She smiled knowingly. "Perfectly oblivious...that's a good way to describe Bianca." Beth chuckled.

"So," I edged forward, "what do you think? Is there any chance that my feelings aren't one-sided?"

Beth contemplated for a moment. Great. She couldn't answer right away. This wasn't a good sign. Maybe I just made a complete ass out of myself. Finally, she answered, seconds short of me losing it. "Actually, I think she does like you."

"You do? Did she tell you that?" My giddiness made me feel like a six-year-old in a candy store with a hundred-dollar bill.

"Not exactly…"

"What do you mean, *not exactly?*"

"Ok, I mean not at all." Beth pulled out her pouty lip. She only did that when she was really frustrated.

"Come on, Beth, you're killing me here." I went from excited to crushed in two seconds flat. I raked my hands through my hair. I was turning into such a girl. I swear someone is slipping estrogen pills into my Red Bull. We pulled into her driveway, and she put the car in park, then turned to me.

"Don't freak out, Cam. I know she likes you."

"How do you know if she hasn't told you?"

"I just do." Beth seemed sure of herself. "Call it my twin sense."

"You guys aren't actually twins, you know." I glared half-heartedly. I was too desperate to be angry.

Beth shook her head. "I know that." My lack of trust was obviously annoying her. "But I also know my sister, and if I say she likes you, then she likes you."

"That's not good enough. I have to know for sure."

Beth examined me. "I have an idea." Sarcasm tinted her

voice. "Why don't you just tell her you like her? You know her whole *the universe hates me* theory. Even if she did like you, which I think she does, she'll never admit it first. Maybe you're going to have to grow a pair and tell her how you feel."

I blinked slowly, mouth agape. Did she just tell me I had no balls? Beth was never so crude. This was quite the challenge, especially coming from her.

I was quick to defend myself. "Your twin sense isn't good enough, Beth." I needed her to understand my predicament. "You think this is just about me being chicken? I'm scared, I'll admit that, but this isn't about being scared. I laid it on pretty thick Friday. I was as forward as I could be without coming out and saying I liked her. And do you know what she did? She laughed at me. She blew me off like it was nothing more than a joke. I know it may have come across a little casual, but being blunt is a risk I can't take right now."

"Why not? If it'll get you what you want in the end?"

"That's just it. I don't know if a declaration of love will end well. What if she doesn't like me? Have you ever thought about that? She's been awfully friendly with Brady lately. What if she's into him and I confess my feelings and she doesn't want me back? What'll that do to our friendship? It would ruin everything." I paused to let my words sink in.

"She's my best friend. I can't risk losing her friendship because you *have a feeling* that she likes me. It would be so awkward. Then you'd have to stop hanging out with me because she's your sister and you'll always put her first. I'd be losing both of you." I sighed. Being so open and emotional was draining on my male psyche.

Beth was quiet. She looked sad. "Ok. I get it. I guess I never thought about it like that before. I honestly think she likes you, but she *hasn't* admitted it. Actually, when I asked her point blank, she full on denied it." I cringed a little, and Beth noticed. "Don't worry; she couldn't look me in the eye while she was doing it, and we both know what that means." Beth was smiling again, and that got a small one out of me. "But if you can't admit you like her and she *won't* admit she likes you, then what do we do about it? You can't go on like this forever."

"I don't know," I answered. "That's why I brought my dirty little secret to you."

We sat in complete silence, thinking. Beth spoke first. "What we need is to figure out for sure that she's into you."

"Thanks, Einstein…" I snapped. "How do you propose we do that?"

Beth gave me a dirty look but ignored my rudeness. "We need to make her jealous," she answered.

"You think I haven't tried that?" I threw up my arms in frustration. "I've been trying to make her jealous for the last *year*. Why else do you think I'm such a flirt? I certainly don't like any of those girls. And yes, I know that makes me a first-rate ass. I thought eventually I could make Bebe jealous. Obviously, it's not working."

"I think the objects of your flirtations are wrong. It's clear to her that you are *just* flirting. You'd never get serious with any of those girls. I know it, and Bea knows it. If she thinks you aren't going to have a relationship, then they aren't a threat. No need to be jealous. She even told me so the other night."

I squashed the false hope that was rising as quickly as I could. "She actually said she'd be jealous if she thought I was hooking up with someone?"

"She did. She said that she'd be jealous if you were really into someone, because it'd mean you'd spend less time with her."

"Well, I guess that's something. Better than her saying she wouldn't care."

"Oh, she'd care all right. And I know how to prove it. You need to ask someone to homecoming, and not any old someone." Beth's look was calculating. "You need to ask me."

"Yeah, that'll go over real well. Then she can be pissed at both of us."

"No, hear me out. It has to be me. It won't be real, of course. We'll just pretend we're going together. We can call it off at the last minute. If we can get her to admit she likes you, then you can take her instead. Think about it: you can't fake-ask someone else. You'd be stuck with a real date to the dance that you *can't* bail on. Not without being considered the world's biggest jerk, at least."

I thought about it. Beth was right. If anything would spark a desperate admission of feelings from Bebe, it'd be the thought of Beth and me going to the homecoming dance together.

"Ok, you may be right. But if we do this, we can't make it look like we're hooking up. That'd piss her off, and then I'd lose her forever. It has to seem casual, accidental, even. Just as friends."

Beth smiled. "I have the perfect idea." She was suddenly excited. "I heard a rumor that Josh Sutton was going to ask me to the homecoming dance tomorrow."

"Josh Sutton?" I interrupted. "The kid from marching band? He's like, king of the dorks."

"The one and only," Beth said, crinkling her nose. "He's nice enough, but I don't really want to say yes. If and when he asks me, I'll just tell him I'm already going with you. Then we can tell Bea that you offered to take me so that I'd have an acceptable excuse to turn Josh down."

The plan sounded simple enough and believable enough. "Beth, you realize if we go through with this, nobody else will ask you because they'll think you're taken. If by some miracle things work out with Bebe and me, you won't have a date to the dance."

She laughed lightly and waved her hand, dismissing my concern. "Don't worry about me. I'll find someone at the last minute. Unlike Bea, I don't have a problem asking a guy out. If worse comes to worst, I'll just go stag. It won't be the end of the world. In fact, I'll enjoy my night as a solitary woman if it means you two finally get together." She smiled, and I could tell she meant every word she was saying.

"Are you sure you want to do this? It has the potential to backfire in a major way." I had to make sure Beth was all in before we did something so stupid.

"Of course," she said as she leaned across the seat and wrapped me in a big hug. She pulled away, grinning as if she were the lovesick fool instead of me. "Operation Cam and Bea Forever is officially underway." I'm not sure I'd have called it something so cheesy, but I had to admit, the name had a nice ring to it.

BIANCA

The team meeting didn't go as long as I'd expected. Coach Lambert dismissed us, and I made a beeline for the locker room. I was going so fast I almost missed Brady coming out as I headed in.

"Hey, Bea, you done already?"

"Yeah, it was a short meeting. You haven't even been over to the library yet, have you? I can find a ride with one of the girls, if you need to go. I totally understand."

"No big deal. I can research now or research later. That's the beauty of the Internet; it'll still be there whenever I get around to using it."

I chuckled. Brady was funny. I wanted to run in and take a shower, but I didn't want to make him wait if he needed to get home. "Are you in a hurry?" I asked, "or do I have time to take a shower?"

"That depends…"

"On what?"

"On whether or not we're still going to 7-Eleven?"

"And why does that matter?" Was he going to tell me I smell bad? I mean, I do, but I didn't think we were at that point in our relationship yet.

"Because if I'm just taking you home, then I know you'll get to shower pretty soon. But if we're going on a Slurpee date, I figured you might want to be clean."

"Are you suggesting that I smell bad?" I teased in mock horror.

"No." He gave me a wry grin. "You're too far away from me to come to that conclusion. What I'm saying is that I don't want to find out if you smell bad. Sweaty basketball player and Cherry Slurpee don't make for an appetizing combination. Trust me, I know."

I laughed at his candid comment. "Well, in that case, give me ten minutes. You've already showered. I don't want to be the only sweaty basketball player ruining the flavor of our drinks."

"Cool." He pulled out his phone. "I'll just wait right here."

I nodded and rushed into the locker room. I showered super quick, even washed my hair. Thank heavens I had some body spray, but I wished I'd had a toothbrush. But nobody goes to school in the morning thinking, *Better pack my toothbrush; never know when you might get some lip action.* I pulled out a stick of cinnamon gum. It would have to do. I strolled out of the locker room nine minutes from the time I walked in.

"Dang, you really meant ten minutes, didn't you?" Brady looked thoroughly impressed.

"Why so shocked? I'm a woman of my word."

"I'm not sure I've ever seen a girl get ready so fast."

"You've seen a lot of girls get ready, then?" I couldn't resist; he'd walked right into it.

Brady turned pink. "That's not what I meant... You know what I meant."

"I know what you meant, silly boy. I guess I'm not like other girls."

"You know, Bianca, I'm starting to realize that." He smiled and threw his arm around my shoulder as we walked toward the parking lot.

Brady drove an almost new Dodge Charger. You can tell a lot about a person based on the condition of their car. Brady's car was immaculate...and *sexy*. I shudder to think what my car says about me. If it wasn't for Beth being part owner and taking better care of it than I did, my car would probably scream *Disaster ahead, turn back now.* We reached the passenger door, and Brady opened it for me.

"Merci beaucoup, monsieur."

"Je vous en prie, mademoiselle."

"Hey. You know French?" I was hoping to impress him with my mad linguistic skills, but I didn't expect him to surprise me with his.

"Not really." He laughed. "I only took one year, then switched to Spanish because I thought it would be more practical."

"Good choice. I took two years to get my language credit out of the way, but now I wish I'd picked something I could use."

Brady hopped into the car and headed us toward 7-Eleven. He got a cherry Slurpee and I picked a Coke one, complaining about how they should have carried a Diet Coke flavor. He offered to pay for my drink but let me buy instead at my insistence. Once we were in the parking lot, we decided it was ridiculous that Cherry Coke wasn't a flavor. That would have been the bomb. So we decided to play Dr. Frankenstein and combine our Slurpees. Brady did the mixing and lost quite a bit on the pavement. He also got a bunch on his arms, which he tried to slurp off while holding both cups.

"I wonder if that's why they call them Slurpees," he said, licking the last bit of sticky juice off his arm. I laughed at his joke, and he handed a now Cherry Coke drink back to me.

"You should have left it. Brown and red arms are a good look for you."

On the way to my house, we decided to see if we could have an entire conversation in French before we reached our destination. This was a total bust because we didn't know how to say much more than *"Ou, est la bibliotheque?"* (Where is the library?) or *"Je voudrais un peu de pain."* (I would like some bread.)

"I'm outraged," I claimed, once I realized we wouldn't be having a sexy French conversation. "Who comes up with the curriculum? A bookworm with a craving for bread? They definitely aren't preparing us for a summer abroad."

"Yes, let's file a complaint with the school board," Brady agreed as he pulled up to my house. He left the engine running but got out of the car to open my door for me. "Thanks for hanging out, Bea."

"Thanks for the ride." I stood there, looking at him, not sure how to end the conversation. Did I shake hands with him? Give him a high five? Were we on hugging terms now?

Luckily, Brady made the decision for me. He leaned in for a quick hug and headed back to the driver's side. "See you tomorrow. It's been fun."

I smiled and waved as he drove down the street. Pretty good for a first non-date, or whatever it was. I hadn't had fun with a boy other than Cam in a long time. It felt pretty nice. I headed toward the front door, when I saw Cam and Beth in our car, wrapped in a tight embrace. They pulled away from each other and Beth said something, but I couldn't make out what it was.

Had they been in the car this whole time? They'd left the school like an hour ago. What could they possibly be talking about? It must not have been a bad thing, because Beth was smiling…and so was Cam. *Don't be jealous. It's probably nothing. Cam and Beth hug all the time. Not usually alone in parked cars, though…*

I walked to the front door and pretended like I hadn't noticed they were there. I'd been having such a good time with Brady, and one look of Cam with my sister put me right into a foul mood. I couldn't let him have control over my emotions like this anymore. As I stomped up to my room and threw myself down on the bed, I made a decision. I was going to move on from Cameron Bates, even if it killed me.

THE NEXT DAY IN GOVERNMENT CLASS, CAM AND BETH MADE me play middleman. As usual, we were seated alphabetically. I was a Bianca sandwich, with Beth seated in front of me and Cam directly behind. It started with Cam whispering in my ear.

"Hey, Bebe, can you pass this up to Beth?" He handed a tightly folded note over my shoulder. It had the end tucked in the way we used to do it when we were kids. So that nobody could "accidentally" peek at what was written inside. I did as I was told and tapped Beth on the shoulder with the note.

She took it from my hand without looking back, opened it, read it, then quickly scribbled something and folded it back up. She did the whole pretend to stretch thing and dropped it behind her on my desk. Before I could pass it back to Cam, he whispered in my ear again, snaking his arm around my side, hand outstretched. "That's for me."

I wanted to tell him a big fat DUH, but I also didn't want to get busted for passing the note, so I slipped it into his hand. A minute later, the note reappeared over my shoulder and I handed it off to Beth once more.

What was going on? I hadn't passed a note since freshman year. Weren't we a little old for this? Why not just text her? What was so important that it couldn't wait until after class? I wondered if it had something to do with them sitting in the car for so long yesterday afternoon. I was mildly annoyed that they'd ask me to risk the wrath of Mr. Collins by passing a note during his lecture. He wasn't dumb, and he wasn't very nice, either. He's the type of teacher who'd pick up the note and read it out loud.

Mostly, I was annoyed they'd folded the note in a way that prevented me from taking a peek before I passed it. If I ran the risk of getting in trouble, the least they could do was include me. Were they even going to tell me what they were talking about after class? I hated it when people kept secrets from me.

After a few more passes, I pulled out a pencil and scribbled on the outside: *I'm not passing this again. Talk to her after class.* Then I handed it back to Cam. I was getting irritated that they had something so secret between them. I know Cam and Beth are friends, but I was feeling selfish. He should have been passing secret notes with me, not Beth. They weren't the *secret note passing* kind of friends. Until yesterday, I didn't think they were the *sit in a parked car for a really long time having a heart-to-heart and hugging at the end* kind of friends, either. Cam didn't even do that kind of stuff with me.

A thought occurred to me. Was Cam having a hard time with something? Who would he go to if he were sad or upset about something really important? I'm not a very good listener, so it makes sense that he'd talk to Beth if he were struggling in some way. I felt a twinge of guilt. Maybe I was too busy being a hormonal teenager to realize that Cam might need me to be a better friend.

I didn't get the note back, so I sat there, trying not to let my mind wander as I listened to the lecture. After class, Beth got up in a hurry. "I've got to run. My lab partner was sick yesterday. I said I'd meet her early so she could copy my notes. See you fifth hour, Bea. Bye, Cam." She slung her backpack over her shoulder and scurried out the door.

I turned to Cam. "What's with all the super secret note passing? You thinking of going back to middle school?"

"Haha, funny girl." Cam's sarcasm was thick. It didn't escape my attention that he hadn't answered my question. Avoidance was never good.

I tried to get serious for a moment. "You know, Cam, if you ever had a problem, you could always talk to me, right? Beth isn't the only good listener in our family."

Cam pulled me into a hug and rested his head on top of mine. "Of course I know I could talk to you. You'd be the first person I'd ask if I needed something or tell if I had a problem." He let go and pulled back to look at me. "The note was just some questions I had about Mr. Collins's lecture." He was smiling, but it also seemed like he was holding back.

Bull crap. If the note was about class, he would have leaned over and asked me the question like he normally did. I wanted to call him out on the lie, but that wouldn't have helped me discover the truth. It would have given fuel for the fib monster to grow bigger. "Ok, whatever," I responded, a little snippy.

I gave him a forced smile. "I'll see you in chemistry," I

called over my shoulder and walked away. I shouldn't be so annoyed. Cam was allowed to have secrets. He was allowed to talk to Beth about them if he wanted to. He was as much her friend as he was mine. Just because I had a sick obsession with him didn't give me the right to act like I owned him. I hated that I was jealous. I wasn't really this person; only when it came to Cam.

At lunch I sat in my normal spot with the team, but I was in a grumpy mood so my participation in the conversation was lacking. I picked at my food, obsessing over what could have been in that note. What was so secret that they needed to exclude me? My feelings were hurt. I needed to stop acting like a spoiled baby.

My eyes had been bouncing between Cam and Beth across the lunchroom. I don't know what I expected to see. Secret hand signals, perhaps? Maybe they were going to sneak off together. But they were focused on their friends like they always were. Like I should be now.

I was feeling bad about thinking something was going on when I noticed Cam trying to get Beth's attention. Her eyes roamed the cafeteria, like she was looking for someone. She finally noticed Cam, and he held up his hands to his shoulders, mouthing something to her. She responded by shrugging her shoulders and shaking her head no. They were having a whole freaking conversation with their eyes. I couldn't do this. It shouldn't be a big deal that there was something between them which didn't involve me. But I was aggravated anyway. I needed chocolate. I got up and left without saying good-bye to my friends, heading for the vending machine outside the locker rooms.

Finally, fifth hour rolled around. We were playing basketball today in PE. This was good news for me, because I needed to blow off some steam. I changed into my uniform and headed out to the gym as Coach Lambert (who was also the phys ed teacher) blew the whistle, signaling the start of our five-lap warm-up. Beth jogged up behind me, Angelica in tow.

"Hey, Bea, how was your lunch?"

"Fine." My answer was clipped. "How was yours?"

"Oh, you know, same-old, same-old."

If Cam wasn't going to tell me what was up, Beth surely would. We didn't keep secrets from each other. Well, if you don't count the fact that I never told her who I liked. But we had an understanding where that matter was concerned, so it didn't feel like I was keeping secrets from her. I looked at her and casually asked, "So what's up with all the note passing between you and Cam in government today?"

"Nothing, really. He'd just heard a funny joke about cheerleaders this morning. He was bored, so he thought he'd tell it to me." She smiled as if she were actually recalling a funny joke.

I was hoping that her story would match his so that I wouldn't have to be mad about them lying to me, but deep down I already knew it wouldn't.

"Oh yeah?" I pushed. "I want to hear it."

"I don't remember how it went. I'd probably butcher the punch line without reading it first. But it was pretty funny."

My ass it was funny. "Ok, well maybe I'll ask Cam to tell

me later."

Angelica picked that moment to grace us with her thoughts. "Speaking of Cam, do either of you know if he has a date for homecoming yet? I was kind of hoping I could get him to ask me…"

Beth hesitantly answered, "I don't think he has a date yet. At least he hasn't mentioned it to me. You know Cam, he never asks girls out. Getting him to ask you might be difficult."

I was feeling vindictive. The words that popped out of my mouth were something I normally wouldn't have said. "You know, Angelica, maybe *you* should ask *him*. If you really want to go with him, that's probably the only way to make it happen."

"Really? You think he'd say yes?" Angelica asked with uncertainty.

Beth whipped her head toward me and gave me a look that screamed *What in the hell are you doing?* We both knew that Cam didn't have the least interest in Angelica Valdez. I think he liked it when she threw herself at him because it stroked his ego, but he'd never go out with her. He'd told us so. I knew it was wrong to set Angelica up for failure, but she bothered me, and right now I didn't care. It'd serve Cam right.

Of course there was the slight chance that he'd feel bad letting her down and actually say yes. It'd pretty much suck if Angelica ended up as Cam's date and I had to listen to her giggle and compliment him all night long. I guess if he said yes, then I deserved what was coming to me for suggesting it in the first place. I was willing to risk it.

"You'll never know unless you ask." My smile was sickly sweet. "But if you're going to ask him, you'd better think about doing it soon. Cam's a hot commodity. You don't want to risk someone else asking him first."

"Oh, you're so right. Thanks, Bianca." She smiled at me as if we were actually friends. We'd finished running, and Angelica headed to the middle of the court to stretch. I started to walk over behind her, but Beth grabbed my arm and held me back.

"*What* are you doing? Cam's going to be so angry if she asks him to homecoming and he finds out you're the one who told her to do it." Her look was a mix of worry and surprise that I'd do something so underhanded.

"Who am I to decide who Cam takes to homecoming? For all I know, he secretly likes Angelica and is dying for her to ask him out. It's not like he doesn't keep *other secrets* from me. Maybe I'm doing him a favor. Besides, you're always getting on my case to be nicer to Angelica. You should be glad that I was supportive." I'm fairly certain the bitterness was seeping from my pores.

"Bea, that wasn't nice. That was just a sneaky way of being mean. Cam will turn her down, and you know it. Then she'll be really depressed and I'll have to give her a shoulder to cry on." Beth was right. Of course I was being mean. But if she had to deal with the fallout of a broken-hearted Angelica, it served her right, too. She'd lied to me just as much as Cam had.

"Maybe he'll turn her down, but maybe he'll say yes.

Guess we'll just have to wait and see." I smiled and left her standing mid court. I always played with the boys on basketball day because it gave me more of a challenge. Beth shook her head and headed over to stretch with Angelica. I knew she was disappointed in me, but right now I didn't care.

Coach Lambert blew the whistle to dismiss us ten minutes early so we could change. I'd worked up a pretty good sweat, so I threw my hair up in a ponytail and went to the shower to rinse off. The extra time it took me guaranteed that I was the last person to leave the locker room. I rushed out the door because I still needed to swing by my locker and grab my chemistry book.

As I approached it, I saw Cam at his locker and Beth at hers, but in addition there was a very flirty Angelica Valdez standing between them. She was leaning in close and had her hand resting on Cam's forearm, no doubt working up the nerve to ask him to the dance. I smirked to myself. *This should be interesting.* I was about to reach my locker so I could have a front row seat for the drama unfolding, when Josh Sutton walked up to Beth, some of his marching band friends in tow.

Josh was a nice kid but kind of dorky. He was super smart, and I knew he had multiple honors classes with Beth. He wasn't really *ugly* so much as his personal hygiene habits could use work. He didn't smell bad or anything, but he had greasy, stringy hair and oily skin, causing some serious acne around the jaw. He always looked like he'd rolled out of bed and come to school without bothering to get ready.

Josh was like the king of the marching band crew. They

all adored and looked up to him. I'm not sure what it was. He was on the drum line, so I guess that was kind of cool. He must have had a really good personality. I'd never had much of a conversation with him, so I didn't really know. The one thing I *did* know is that he had a super huge crush on Beth. For once in my life, I wasn't envious of her.

Everyone stopped talking as Josh cleared his throat and said, "Hey, Beth."

"Hi, Josh, what's up?"

"Well, I wanted to ask you…" Josh looked around at the crowd and then down at the floor. "I mean, um, would you be interested in going to the homecoming dance with me?"

I saw the stressed out look in Beth's eyes. It was so slight that I bet nobody else picked up on it. I had to hand it to Josh. He had some major balls; kudos to him. However, I knew Beth didn't want to go to homecoming with Josh. The dance was a formal and supposed to be a magical night full of romance. Not an evening of small talk designed to keep your date from getting his hopes up about a good night kiss.

For a second I forgot about being pissed at her, and my instincts to jump to her rescue kicked in. Beth never said no to a boy who asked her out. I had to keep her from ruining her evening just to make sure Josh's feelings weren't hurt. My mind was searching for a good excuse when Cam stepped up first.

"Oh man, Josh dude, I'm sorry." Cam linked his arm with Beth. "Beth already has a date. I asked her this morning." Beth didn't look surprised by this revelation. I thought that Cam just said that as an excuse to get Beth out of a date with Josh. Seeing her reaction made me wonder if she knew it was coming. Is that why they were passing notes this morning? Was Cam asking Beth to homecoming? Kind of lame for Cam to do it in a note.

Beth smiled sweetly at Josh. She placed her hand on his arm as she spoke. "I'm so sorry, Josh. I would have loved to go, but you're just a day too late. Bad timing, huh?" Beth's apology seemed sincere. Probably because it was. She may not have wanted to go to the dance with him, but I knew it was killing her to disappoint and embarrass him in front of his friends.

Josh looked crestfallen, but he held his chin high and took the rejection like a man. "It's ok, Beth, no worries. I'll just have to make sure I ask sooner next time." His smile was forced. I was gaining a newfound respect for Josh Sutton. He was being very big about this.

Josh turned around and started to leave, but Beth kept hold of his arm. "Will you at least save me a dance?" she asked as she nodded her head toward Cam. "This big lug might have asked me first, but he doesn't have to monopolize my whole evening." There's the Beth I know. She was a fixer, and she wouldn't be ok with just telling him no.

Cam threw his hands up in surrender. "If the lady wants to dance with you, I won't be able to stop her. Go for it, man."

Josh smiled for real this time. "Well, since I'll have to ask someone else now…" His eyes deliberately shifted to Angelica as he looked her up and down. "I don't know how my date will feel about me ditching her to dance with you. I guess we'll have to play it by ear." I was surprised by his casual *who cares* response. Like he wasn't just rejected by the prettiest girl at school in front of all his friends. Damn. He was good. I was starting to see why the band geeks worshiped him. Josh had mad confidence.

"Fair enough." Beth laughed, and somehow the world was right between them. I don't know how she does it. They said their good-byes, and Josh left with his friends. That's when I remembered that Angelica had witnessed this whole exchange. She stood there, stiff as a board, face so red I thought her head might explode. She looked at Beth and opened her mouth to say something, probably to call her a nasty name, but then closed it quickly. Tears were welling up in her eyes, and it was clear that she'd felt betrayed. Then Angelica did something completely uncharacteristic. Instead of throwing a temper tantrum like I'd expected, she turned around and walked away.

"Angelica, wait..." Beth called after her, but she was already halfway down the hall.

"You asked her this morning, huh, Cam? When were you guys going to tell me? Is that what all your secret note passing was about?" I glared at both of them, then took the cue from Angelica and turned around, heading for the chemistry room. As I walked away, I heard Beth mutter something about damage control, and she took off after her friend.

"Bebe, come back here," Cam pleaded. I stopped walking but didn't turn around. "Bianca, please come back so I can explain." He never called me Bianca unless he was being really serious or he was really in trouble. I almost caved. His voice sounded pained. But I was hurt and angry, and that was enough to help me resist his request. I shook my head no and called out to him without turning around. "I'm going to be late for class." Then I walked away.

CAMERON

"Bianca, please come back so I can explain." I rarely called her Bianca unless I was in trouble with her, and right now, I'm pretty sure I was in very hot water. She ignored my request and left for class without me. Damn it. I turned around and banged my head against my locker. Angelica had looked super pissed. I'm not sure what that was about, but Beth took off after her before I could ask. I knew this whole homecoming date thing was a bad idea. I picked up my backpack and headed for Mr. Gardner's class. This wasn't how today was supposed to work. At least we were lab partners; she couldn't ignore me for the whole class.

I walked into chemistry as the bell rang, and I noticed that the lights were dimmed and the projector was turned on. Crap. I totally forgot that we were watching a movie today. Mr. Gardner always told us that we could sit wherever we wanted when we watched a movie—as long as we stayed quiet and paid attention. I looked at our table, and sure enough, Bebe wasn't at it. She was sitting between Brady and Mike. Great, not only had I pissed her off, but I'd pushed her straight into the arms of my competition.

"Mr. Bates, please find a seat; we're ready to start."

"Yes, sir." I stared at the table where Bebe sat. It was already pretty small, and having three people at it didn't leave much room. Not to mention that Bebe was sitting *between* Brady and Mike. Clever girl. Even if I pulled up a stool to the end of the table, I wouldn't be able to have a private conversation with her. I slumped down at my own table, resigned to defeat.

While the movie played, I kept glancing at Bebe and Brady. They were whispering quietly, and she was laughing like he was the funniest guy on the planet. They were sitting pretty close, touching shoulders, actually. Probably so that they wouldn't get caught talking. Luckily, Mr. Gardner noticed.

"Bianca, do I need to send you back to your seat?" Bebe shot me a glance. *Yeah, she's breaking the rules. Make her haul her ass back over here.*

"No, Mr. Gardner. Sorry. I promise we'll be quiet." She looked at me again, just to make sure that I got the point. She really didn't want to talk to me right now. True to her word, Bebe stayed quiet for the rest of the movie. She and Brady continued flirting back and forth by writing notes on a piece of paper in front of them. Maybe they'd be stupid enough to throw it away at the end of class so I could see what was so damn funny. The bell rang, but Bebe picked up the note and shoved it in her backpack, then walked out with Brady by her side.

Today was a drill day at basketball conditioning. We alternated each day between running/lifting and basketball skills. Normally if there was partner work, we were encouraged to pair up with someone from our team. But today, Coach Lambert asked us to pair up boy/girl. She wanted the girls to practice shooting around an opponent that was taller.

I looked at Bebe, but she ignored me and walked straight over to Brady. I guess I knew that was coming. At least during practice she was all business so I didn't have to witness them fawning all over each other. My frustration was wearing on me. I couldn't fix the problem if I couldn't get her to talk to me. She couldn't ignore me forever; I'd corner her in the car. Even if she wouldn't talk back, she'd be forced to listen.

Coach Adams blew the whistle and called the practice. I showered as fast as I could and hurried out the door to catch Bebe before she escaped. I stood outside for fifteen minutes, but Bebe didn't immerge. She couldn't hide in the locker room all day. I was getting ready to send one of the girls back in after her, but Beth walked up behind me. "Don't bother; she's already gone."

"She can't have gotten ready that fast; there's no way I missed her. I was in and out in like five minutes, and I've been standing by the door since I walked out." There wasn't another door exiting the locker room, unless she snuck out

113

through the gym. Darn, I didn't think about that. Beth opened her phone, scrolled through her texts, and read one out loud.

Bea: Skipped a shower. Don't wait for me. I'm catching a ride home with Brady.

I slid down the wall in frustration and parked it on the floor with my head in my hands. "It wasn't supposed to happen like this. She was *supposed* to hear about the homecoming arrangement from us, after the fact. When we could control how the story was presented. Not witness it unfolding firsthand. She's so pissed she won't even look at me, much less talk to me. She practically leapt into Brady's waiting arms. I don't think she's very jealous right now."

"I wouldn't say that." Beth sat on the floor next to me. "I think jealousy is half of the problem. The other half, I'm pretty sure, is the note passing, for some reason. She gave me the third degree during fifth hour, wanting to know what we were talking about. I didn't know what to tell her, so I made up something about you being bored. Said you were telling me a funny cheerleader joke you'd heard."

"Damn." I banged the back of my head against the wall repeatedly as I sighed. My poor head was taking a beating today. I probably deserved it. "I guess you and I don't have a super special neighbor sense, do we?" I asked. Beth looked confused. "Bebe asked me about the note passing, too, right after you left government. I told her that I was asking you some questions about the lecture."

"Ah, I see," Beth said. "We were caught in our lie. No wonder she's upset. I don't know who's more mad at me,

Bea or Angelica." Beth looked like someone had kicked her puppy.

"What's up with that, anyway? What was Angelica so pissed about?"

"She was getting ready to ask you to homecoming, right before Josh showed up."

"She what?"

"Yeah, she was asking Bea and me during PE if you had a date for homecoming yet. I told her that I didn't think you did. Bea suggested that she should go ahead and ask you, since you have that *no asking girls out* rule."

"Why would she do that? She doesn't like Angelica any more than I do."

Beth gave me a look, suggesting I was less than intelligent. "I'm guessing she did it to retaliate. She only told Angelica to ask you to the dance after she realized that we'd been lying to her about the note. Bea can be pretty mean when she's angry. I'm kind of mad that she dragged Angelica into it. I deserve it, but she doesn't." I wasn't following, so I waited for her to expound.

Beth sighed. "Why do you think Angelica was so angry? I told her that you didn't have a date to the dance, and then thirty minutes later you told Josh that you'd asked me this morning. Right in front of her. She thinks I flat-out lied to her."

"Ouch." I winced. "I'm so sorry, Beth, I didn't know."

"I know you didn't, you couldn't have. Don't worry about it." Her smile was sad. She put her hand on my knee and used it to provide leverage as she stood up. Then she turned around and offered me a hand. "Let me worry about Angelica. I know the problem with Bea is just as much my fault, but I think she's more likely to listen to you."

"I'm not so sure about that." I let Beth help me up, and we walked to the car.

"Please, you got that girl whipped. Why do you think she's so mad at you? She wouldn't be ignoring you if she didn't care...a lot. Just give her a few hours to calm down. You need time to figure out how to beg for forgiveness anyway." She elbowed me playfully in the side.

"What should I say to her? I'll probably only get one chance to make this right. I can't screw it up." Fear was creeping into my gut. It might already be too late.

Beth hooked her arm through mine as she spoke with sympathy and determination. "Cam, there's only one thing you *can* tell her. If you want to fix this, you're going to have to tell her the truth."

My heart sank. That's what I was afraid of.

I SPENT THE AFTERNOON CHECKING MY PHONE. WAITING for some indication that Bea was ready to talk. But she didn't call, and neither did Beth. I stalled as long as I could. At eight o'clock, I sent Beth a text. I wouldn't be able to sleep until this was taken care of.

C: Have you talked to Bebe yet?
B: Nope. It's been radio silence all afternoon.

C: Do you think she's cooled off at all?

B: She's sitting on the couch with a quart of rocky road and watching *Love & Basketball*...

B: What do you think?????

C: Crap that's bad.

B: Yep.

C: I'm coming over. Don't let her slam the door in my face.

B: Not sure I can stop her. Good luck.

I put my phone back in my pocket and looked in the mirror. I changed into her favorite shirt of mine, and sprayed on some of the cologne she liked. It couldn't hurt, right? Then I walked across the street to pay the piper. I took a deep breath and knocked on the door. Bianca's dad answered.

"Well, hello, Cameron, what can I do for you at this hour?"

"Sorry it's so late, sir. I need to talk to Bianca; is she home?"

He called into the family room, "Bianca, sweetheart, Cameron is here."

"Tell him I'm not home!" she yelled back, with the obvious intent for me to hear. Mr. Barnes eyed me suspiciously.

"We had a fight today. I came to apologize." Mr. Barnes's smile was sympathetic. At least one person in their house still liked me.

"Bianca." He used his *stern parent* voice. "Don't be rude. Please come to the door."

I heard the television pause, and she walked into the kitchen, probably to put the ice cream back in the freezer.

She was in fuzzy pajama pants and a T-shirt that had a picture of a stick figure with a basketball in its head in place of a brain. She had big, furry slippers on her feet and her hair piled high on her head. I couldn't help but smile, she looked so adorable. Even when she was mad at me. She came to the door and stood there with her hands folded across her chest, silent and staring.

Mr. Barnes cleared his throat. "Ahem… Why don't you two go out on the porch so you can have some privacy?" He flipped on the front porch light and pushed us out the door, shutting it behind us. Bebe walked over to the porch swing and sat down. I followed and stood in front of her. "Can I sit?" I gestured to the swing beside her.

"Depends; are you here to feed me more lies?" The question still hurt, but it didn't have as much bite as I expected. Maybe she *had* cooled off a little. I took a seat next to her.

"Bebe, you didn't see what you thought you were seeing, and you didn't give me or Beth a chance to explain." She didn't argue, so I pushed on. "I *am* going to explain everything, but first I owe you an apology for not being truthful with you about the note." She made a grunting noise but otherwise stayed silent. "The only reason Beth and I lied was because we didn't want to hurt your feelings."

"Lot of good that did," she muttered as she pulled her knees up to her chest and hugged them.

"Beth came to me with a problem yesterday. She heard a rumor that Josh Sutton was going to ask her to homecoming this morning. She was freaking out because she didn't want to say yes, but she didn't have an excuse to say no, either. I told her that if Josh asked her, she should tell him that she was already going with me."

Bebe looked up at me. "Is that the truth?"

"I swear. The note we were passing this morning was me finding out if Josh had asked her to the dance yet. I needed to know if I should pretend we were going to homecoming together or not. She told me he hadn't, and I asked her if she knew when it was going to happen. That's what the entire conversation was about, nothing more."

"If that's all you were talking about, then why the big secret? Why lie to me?"

"We were afraid that if you thought Beth and I were going to the dance together that your feelings would be hurt. We'd planned to tell you that the arrangement was just an excuse, if it happened, but figured there was no point bringing it up until then. We weren't even sure Josh would ask her. If he didn't, then she wouldn't need a fake homecoming date."

Bebe scoffed. "You were afraid my feelings would be hurt if you asked Beth out? That's what all of this was about? I don't care if you go to the dance with Beth. I don't give a rat's ass who you go with. Geez, Cam, you're such a conceited asshole." My heart was ripping in two. She tried to slap me on the arm, but I grabbed her hand and held it to my chest so she couldn't pull it away. She struggled against me, but I gripped harder. Then she turned her head so I couldn't see her face.

"Bebe, look at me." She shook her head no. "Bianca, please?" My voice was soft now, pleading. She finally gave in and turned her head to me, her eyes glistening with tears. I wanted to kiss her in that moment, kiss all the sadness away. I wanted to hold her and tell her that I was being such an idiot because I loved her and she didn't love me back. I was so close to telling her how I felt. But she'd just told me that she didn't care who I was with. How could I take that chance now? I'd rather have her friendship than not have her at all.

"I wasn't *trying* to be a conceited asshole. I guess that's just one of my many natural talents." I gave her a small smile. She arched an eyebrow at me and I let out a single laugh. "I wasn't. If *you* asked someone besides *me* to the dance, my feelings would be hurt. You're one of my best friends. You never ask guys out. If you finally decided to break your rule and you chose to blow it on another guy, I'd probably turn into a jealous lunatic."

She really laughed at me then. "You're so full of crap."

"That's what you think, but I know the truth." I winked at her, needing to lighten the mood. I finally let go of her hand on my chest, and she pulled it into her lap. "So, am I forgiven?"

"I don't know. I guess I should forgive you, since you went through all the effort of wearing my favorite shirt and cologne." She smirked.

"You noticed that, huh?" I couldn't hold back my smile. "I was kind of hoping it'd be sort of a subliminal peace offering."

She nodded her head. "It *was* a good idea." Bebe paused for a long moment, then got serious again. "Do you promise you'll never lie to me again? I might not have cared if you and Beth were going to homecoming together, but it was eating me up that I thought you were sneaking around and lying to me. You and Beth are my best friends; I need to believe that I can trust you."

I held up my hand like a Boy Scout. "I promise you, Bianca Olivia Barnes, that I will never lie to you again. Cross my heart, hope to die, stick a needle in my eye."

"I'll hold you to that. If you lie to me again, you might as well walk around with eye patches on to protect yourself." She smiled at me, and I knew I'd been forgiven.

I put my arm around Bebe and leaned in to kiss the side of her head. "I'm sorry." I breathed into her hair.

She wrapped her arms around my waist and sighed. "I'm sorry, too," she whispered.

We sat like that for a while, rocking on the porch swing in companionable silence. Me holding her, and her snuggled up against my chest, the smell of her orange blossom shampoo tickling my nose. *I love you, Bianca*, I whispered to her in my mind. And just for a moment, I pretended that she whispered back to me...*I love you, too.*

. . . . .

B: How'd it go?
C: I think I've been forgiven :-)
B: Did you tell her the truth? Because I don't want to tell her the wrong story again. LOL
C: Yes I told her the truth.

B: Which was?

C: That we'd planned the fake homecoming date so you wouldn't have to go with Josh. And that we didn't tell her the truth because we didn't want to hurt her feelings.

B: Ha! And how'd that go?

C: She hit me and called me a conceited jackass.

B: ROFL!!! Did you tell her how you feel?

C: I couldn't.

I waited for another text, but my phone rang instead. Beth's name flashed on the screen and I picked it up. "Hello?"

"Sorry, I wanted to scold you and I didn't think the full effect would come through over a text message."

"The proper response to someone when they say hello is to say hello back."

"Cam, this isn't funny. Why didn't you tell her how you feel?"

"You weren't there; you didn't hear her. I was going to tell her, I swear. I told her everything else that happened. I came clean about the note, and that we knew Josh was going to ask you to the dance so we planned a fake date to get you out of it."

"Did you tell her that the real reason we were faking a date was to make her jealous?"

"Well, no, but..." I was cut off before I could defend myself.

"Then you didn't tell her the truth. If she ever finds out that you kept something from her, she'll never forgive you. Bea can hold a grudge for a really long time." I was definitely feeling her scolding right about now.

"Do you know what she said to me right before she called me a conceited jackass?" I asked. "She said that she didn't care if you went to the dance with me. That she, and I quote, 'didn't give a rat's ass who I went to the dance with,' only that she'd been lied to. How was I supposed to tell her my real feelings after that?"

"I don't know? You open your mouth and words come out? Truthful words..." Beth was getting frustrated. That seemed to be happening a lot lately.

"Bethany," I said her name as gently as I could so that she'd calm down and listen to reason. "She doesn't like me. She basically said as much. There's no point in telling her how I feel and making everyone awkward."

"Cameron." She used my full name, too, but with none of the gentleness that I'd used with hers. "I can't just stand around and watch you self-destruct because you and Bianca are prideful idiots. She likes you, I know she does. I'd be willing to stake our friendship on it. I'd even be willing to bet you and Bea's friendship. This has to stop. If you don't tell her how you feel, then I'm going to."

"You can't. I'll lose her." I was on the verge of tears. I'm not much of a crier. Not over my feelings, at least. I cry in movies when little kids die or underdog teams win champi-onships. You know, the kind of stuff you're *supposed* to get teary-eyed for. I'm man enough to admit it. But this was too much. I'd been holding in my feelings for two years. If I tell her now, I risk losing her, but if I don't tell her at all, I'll lose her anyway when we graduate. Maybe I'll get lucky and she'll change her mind once she knows how I feel.

Beth's voice took on a kinder, softer quality. "I know it'll be hard, but I promise you it *will* be worth it." She was using her mom voice on me.

"Ok, Mom." I couldn't help the jab, and it made me smile. A tiny, pathetic smile, but a smile nonetheless. There was a long silence before I spoke again.

"I'll tell her. I promise. I just need a little more time. I need to find a way to show her how I feel before I tell her. That way she'll believe me when I do."

"Fine." Beth had switched from her caring and concerned mom voice to her no-nonsense mom voice. "I'll give you one week."

"A week? What can I possibly accomplish in a week?"

"A lot more than you think. You need a deadline, Cam, or you'll never actually do anything."

"But a week?"

"Fine," she conceded. "Ten days. Tomorrow is Wednesday. I'll give you through next Friday night. If you haven't told her how you feel by then, I'm marching into her room first thing Saturday morning and telling her for you."

I knew she'd do it, too. "Crap, Beth, you really *are* starting to sound like my mom."

"That's because you're desperately in need of a little tough love." We were on the phone, but I could hear her smile through the receiver. I guess she was embracing her role as my third parent.

"Ok. I'll figure something out."

"Good boy." She was really running with this mom thing. "Now I better go, because I just heard Bea come upstairs and I have some groveling of my own to do. Thank heavens you went first. I'll probably dodge the conceited jackass accusations."

"Did you just say ass?" I laughed in disbelief. Beth never swore.

"It was a direct quote. Don't make me use it again."

"Yes, ma'am. I guess you better go make your peace."

"It *will* be all right, Cam, I promise."

"Thanks. Good luck."

We hung up the phone, and I lay back on my bed with my basketball, tossing it into the air and catching it over and over again. I sure hoped she was right.

BIANCA

I'D WANTED TO STAY MAD AT CAM FOR LONGER. I TRIED, really I did. I can usually hold a grudge like nobody's business. But where Cameron Bates is concerned, somehow my defenses are weakened. He's my kryptonite. The only other person that I can't stay mad at for long is Beth, and since I'd forgiven Cam, I guess I needed to forgive her, too.

I'd come upstairs and lain down on my bed after talking to Cam out on the front porch. I needed to think before I spoke to my sister. They'd been worried about making me upset with a fake homecoming date scheme. That was utter nonsense, because I'd have been totally fine. It even sounds like a plan I'd have come up with myself, had they bothered to involve me in the plotting.

Their worry over my feelings could only mean one thing.

One, or both of them, suspected how I felt about Cam. My money was on Beth. I've never been able to hide much from her. She calls her ability to read me her *Super Secret Twin Sense*, but I've always thought of it more as a mother's intuition. Her powers seemed to amplify whenever I was about to do something stupid that would get me in trouble.

If Beth thought I had feelings for Cam, then I hadn't been playing it cool enough. Fake date to homecoming my butt. Their dumb plan was pushed into motion by fate. It was the universe, telling me it was on to me. Letting me know that my daydreams had been written across my face. I knew how to convince Beth that I wasn't deeply, madly in love with Cam. Their fake date to the homecoming dance needed to be a real one. If I pushed for them to go together, maybe they'd believe me when I said I was ok with it.

It would suck, of course, watching them dance all night, wishing it were me in Cam's arms. Unfortunately, it may even plant a seed that hadn't been there before. I didn't *really* think Cam and Beth were into each other, but forcing them together in such a romantic situation might light a spark. Coming clean about my feelings so I could take him to the dance myself would definitely ensure they went together. Their date to the dance was inevitable. But if they went at my insistence, maybe the night wouldn't end with a goodnight kiss…or something more.

Fate was a cruel master. I had to push Cam and Beth together in hopes of keeping them apart. I sat up on my bed, knowing what I had to do. I was getting up to talk to Beth, when I heard a knock on my door. "Bea, can I come in?"

Beth's voice was hesitant.

"Sure," I called as I leaned back against my headboard. Beth entered the room with an apologetic smile.

"So...Cam talked to you already?" She asked it like a question, but I was pretty sure she knew the answer. Beth probably sent him first so I'd be less mad when I got to her. It's what I would have done.

"Yes, we had a talk."

"And?"

"*And* you guys are both idiots. Why didn't you tell me about Josh Sutton? I can't believe you went to Cam first. I'm your sister, for crap's sake. Your best friend. Your freaking twin. Me, *I'm* all those things, not Cam. You should always come to me first." I pouted, but it was clear that I wasn't mad at her anymore.

Beth had the decency to look really guilty. "I'm sorry, Bea. I was freaking out because I really didn't want to say yes to Josh, and I didn't have a good enough reason not to. You'd stayed for that basketball meeting and Cam was the only one around, so I told him because I was desperate to find a solution."

Well, that explained the long car conversation I stumbled across yesterday. "Why didn't you say something to me when I got home?"

She'd sat down cross-legged on the end of my bed, and now she was looking down at her lap, playing with the hem of her shirt. "Well..."—she started—"I still think you like Cam. I worried that if you thought we were going to the dance together, you'd feel like I'd betrayed you. We were going to tell you about the plan so you didn't get the wrong idea, but then Josh asked me while Cam was actually standing there. Cam had to spill the beans before we'd gotten the chance to let you know."

Ok, so Beth knew how I felt. *Don't stress about it, Bianca. Deny, deny, deny.* "Beth, I've already told you…" She didn't let me finish, holding up her hand to stop me.

"I know, I know, you don't like Cam. Say it as many times as you want; I'll never believe it. You may not fess up, but I know the truth. You can't fool me."

"Well, if you really believe that I like Cam enough to be worried over a fake dance proposal, then you were very shortsighted in your plan."

"What are you talking about? It's not like we're actually going to the dance together."

"That's my point exactly. Now you *have* to go together." Beth looked confused. "Think about it, brainiac. Boy, for a smart girl you really are slow sometimes. You still have to go with Cam, or Josh will know you lied to him and you'll hurt his feelings anyway. Either that, or he'll find out you're free that night and ask you to go again. You probably let him down a little *too* gently." I smirked. I was kind of enjoying her predicament. "Not to mention Angelica will just think you lied to her…again." At the mention of Angelica, Beth groaned and threw herself across my bed, burying her head under my pillow. "How's that going, by the way? Did you tell her what was really going on?"

Beth rolled on her back and put the pillow behind her head. "Yes, but she's still super mad. I told her that Cam lied to Josh and we hadn't actually decided to go together that morning. It's not like she's never done the same thing to avoid a date. Of course, she says no to the guy's face sometimes, too. She still thinks you told her to ask Cam so that she'd look stupid when he turned her down."

"That's probably because I did."

"I know that. You're a big fat jerk by the way, but I still stuck up for you with Angelica. I told her you didn't know about the arrangement either." Beth put the pillow over her face and screamed into it. I tried not to smile, but I couldn't help feeling that she was getting what she deserved. *I'm a horrible sister.* "If I show up at that dance with Cam, she'll never speak to me again. I'm screwed either way."

I couldn't help but dish a little of her own motherly advice. "I guess next time, you'll have to think about the potential consequences of your decisions *before* you act on them." I delivered my wisdom authoritatively.

Beth rolled her eyes at me, her voice dripping with sarcasm. "Thanks, Mom."

She quickly realized what she'd said and slapped her hand over her mouth in shock. That was my line; she'd never used it. We looked at each other, then erupted in a fit of giggles. Beth looked up to the sky. "Sorry, Mom." She sighed and cast her eyes in my direction. "Our mother is probably looking down on us and wishing she could spank our butts for all the times we take her name in vain." The smile slipped from her face, and her eyes glossed over.

I crawled over to Beth and put my arm around her. "Well, since you obviously got your practical and responsible nature from our father, I like to think that I got my wicked streak from Mom. I bet she appreciates all the mom jokes; she probably even laughs at them. I think it makes her happy to know that even though we don't remember her, we haven't forgotten her."

"You really think so?"

"Yes, I do. And I also think she's incredibly proud of the person you are. You're an excellent mother." She elbowed me lightly in the side, but her smile was back. "I couldn't have our real mom, so God blessed me with the best sister-mother anyone could ask for."

Tears spilled from Beth's eyes. "I'm so sorry I hurt you, Bianca."

I laid my head on her shoulder. "It's ok. You're my twin *and* my surrogate mother. I'll always love you. No matter what."

Cam must have still been feeling guilty, because when he met us at the car Wednesday morning, there were no sassy remarks. Or maybe it was because he was running behind and needed to stay on my good side. If we didn't hurry, we'd be late for school.

"Good morning, Beth; good morning, Bebe." He gave Beth a hug, then wrapped an arm around me, in sort of a side hug, while kissing me on the temple. Weird. *But* amazing-*weird. Is that even a thing?* The weirdest part wasn't that he had kissed me; it was weird because even though it was unexpected, it didn't *feel* weird. It felt natural.

Of course I couldn't let it slide. "What was that for? Still trying to get back in my good graces? I already told you that you're forgiven."

"Can't a guy hug his friends?" I gave him a pointed stare. I was referring to the kiss, and he knew it. He smiled and answered the question that I'd sent with my eyes. "I'm just glad you aren't mad anymore, so I'm in a good mood." Cam opened the passenger door but didn't get in; instead, he held it wide and stepped away. "In fact, I thought I'd offer you the front seat today, if you want it." His eyes were sparkling with mischief.

"Don't do it, Cam," Beth warned. "If you give her an inch, she'll take a mile...or two...or ten."

"Is this some kind of a trick? Do you have a water balloon, or an egg, in your pocket that you're waiting to smash over my head?" I wanted the front seat, but I was very skeptical.

He pulled his hands out of the pocket of his hoodie and held them up to show they were empty. Then he patted his pockets down. "No tricks. I promise. Just consider it part of my apology. A peace offering."

"You worried that the shirt and the cologne weren't enough?" I smirked at him as I got into the front seat. Beth looked confused but got in the car without asking for me to elaborate. The seat was really far back because Cam had been the last one to sit in it. I looked at him in the rearview mirror and laughed out loud. His knees were practically in his chest. I guess Beth's rule about the front seat might have been a fair one. I pulled my seat up all the way and I buckled my seat belt.

We got to school a little later than normal, so I had to go straight to English without stopping at my locker. I sat down at my desk and Cam slid in behind me.

"All right, class, please take out your books and turn to chapter three on editing," Ms. Cutter announced from the front of the room. She was writing something on the whiteboard.

"Crap. I forgot my book. We didn't have time to go to our lockers." I groaned. Ms. Cutter had a strict *come to class prepared or don't come at all* policy. She'd give you a pass to your locker, but it would usually be accompanied by a pass to detention.

"I don't have mine, either." Cam frowned. "What are the chances she won't notice?"

"Considering she walks up and down the rows to make sure we're working, I'd say they're slim." I didn't really want to miss conditioning because I was in detention. Coach Lambert would have an aneurysm, and then she'd torment me with extra suicides. The boys' coach was much more forgiving. Adams would give the guys a slap on the wrist and tell them not to let it happen again. I turned in my seat. "Ms. Cutter loves you. You're way less likely to get detention than I am. Plus, Coach Adams won't punish you eternally if you *do* get detention. Tell her you need your book, and grab mine from my locker, while you're at it. Please?" I gave him big, sad puppy dog eyes. "I'll owe you a favor, anything, anytime."

Cam watched me, weighing his options. "Ok, fine, but if I get detention, you owe me a lot more than a favor." His eyes filled with mischief just like they had this morning, and I had a feeling I could end up regretting my answer. "I'm thinking a backrub or a home cooked dinner. Maybe a make-out session?" He raised his eyebrows in question, waiting for me to freak out. I kept my face unreadable, but my mind wandered to thoughts of making out with Cam. Was it wrong to hope he got detention?

We were quickly running out of time, so I agreed to his terms. "Fine, fine. Just go get the books before it's too late." I grabbed his hand and wrote my locker combination on it in pen.

Cam cleared his throat, and he raised his hand. Ms. Cutter turned from the whiteboard to face him. "Yes, Mr. Bates?"

"Ms. Cutter, I don't have my book." He frowned, a penitent student. "My ride was having car troubles this morning, and I didn't have time to go to my locker." *That's right, Cam, charm her pants off.* "I thought you'd appreciate it if I was at class on time, so I came straight here." He turned on the hundred-watt smile, bringing the dimples out in full force. Nobody could resist the dimples, especially Ms. Cutter.

"I'd have appreciated it if you'd been in class on time *and* prepared." She scolded him, but it wasn't very convincing. Ms. Cutter picked up her slip of hall passes and scribbled on one, then held it out to him. "I'll let it slide this time, since it's your first infraction of the year. Next time, you'll get detention. You have three minutes to be back."

"Thanks, Ms. Cutter, you're the best." She tried to hide her smile as he grabbed the slip from her hand and headed out the door.

Two minutes and forty-eight seconds later, Cam walked back through the door, two books under his arm. Ms. Cutter was rummaging through her desk drawer for something, so she didn't notice that little detail. Cam's eyes found mine, and he winked as he put the pass on her desk and headed for his seat. I grinned. I knew he wouldn't get in trouble. He handed me my book as he sat down.

Cam leaned over his desk and whispered into my ear. I'd worn my hair in a high ponytail that morning, so his lips were practically touching my earlobe. His warm breath was tickling the skin on my neck. My eyes closed involuntarily, and I had to repress the shudder that ran through my body. Luckily, I was wearing a long-sleeve shirt, because goose bumps were covering my arms.

"You were right; no detention. Guess you're off the hook, Bebe." I could feel his lips turn up in a smile.

Well, that's unfortunate for me, now isn't it?

"Also, there was something on your locker when I got there."

"Mr. Bates, are you following along?" Ms. Cutter knew he wasn't, but he could do no wrong in her eyes.

Cam sat back in his seat and opened his book. What did he mean, there was something on my locker? Did he mean someone had vandalized it? Did Angelica decide to retaliate by writing filthy names on it with permanent marker? I wouldn't put it past her and wouldn't say I didn't deserve it, either.

Cam couldn't just tell me something like that and then not tell me what he'd seen. I ripped a piece of paper from my notebook and scribbled on the top.

What was on my locker?

I folded the note hastily and slipped my hand behind me under his desk so that it was resting on his knee. Ms. Cutter would've definitely noticed the old stretch and drop.

Cam's hand reached out for mine and grabbed the note. The brief touch of his fingertips tangling with mine made me feel warm all over. *I'm pathetic.* I waited for a minute, pretending to be engrossed in my text, when he leaned forward and his hand wrapped around my waist from behind. He dropped the note in my lap. I waited until Ms. Cutter looked away and unfolded the paper on my open book.

It was an envelope taped to the front of your locker with your name printed on it. Looked like it was a card or something. I didn't grab it because I didn't know if you'd want me to leave it for you. Ms. Cutter keeps looking back here, so let's talk about it after class.

I left his message open on my textbook and started taking notes on the paper below it, periodically glancing back up at Cam's writing. A simple letter taped to my locker? Or an envelope filled with anthrax spores from a pissed off cheerleader seeking revenge?

I looked at the clock. Thirty-five minutes left of class. The worst part was that I didn't have time to visit my locker between first and second period. I'd have to wait until just before government to find out what it was. Hopefully it was still there. Unless it really was anthrax. This was going to be a long hour and a half.

The bell finally rang, and I looked at Cam. "So this letter on my locker, was there anything suspicious about it? Was my name pasted on it with letters cut from a magazine, or was it written in blood perhaps?"

He laughed at me. "What kind of letter are you expecting? A death threat?"

"Something like that. I'm pretty sure Angelica is going to have it out for me after yesterday's little homecoming exhibition."

"Well, if it makes you feel any better, your name wasn't written in blood. But the handwriting actually *did* look kind of girly, and the envelope was pink."

So the envelope was supposed to look enticing? Anthrax spores were seemingly more likely by the minute.

I made it through second hour just short of being killed by curiosity and dashed out the door, straight to my locker. I stopped and examined the envelope. It looked harmless enough, and Cam was right; the handwriting was kind of girly. I'm pretty sure Angelica isn't smart enough to really booby trap an envelope. She's more the emotional damage type. I was snapped out of my analysis when Cam and Beth walked up beside me.

"Ooh, Bea, what's that?" Beth sounded excited, much more than I was.

"I don't know. I'm in the middle of trying to decide if it's a death threat from Angelica."

"Don't be ridiculous, Bea; Angelica would never send a card with a death threat." Beth smirked. "She'd just say it to your face. Open it already, would you? I'm dying to know what's in it." Beth was bouncing on her peppy little cheer toes.

She was right. Angelica probably wouldn't waste her time threatening me so discreetly. She'd do it loudly and in front of a lot of people for maximum attention. I reached up and grabbed the envelope off my locker, then turned it over. It'd been sealed shut. *Here goes nothing…* I carefully opened it and pulled out a piece of plain white cardstock, cut and folded to the shape and size of a card. On the inside was a note, typed on plain printer paper.

Dear Bianca,

I hope this letter doesn't freak you out, but I've wanted to tell you for a while now how I feel about you. I know it's a little cowardly to tell you in a note. I'm sorry I don't have the nerve to tell you in person. Hopefully I will sometime soon, but for now, this will have to do.

I'm not really sure where to start, so I guess I'll begin by letting you know some of the things I like about you. You're an amazing person. Funny and witty and sarcastic. You make me laugh whenever I'm with you. You're so talented as a basketball player, which I have to tell you is super hot. You're wicked smart but play it down because you're real, not pretentious. You're loyal to your friends and your team, and no matter what, you'd have their backs.

To top it all off, you're one of the most beautiful girls I've ever known. I saved this for last because it's not the only reason I like you, but it's definitely a bonus. I can't help but stare when you walk into a room, because you light it up. I have to admit I   find myself thinking about you more often than I probably should.

I know I may sound like a stalker, but I promise I don't have any creepy stalker tendencies. I'm not some sappy girly dude, either. Maybe that's why this is too hard to say in person. :-) I just needed to get all of this off my chest. Sorry it's taken me so long to admit my feelings. You deserve to be told how wonderful you are every day.

Yours - ?

Oh. My. Gosh. It's a love letter. I looked over my shoulder and up and down the hallway. Maybe the writer was standing close by, watching me read it. *Holy Crap. What if he IS watching me read it, right now? What if he's a weirdo? What if he's not a he? No, no, no, he said he was a dude.* I shook my head, mind racing. Who in the world would send *me* a love letter?

"Eeeek!" Beth squealed over my shoulder, her bouncing now uncontrollable. Guess she'd been reading along. She grabbed me by the arms and started shaking me. "Oh my gosh, Bea. You have a secret admirer. That's so romantic." She was grinning from ear to ear. "I wonder who it is? From what he said, it must be someone you know and talk to, at least a little."

Cam was standing over my shoulder, reading the note, too. Maybe I should have concealed it better. Who knew what kind of ribbing I'd get from Cam about this. "Guy sounds like a loser to me. He should have had the man parts to come tell you himself." I looked up at him, and the faintest of smiles played on his lips. He'd definitely be making fun of me.

"What?" I asked him sarcastically. "You don't think it's romantic?"

"Oh, sure. It's romantic…If you're a sissy."

"Well, what would you have done differently? *Mr. I'm the bomb at expressing my feelings, which is why I've had plenty of steady girlfriends?*"

"Dang, why don't you tell me what you really think?" Cam's words were accusatory, but it was clear that he wasn't upset. He looked like he was going to laugh. "I don't know, *Bianca*. Maybe I wouldn't have done it differently. For all you know, I would have done the *exact. Same. Thing.*" Cam stared at me, his eyes boring holes into mine, waiting for a reaction. Then he turned the conversation back to me. "You know, Bebe, you've conveniently avoided telling us how *you* feel about having a secret stalker."

I *had* avoided it, because I wasn't sure how I felt about it yet. I was still stunned by the fact that someone actually liked me and not Beth. I wouldn't say that, so instead I offered, "I don't know. I'm still trying to decide if it's a practical joke. I mean, there haven't been any guys acting interested in me lately."

"I think that's the point, Bebe; he's telling you in a letter because he can't tell you how he feels in person." Cam was giving me the *duh* look.

"I know, but this letter was delivered completely out of the blue. Forgive me if I decide to wait a day or two for the hidden camera host to pop out and tell me I'm being pranked. I suppose by then I'll know what to think, once I've decided it's the real deal."

The warning bell for third period rang. "Bea, you're completely hopeless." Beth sighed. "Why can't you just accept it for what it is and be excited that somebody *loves* you?" She said the word *loves* as if she were an eight-year-old telling me I was k-i-s-s-i-n-g someone in a tree.

"I don't know," I answered as the three of us headed toward government. "I guess I just think that it's too crazy to be true." I had no clue who'd left the note, and I wasn't sure I could believe their words until I knew who my mystery man was.

CAMERON

LAST NIGHT AFTER I'D SPOKEN WITH BETH, I WAS A HOT mess. She'd given me an ultimatum: either I tell Bebe how I felt, or she would. So I wrote a letter. I'd spent most of the night writing and rewriting that stupid note. I hadn't been able to sleep because I was stressed about delivering my message, so of course I overslept the next morning.

I thought I was busted when Bebe asked me to prove I wasn't hiding anything destructive in my pocket. I was sure she'd ask me to show her the inside. Luckily, she was satisfied with the pat down. Even luckier, we needed our English books and I had an excuse to go to her locker. That dumb envelope was burning a hole in my sweatshirt. Still, I almost chickened out.

I observed Bebe carefully as she read my sappy love

letter. She looked overwhelmed, not at all excited. I'd hoped for a better reaction than a blank stare. Trying to play it cool, I told her the letter writer was a loser. In hindsight, I realize that was probably a bad idea. I really needed to stop giving her mixed signals. And, I needed to know what she was thinking. So I turned the conversation back on her.

"I'm still trying to decide if it's a practical joke. I mean, there haven't been any guys that have acted interested in me lately." She answered, truly mystified.

Yes, there had been. Brady had been all over her ever since school started. She really was oblivious if she didn't notice that. I wanted to scream and pull my hair out. Why couldn't she see what I saw in her? She was perfect, and I'd just told her so. Bebe had Beth on such a high pedestal that she couldn't see her own amazing qualities. It was maddening. I was going to have to do a lot more than write her a love note, if I wanted to get her out of her own head.

We had a test in government today that took up the whole hour, and Bebe was done long before me. I was still finishing my last question as the bell rang. She gathered up her stuff and patted me on the arm. "See you in sixth," she whispered, then headed out the door. Beth had gone without me, too, so I wasn't able to talk about the situation until lunchtime. She texted me.

B: That letter on Bea's locker WAS from you, right?
C: Who else would it be from?
B: Just checking. :-) Cam, it was so good!
C: I don't think Bebe would agree.
B: Don't freak out. She just needs to process.

C: She didn't seem too impressed or very happy to have a secret admirer.

B: Chill. Bea's probably obsessing over who it is as we speak.

I looked over at Bebe's lunch table and caught her staring back at me. I smiled and waved. Did she suspect that I was the one who sent the note? Part of me hoped so. That'd make this whole charade a lot easier. She smiled back, like she felt guilty she'd been caught, then turned her attention to her friends.

C: I don't know...

B: Trust me. So what do you have planned next?

C: I'm not sure yet, but I know it has to be better than my lame note.

B: I already told you, the note wasn't lame. It was perfect.

C: I guess we'll see tomorrow when I make my next move.

B: I can't wait. You better make it good.

C: Geez, Beth. No pressure or anything.

B: I know you'll come up with something awesome. I have faith in you. :-) <3

C: Well, at least that makes one of us...

I spent the rest of lunch in La-La Land, racking my brain for good ideas. Something that would prove my note was sincere without making me look like a sap. Maybe I could leave something in her locker. I had her combination now. Flowers...candy...doves? Ok, I was reaching with that last idea. A present could work, but what should I give her?

If it was something too personal, she might know it was me. I wasn't ready for that. Not personal enough, though, and it wouldn't seem thoughtful.

What does Bianca Barnes like? What makes her excited? The obvious answer was basketball, but I don't think even Bebe would consider basketball a super *romantic* subject. I know she's been wanting to get some sweatbands for practice. *Because nothing says I love you like new sweatbands. Cam, you're such a guy.* Maybe I should head to the store after school and walk around until inspiration strikes? Yeah, that sounded like a good plan.

By the time chemistry class rolled around, I was dying to see if Bebe had formed more of an opinion on her secret admirer. Beth was right about one thing; knowing someone had a crush on her, but not knowing who it was, would be driving Bebe nuts. I tried to act casual as I strolled into Mr. Gardner's class and pulled up a seat next to her. "So how's your day been, Bebe?"

She looked at me with exasperation. "How do you think it's been? I'm going freaking cuckoo. I can't stop thinking about that stupid letter and who might have written it. At this rate, you're going to have to commit me to the loony bin by the weekend."

I loved that she was so flustered. My confession must be having a bigger affect on her than I initially thought. This was good. I decided to push her a little harder. "Stupid letter, huh? You didn't like it? I think most girls would be pretty excited to be given something like that. I know if some chick had done the same for me, I'd be extremely flattered. Not surprised, but definitely flattered…"

Bebe punched me in the arm. "I swear, if your head got any bigger, we wouldn't be able to fit you in the car every morning. Of course, you could use your big noggin full of hot air to float yourself to school…" she trailed off.

"Hey, you're the one who made me promise never to lie to you again." I held my hands up in mock innocence. "I'm just being honest, per your instructions." Bebe rolled her eyes, letting me know exactly how monstrous she thought my ego was. I loved it when she gave me attitude; it made me want to sweep her up and prove to her that she wasn't immune to my charms.

"Seriously, though," I continued, "aren't you at least a little flattered?"

Bebe's face turned pink, with embarrassment. "*Flattered* doesn't even begin to express how I feel. I'm completely flabbergasted." She looked down at the table. "I'm having a hard time believing that someone really thinks those things about me."

"Don't be so humble. I'm sure there's plenty of guys who think that about you."

"Oh yeah? Name one."

"Well, for one, *I* think you're all the same things that Mr. Mysterious does." *Holy flaming bag of cow dung. Did I just say that out loud? Please tell me I didn't say that out loud.*

Bebe looked startled for a moment, then shook her head and laughed. "Yeah, but whoever wrote that note thinks those things in an 'I want to have your babies' kind of way, not an 'I love you like my baby sister' kind of way. Two completely different kinds of babies here."

What the freak? If I wasn't a gentleman, I'd have bopped her on the top of her cute little head. Jog some sense into her brain. Nothing I thought about her had *ever* put her in the little sister zone. I'd wanted her to have my babies since I was fourteen years old. I can't believe I was about to say this, but clearly the thought of *me* loving her wasn't going to prove her worth to her. I nodded my head toward the table where Brady and Mike were getting settled. "I'm pretty sure Brady doesn't think of you in a strictly platonic manner…"

Bebe bit her lip as she turned her head to look at Brady. I was probably going to regret that comment later, but she looked ready to concede.

"You think Brady likes me?" she asked, as if the thought hadn't ever crossed her mind.

"Bebe, the guy's not even subtle about it."

"Do you think he's the one who wrote the note?"

"Hold on now, I didn't say that." I wasn't about to let Brady get the credit for my swoon worthy literary master-piece. "Brady doesn't seem like the secret admirer type. I think if he liked you, he'd just come right out and say it."

Bebe thought for a moment longer and then turned back to me. "I guess you're right. I mean, he's always been pretty direct whenever we talk, and he isn't very shy about flirting."

"I think he's absolutely shameless around you. He's way too forward," I complained.

"Oh hush, Cam. Brady's a nice guy. It's nothing but harmless flirting."

"As harmless as mine?"

Her face got pink again. I couldn't tell if she was thinking about my flirting or boy wonder's. I'd had enough of this conversation. If I couldn't rein it in, she'd go home and start pining away for the wrong guy. "I don't think your admirer is Brady. Actually, I'm sure it's not Brady."

"Well, if it's not Brady, then who could it be?" She looked genuinely puzzled, and I sighed inwardly.

"I don't know, Bebe. Maybe you'll get another clue tomorrow?" *She'd definitely get another clue tomorrow. One that was way too awesome for the walking toothpaste ad to come up with.* Honestly, Brady was a decent guy. I shouldn't be such an a-hole to him, even if it was mostly internally. Any other girl, and I wouldn't give two craps about it. I'd even be ok if he dated Beth. But Bianca Barnes was off limits.

AFTER THE GIRLS AND I PULLED INTO THEIR DRIVEWAY, I headed straight home, spouting off a half-truth about tons of homework. I went in the front door and looked out the window until I'd seen that they were gone. Knowing Bebe, she probably headed straight for the kitchen. She could hold her own when it came to eating after a hard workout. Since the kitchen faced the backyard, I had a very small window where I could sneak out without being noticed. I went to the garage and pulled out the old bike. The store was only a mile away, but I really did have a lot of homework, and I had no idea how long this would take.

As I walked in, my mind was drawing a blank. I strolled through the food aisles. Candy seemed so cliché. Then I headed past the ultra tiny floral department. Flowers were kind of cliché, too. Besides, if I wanted to get her flowers, I'd have to get them from somewhere else because the selection here was puny.

I walked through clothes and toys, but those were an obvious no. Then I headed to sporting goods, where I contemplated for a while before deciding that my original assessment was still accurate. Basketball paraphernalia, while practical, was not likely to send the right message. Neither were housewares, so I skipped the entire middle of the store.

I was about to complete the perimeter lap as I approached the media section. I walked past books and magazines and started thumbing through the DVDs. That's when I saw it: a copy of *Hoosiers*. It was Bebe's second favorite basketball movie, right behind *Love & Basketball*. I happen to know that her current copy has so many scratches that it's pretty much worthless. It's an iconic movie. Anyone who knows Bebe's into basketball, which is *everyone*, could have picked it. That means I wouldn't be completely revealing myself.

It was the best idea I'd come up with so far, but it still seemed kind of lame to give her only a movie. I grabbed the DVD and kept walking, making my way to the front of the store where there was a vending machine. All this thinking and wandering was making my brain hurt. Maybe some caffeine would help me gain inspiration.

I put my money in the machine and pushed the button

for a Dr Pepper. If Bebe was here, she'd have insisted I get Diet Coke so she could drink most of it. And I'd have done it because I'm whipped. Maybe I should put the movie back and buy her a few two-liters of Diet Coke. Or maybe I could get her the Diet Coke to go with the movie? Heck, why not grab some popcorn, too?

The idea hit me like a ton of bricks. Instead of just getting her one of her favorite movies, I could get her a whole date package. To be shared with me upon revealing who I was, of course. I could make it fancy, like a gift basket. Chicks like that kind of stuff, right? I know my mom did, but I'm not sure she was young enough to be considered a chick. I needed confirmation from a less geriatric source. I pulled out my phone to text Beth.

C: So I want to get Bebe a gift, but I'm not sure what to get. I was thinking of putting together a gift basket with her favorite movie, popcorn, candy, Diet Coke, etc. Then suggest we use it together. Is that a lame idea?

B: No way. I love it. Totally cute. You come up with that all by yourself? ;-)

C: Yes, I'm not completely useless.

B: I think she'll like it. Not too sappy or overwhelming, but personal and fun.

C: Glad you approve, cuz assembling a gift basket will challenge my membership in the man club. If anyone finds out, they'll pull my card for sure.

B: Well, then, I guess mum's the word.

C: Thanks.

I put my phone back in my pocket and grabbed a

shopping cart. I had the movie; now I just needed the snacks. I'm a Dr Pepper junkie and Bebe knows that, so just to be safe, I grabbed a regular Coke to go with the diet one I'd picked up for her. I also grabbed a three-pack of microwave popcorn and some candy. Bebe's favorite is Junior Mints. I know this, but I don't think it's as common knowledge as her Diet Coke addiction. If I picked up the Junior Mints, would she realize it was me? I decided to play it safe and went with a random assortment of chocolate. Now I needed a basket.

I figured I could find something in the home decor section that I'd previously skipped. When I got there, I looked around, making sure the coast was clear, as if I were about to commit some heinous crime. Then I pulled the hood of my sweatshirt up over my head. If I ran into someone I knew, it would be *very* bad. I'm not sure how I'd explain the fact that I was shopping for a decorative basket. I headed up the aisle, grabbed the first thing that looked big enough, and got out of there as fast as I could.

Once I was safely away from the home decor, I stopped and arranged my items in the basket to see how it would look. All the important elements were there, but it was still lacking appeal. It looked too plain. Like a helpless teenage boy put it together. What was I missing? I thought back to all the gift baskets my mom had received or put together over the years. They always had something fluffy in the bottom, like dried grass or fancy paper pieces for the gift items to sit on. And every last one of them had a big-ass bow on the top.

"Damn it. You have *got* to be kidding me." I swore

out loud as I realized what I'd have to do. I'd already risked enough by shopping for home decor, and now I had to go to the craft section and buy ribbon? I hope Bebe appreciated this dumb basket. Once I picked up some ribbon and fake grass, I'd need to head to the women's underwear section and buy myself a bra.

After securing the last items I needed, at great risk to my reputation, I went to the checkout and placed everything on the belt. The cashier was a college-age guy. Why couldn't it have been a girl? I could've told her what I was doing and probably ended up getting her phone number. Instead, some douche who looked like the long-lost member of One Direction looked at me, looked down at my purchase, looked back up at me, and raised his eyebrow in question.

"It's a present for my best friend…who happens to be a girl…" I don't know why I felt like I had to defend myself. I should be confident enough in my masculinity to buy all the pink polka-dot ribbon I wanted.

"Riiiiight…" the cocky cashier responded with a smirk.

What the hell? Could this be any more horrifying? The guy bagged my items and then looked up at me, considering something before he spoke. "I better double bag these for you. You know, so nobody sees what's inside. Hate for you to run into your 'friend' and ruin the surprise."

His hands were busy with my bag, but his voice clearly suggested the air quotes around the word *friend*. I didn't bother thanking him as I took my bag and headed out the door. I hoped Bebe responded well. I'd hate to think I'd made a fool of myself for nothing.

BIANCA

CAMERON HAD TOLD ME I WAS BEAUTIFUL. AND FUNNY AND amazing. Ok, he didn't actually say it, but he openly agreed with my mysterious letter writer, and I thought that should count. I know it's not the same when you say those things about a friend as it is when you say them about someone you're romantically interested in. But for the rest of the day yesterday, I'd pretended that Cam was my secret admirer. That he'd been pining away for me since the day we met. I fantasized about him telling me in person and then sweeping me into his arms and kissing me senseless. I'd told myself that I could have one afternoon of daydreams before I had to come back to reality. It wasn't very fair to my real secret admirer if I pretended he was someone else.

I woke up Thursday morning with the letter still on my

mind, or more accurately, the letter writer. Who was he, and would he ever reveal himself? The unknown was driving me nuts. No one came forward about it being a joke, no TV host jumping out when I least expected it. It seemed that someone out there really did like me.

I was a little worried that my secret admirer would be somebody weird or gross. Or maybe a super nerd like Josh Sutton. I know it's shallow, but was it too much to hope that he's super hot and cool? Or, at the very least, just super hot? What if the guy asked me out? After pouring his heart out to me, I couldn't say no. That would majorly suck. I got ready for the morning on autopilot and went down to the kitchen. Cam walked in as I was spreading cream cheese on my bagel.

"Good morning, sunshine." He greeted me, then plucked the bagel out of my hands. Rather than complaining, I put another one in the toaster. "Wow. No argument? No physical abuse? No nasty name calling?" He took a bite of my breakfast as he placed his free hand on my forehead. "Are you feeling ok this morning?"

I swatted it away. "I'm fine. Just distracted, that's all."

"Could it have something to do with a certain love letter?"

"Could it? How could it be anything else? You read it. Either this person is a sociopath or the sweetest guy on the planet. I hope for my sake it's the latter, but with my luck, you never know…"

Beth responded as she rushed into the kitchen. "I'm sure it'll be fine, Bea. He's probably totally normal, and when you find out who it is, you'll feel silly for worrying." She grabbed an apple and banana out of the fruit bowl and headed for the side door. "Come on, slowpokes; I was late to first period yesterday."

I grabbed my new bagel, then shot Cam a glare, warning him of imminent death should he touch this one. He followed me to the car. "Maybe now that he got the hard part out of the way, he'll tell you who he is?" Cam reassured me as he put his arm around my shoulder. "Besides, you're forgetting something very important."

"Oh yeah? What's that?"

"You have me. And I have it on good authority that I make an excellent fake date." His dimples came out. "If he's a weirdo, you can tell him you already have a boyfriend, but thanks anyway." He seemed pleased with his idea.

"And you, my friend, are forgetting something important as well," I countered.

"Which is?"

"That your fake homecoming date turned into a real one because you had to keep up pretenses. If I told this guy we're dating, we'd have to *actually* date. At least for a little while, so I didn't look like a lying jerk."

We'd reached the car, and Cam opened the back door for me. He leaned on it, pinning me with his stare. "I could think of a lot worse things than dating you."

I held his gaze. Call me crazy, but in that second, he looked sincere. Like he might actually want to be my boyfriend. My brain melted, and my heart pumped faster. I could feel the heat in my cheeks. After a second, I realized that he was still staring at me and I was staring back. I shook my head. *It isn't real, Bianca. Don't let your heart play games with your head. It will only make you miserable.* I had to stop thinking like this. I was a victim of torture, but the torturer was myself.

I slid into the backseat. Cam shut the door, then got in front. I was quiet as we headed to school. Determined to focus my thoughts on healthier things. I thought about Brady. Cam had suggested that Brady liked me. I assumed that all the flirting and joking was a friendly gesture, but what if it wasn't? What if he really did like me? What if he was my secret admirer? That wouldn't be so bad.

Brady is fun, sweet, and way good-looking. His smile is amazing. Plus, we have quite a bit in common, even besides basketball. I enjoyed talking to him and spending time with him. I decided right then and there that I was going to stop living in the clouds and start dating in reality. I was going to show Brady I was interested in him. Besides, I still needed a date to the homecoming dance. Maybe if I played my cards right, he'd ask me.

We pulled into school and parked in our usual spot. Cam opened my door for me again, and I thanked him as I stepped out. He'd been quite the gentleman this morning. What had gotten into him? "What's with all the special treatment this morning?" I asked. "Opening my doors for me? Who are you, and what have you done with my Cameron?"

"Your Cameron is still in here. He's just decided not to let some dumb secret admirer outdo him." His comment was playful, but if I didn't know better, I'd think there was a hint of jealousy in it.

The three of us arrived at our lockers, and when I opened mine, I gasped at what I found. "What the heck?" Sitting inside, on top of my books, was a gift basket.

Beth leaned around my door and started squeaking. Her words were indecipherable other than to convey a heightened sense of excitement. "Oh, Bea." She finally got out, "He got you a present."

Somewhere in the back of my mind, I assessed that I should be reacting similarly to Beth. What if he was watching? He'd be disappointed at my lack of enthusiasm. But all I could think about was how he got into my locker. Another note would have been easy to slip in through the vents, but to put a whole basket in means that my secret admirer needed my combination. I did a quick scan of the hall. There were loads of kids, but nobody seemed to be paying particular attention to us.

"Hang on a second, Beth," Cam spoke up. "Maybe we should check and make sure it's actually from the same guy."

"Get real, Cam." Yes, I snorted... "You honestly think this could be from someone else? One secret admirer is shocking enough, but two of them fighting for my affections is a physical impossibility."

I reached into my locker and pulled out the basket. It was really sweet. Someone had gone through a lot of effort to make it personalized. It had a DVD of the movie *Hoosiers*, one of my favorites, along with all the provisions for a movie night: popcorn, candy, and even a Diet Coke. It was so personal that there's no way he bought the basket as is. Whoever this guy was, he actually put it together himself.

Complete with decorative grass in the bottom and a big pink polka-dot bow on the top. A bow that'd been handmade. The contents of the basket were thoughtful, but I was even more impressed by the effort. Hanging from the basket was a little note card. I read it out loud.

I hope you like this movie as much as I do. I'm also hoping you'll keep the basket and   goodies someplace safe for now. Maybe we can get together soon for a movie date. :-)
Yours -?

"Well, that didn't help solve the mystery," I grumbled.

"Bea, why are you always so negative? You focused on the one bad thing. This guy just asked you out. In the sweetest way imaginable. Aren't you at least a tiny bit excited?" Beth's bottom lip stuck out in a serious pout, and I gave in a little.

"Of course I'm excited." I smiled at her. "It's one of the nicest things anybody has ever done for me. And I really love the basket. I only wish I knew who left it, so that I could give him a proper thank-you." I put the basket down and faced my locker mates as I continued speaking. "So, which one of you gave him my locker combination?"

Beth and Cam both faked innocence. At least, I think they were faking. Beth responded first. "What are you talking about?"

"Oh, don't play dumb with me," I scolded, pointing my finger back and forth between them. "I know one or both of you knows who left this. In order to put it in my locker, mystery man would have needed the combination. There are two people in this school, besides myself, that know my locker combo. And they both happen to be standing right in front of me. Unless he's been spying on me with binoculars while I open it, one of you gave him the info." I stood there, hands on my hips, taping my foot, channeling my inner Nancy Drew.

They both gawked at me, stunned and silent, before Cam spoke up. "Bebe, I swear I didn't give your locker combination to anyone."

"Me, either," Beth agreed, shaking her head.

"Come on, guys. I'm not buying it. I wasn't born yesterday, you know. I'm not leaving this spot until I get the truth."

"Maybe someone really was watching you open your locker so they could get the combo?" Beth reasoned. "It's not impossible. You wouldn't even have to get that close to figure it out. If it was at a time when the halls were really crowded, he could've seen you open it from just a couple feet away. You probably wouldn't even have noticed he was watching."

Beth made a valid point. I frowned.

"Plus, Bebe, you know the office secretary keeps everyone's combo on her desk in a manila folder," Cam added. "So that she can look them up if people forget. Or break in if Principal Davis thinks someone has contraband stashed. It wouldn't be very hard to lean over the counter while she was gone and peek in the folder." Cam looked thoughtful. "It's actually a little disturbing how easy it would be for someone to get another person's locker combination."

My determination was fading. Another good point. Maybe they really didn't know who was doing this. And if that was the case, who knew when I'd find out the truth? "You guys promise you didn't give out my locker combo to someone? And before you answer, remember that you both recently swore never to lie to me again. Cam, under penalty of eye gouging."

"We promise," Beth answered for both of them. She looked at Cam, and he nodded in agreement.

The bell rang. Cam and I said good-bye to Beth as we headed off to English class. I hoped my secret admirer wouldn't wait too long to reveal himself. There was a stack of candy and some Diet Coke in my locker that were calling my name.

Ms. Lambert let us out of PE a little early, and I didn't need to rinse off, so I got to chemistry class right as the fifth-hour dismissal bell was ringing. I went in to the empty classroom and plopped down on my stool, opening my backpack. I was pouring over yesterday's notes to brush up for today's quiz, when I felt someone walk up beside me. Brady was standing there, looking as handsome as ever, and flashing his beautiful smile.

"Hey, Bea. How's it going?"

"It's going ok. How are you today?" I smiled back at him

and closed my notebook.

"Pretty good," he answered, then paused before speaking again. "I was wondering... Were you planning on going to the football game tomorrow? It's an away game. I was thinking that if you weren't already going with someone else, maybe you'd want to ride up with me? We could get some food after. If you're up for it, maybe even catch a movie?"

Cam and I usually went to the home football games together, but we rarely made the effort to attend away games. And we hadn't discussed the possibility of going to this one, so I didn't see any reason not to say yes.

"I'd love to," I answered, sincerely excited about the invitation.

"Awesome. The game starts at seven, so I guess I'll pick you up at six?" Brady asked.

Cam had come in during our exchange and was trying to pretend like he wasn't eavesdropping. Brady glanced at him with a worried expression. Like he was poaching on Cam's territory. Definitely something he didn't need to worry about. Cam already knew that Brady liked me and didn't say he objected. As far as I was concerned, that was the equivalent of giving his blessing.

"Sounds like a plan. I'll text you my address right now." I whipped out my phone to send the message before Mr. Gardner could yell at me to put it away.

"Cool." Brady flashed one last smile, then headed for his seat.

I put my phone back in my bag and I turned to Cam. He was sitting on his stool, staring at me with his mouth hanging open. "What?" I asked, raising my eyebrows expectantly.

"You're going to the football game with Brady tomorrow? On a date?" He closed his mouth, scrunched his eyebrows, and stuck his bottom lip out in a pout. "We always go to the games together."

"We almost never go to the away games. I didn't think you'd care since we hadn't even discussed going to this one."

"But you're going with Brady...on a date..."

"Yes, I think we established that already. You know, I *do* go out on dates from time to time."

"But not with Brady."

"What's your problem? I thought you liked Brady? I thought you guys were friends? For crap's sake, Cam, you're the one who pointed out that he might like me." I was irritated by his reaction, so I decided to poke the bear. I spoke in baby talk. "What's wrong, little Cam? Is somebody jealous?" My taunt was mostly meant to be a joke, but he crossed his arms and grunted.

"No. Well, not that much really."

I laughed and slapped his back. "If it bothers you so much, why don't you get a date and join us?" I knew he wouldn't, so my offer was completely benign.

"You know I don't do that."

"Come on, Cam, you go out with girls all the time."

"Yes, but I don't ask them out. It's against the rules."

"I know; it's a stupid rule."

Cam looked like a three-year-old ready to throw a temper tantrum, so of course I couldn't resist pushing him a little more. "You know, if you really wanted to join us, I could tell Angelica that you're looking to double. All she needs to do is ask."

His head snapped up and his eyes narrowed. "You wouldn't dare."

Yes, I would; I already had. The thought made me snicker. "I'm just trying to help a brother out." I held up my hands. Cam knew better, and I knew he knew. That's what made our relationship so fun.

"Fine, you win. Go on your stupid date with Brady. Leave me home, all alone on a Friday night. Maybe I'll borrow your copy of *Love & Basketball* while I cry into a gallon of ice cream." He'd gone back to pouting.

"Oh my gosh, don't be so dramatic." I laughed. "One Friday won't kill you."

"That's what you think," he mumbled as Mr. Gardner spoke, putting an end to our twisted conversation.

"All right, everyone, clear your desks and take out a pencil. It's quiz time!"

Why did our teacher always sound so excited about quizzes and tests? I guess he loved to torture us. Maybe almost as much as I loved torturing Cam.

13

CAMERON

BRADY. FREAKING. JONES. HE DIDN'T KNOW IT, BUT HE was becoming my new arch nemesis. The Larry Bird to my Magic Johnson. Yes, I know as far as looks were concerned Brady should be Johnson and I should be Bird, but forget that. Nobody is better than my man Magic, so Brady is the Bird. The big, dumb Bird. Big Bird. The thought of that goofy *Sesame Street* character made me smirk. From now on at practice, I'd just call him Big Bird. The nickname wouldn't make sense to anyone else on the team, but it wouldn't matter. If I started it, the name would stick. Serves him right. Nobody tries to snake my girl from me.

I'd walked into class at the absolute worst time. And yet it was also the best time. I hated that I had to watch Bebe get all excited over a date with some other dude. On the other hand, I had gotten the information firsthand. I knew exactly what his plan was for Friday night, which meant I knew exactly how to sabotage their date. I was being juvenile, but I couldn't help it. After all my hard work, if she ended up with someone else... It wasn't an option. Period.

I was in a grumpy mood, so when I asked my mom if I could take my dinner upstairs and eat in my room, she didn't argue. Now, I sat at the computer wondering what my next move should be. Obviously I had to know what was happening on that date tomorrow. I didn't trust them to be alone together. What if he tried to kiss her? Even worse, what if she kissed him back? What if there was *more* than kissing? Good heavens. I couldn't think about that.

C: Bebe is going out with Brady tomorrow night.

B: I know. She told me at dinner.

C: What am I supposed to do?

B: I don't know, what can you do?

C: Well, I have to stop it.

B: I don't think that's a good idea. She'd be pretty mad.

C: I can't sit around and do nothing.

B: I don't know what to tell you.

C: We should go with them.

B: Still a bad idea.

C: Fine, whatever. I can see you aren't going to be any help.

Ten seconds after I sent my last text, my phone rang, Beth's name on the screen. I picked it up and went straight into my rant.

"I know I sound like a jerk, but I can't handle the thought of them going out."

"I clearly remember someone telling me recently that the proper response when answering the phone was *hello*," Beth lectured me without responding to my comment.

"Hello, Mom." I didn't have time for a tongue lashing, so I moved on. "What if he puts the moves on her? If they hold hands, or kiss, or make out… I'm going to freak out. Do you hear me? What if he asks her to homecoming? I can't watch her dancing with another guy all night. It would be torture."

"What did you think would happen? You already have a date to the dance, remember? And even if you didn't, you refuse to ask Bebe. You blew your shot there." There wasn't an ounce of sympathy in her voice.

"I thought you were on my team, Beth?"

"I am. Really, I am. But I'm not going to sabotage Bebe's date, if that's what you're thinking of doing. That is what you're planning, isn't it?"

"If I promise to go undercover, will you go with me? Just reconnaissance work. Spying only, no interference, no sabotage, no fighting Big Bird."

"Fighting who?" Now she was confused.

"Never mind." I didn't feel like explaining the nickname. "Will you come with me?"

"I don't know. If she saw us, we'd be back on her black list. She's barely forgiven us for the last infraction."

"That's why we won't let her see us. We'll get disguises." I was starting to sound like a maniacal mad man. Sooner or later, my sinister laugh was going to break free.

"Yeah, because that won't be obvious. Good idea, lover boy."

"Ok, no disguises. But we can wear sweats and hoodies and keep them up over our heads so we're less noticeable. Please? I have to know what happens. It could be fun. You don't have other plans, do you?"

"You mean other than needing to be at the game to cheer?"

"Yes or no, Beth?" I was losing my patience.

"If I say no, will you go without me anyway and cause a big scene?"

"Potentially…" Ok, I probably wouldn't, but she didn't need to know that. I needed a wingman, and she was my only option. There was silence on her end of the phone, and then she finally released a big sigh.

"Fine. I'll go with you. But if we get caught, I'm throwing you under the bus."

"Beth, you're the best."

"I know. You've said so a lot lately. I have to ride the bus over with the cheer squad, and obviously I can't sit with you at the game. But I'll get a note from my dad excusing me from the bus ride home. That way I can leave with you. You'll have to keep tabs on them, because we'll need to follow them from the stadium to wherever they're going. I'll try to get some clues about their plan beforehand, but I can't give her the third degree. She'll know something's up."

"That's ok. I'm an expert at tailing people." I was already in spy mode, and Bebe's date was still a whole day away.

"When's the last time you tailed someone?" Beth's tone said I was full of crap and losing my marbles. Maybe I was.

"Ok, well I'm sure I *will* be excellent at it. I'm good at most things."

"Humble, too." Her eye roll was implied. "Make a plan, and I'll go with the flow. But seriously, Cam, do not get us caught. You hear me?"

"Yes, Mom."

Beth laughed and hung up the phone without saying good-bye. I didn't care if I promised not to interfere. If it looked like things were going to get serious, I'd find a way to break them up. Knowing I had a plan lifted a huge weight off my chest, and I was able to focus on the other task at hand. I still had to come up with a way to show Bebe that I was thinking about her tomorrow. Another item in her locker would probably be pushing it. I didn't want to get caught yet, so my gesture needed to be on a different turf and much bigger than the last.

After thirty minutes of nothing but super dumb ideas, I did what no man should ever do. I had no choice; I wasn't that creative. I opened a Pinterest account. My mom was on that stupid website all the damn time, so I knew there'd be plenty of ideas. I just hoped that nobody ever found out. I should be safe because I didn't link it to my Facebook, and I was pretty confident none of my guy friends were on there. To be sure, I made my username *Magic-J* and skipped a profile picture. Hopefully that would be enough to keep my dirty little secret.

Ten minutes later, I found the perfect idea. Something

called a heart attack. It's where you cut out all kinds of paper hearts and hot glue them to popsicle sticks. Then you shove the sticks in the ground at the yard of the person you want to heart attack. When they come out in the morning, their lawn is covered in hearts. It was going to be a lot of work, but I knew that my mom had all of the necessary items in her hobby room. That would save me another embarrassing trip to the craft section at the store. Plus, this would definitely make the grand statement I was looking for.

After hunting down the supplies and asking my mom how to work the glue gun (yeah, that was an interesting conversation), I got started on my project. Three hours later, I had five hundred construction paper hearts in all colors and sizes glued to popsicle sticks. I'd also made one giant heart to tape to Bebe's front door, with a simple message that I'd typed up on my computer.

Bianca,
I wanted you to know that you have my hearts.
Yours - ?

You have my hearts…plural… Get it? Because there were five hundred of them going on her lawn. Damn, I was clever. I was also getting good at this whole secret admirer thing. I looked over my room, paper scraps everywhere. If my career in the NBA didn't pan out, maybe I could do this for a living.

I peeked out my window, then at my clock. It was

midnight and all the lights were off across the street, but I decided to wait a little longer. Just in case. Finally, at one o'clock, I threw on my black sweatpants and black hoodie. I even added a black ski mask for effect. Then I dumped my laundry basket out on my bed, put the paper hearts in it, and snuck across the street.

I bent over to put the first stick in the ground, but it was much harder to get in than I expected it to be. Damn popsicle sticks; the ends were blunt. What were the manufacturers thinking? They should have made the ends sharp. Forget that it'd be a hazard to small children; it would have made my night a hell of a lot easier.

An hour later, I stuck my last heart in the ground, then tiptoed to the front door and taped my note to it. I hurried across the street and into my house. Then I ran straight up the stairs and looked out my window to survey my work. The moon was pretty bright, and I had a clear view of the yard. For the first time, it dawned on me how lucky I'd been that I hadn't been caught.

Bebe's yard looked awesome; I mean, it seriously kicked butt. If this didn't knock her socks off, then there was no hope of impressing her. I shucked off my clothes and buried myself under my blankets. For the third time this week, I fell asleep with a huge grin on my face.

Morning came quickly, and when my alarm went off, I started to snooze it before remembering last night. I shot out of bed. Had Bebe seen her front yard yet? I kind of wanted to be there when she did, if I wasn't too late already. I jumped in and out of the shower, threw on the first outfit that looked clean, brushed my teeth, gathered my school books, and headed down stairs. I was getting ready to walk out the door, when I noticed the clock. I wouldn't normally head over for another twenty minutes. I guess I should've enjoyed my shower a little longer. If I went over now, I'd look suspicious.

I sat on the couch in the front room, my stare alternating between the window and the clock. After the longest ten minutes of my life, I decided to give up and headed over early anyway. I walked through the side door and into the kitchen, where Bebe was making her customary bagel and Beth was blending a smoothie. *All right, Cam, don't give yourself away.* I waited until the blender was done, took a few deep breaths, and put on a casual expression.

"Hey, guys. What's up with the front yard?" I suppose I could have had a better segue. Guess it's too late now.

Bebe gave me a questioning look. "What do you mean, what's up with the front yard?"

I pulled an apple from the fruit bowl and took a big bite. People always looked like they didn't give a crap when they answered a question with their mouths full of food. That's a thing, right? "You mean, you haven't seen it yet?" Sweet. Now I could see her reaction as it happened.

Beth shot out of the kitchen. Five seconds later, there was a scream from the front door followed by a very dramatic "OH. MY. GOSH! Bea, get your butt out here!"

"What in the heck is going on?" Bebe looked puzzled and walked out of the kitchen. I followed at a leisurely stroll. When we reached the front porch, Beth stood there, taking it all in. Bebe froze in place when she saw the artfully decorated yard before her.

"Oh my gosh." Bebe's words were the same as Beth's, but instead of a scream, they came out in a whisper. Her look of surprise was priceless as she scanned the lawn in wonder. "I can't believe this. Is it from him?"

Neither of the girls had noticed the message taped to the door yet, so I cleared my throat. They were so entranced by the hundreds of hearts that they probably wouldn't see it until I pointed it out. "Ahem... It appears his royal smoothness *is* to blame for the scene before us."

Bebe turned, and I nodded toward the door. As she walked to it, Beth caught my attention and mouthed, *"You did all this?"* My answering grin was enough for her, and she stared at me with a look of hero worship.

"You have my hearts..." Bebe was reading the note out loud.

I couldn't help my snarky response. After all, it was completely in character for the Cam that *wasn't* her secret admirer. "I'll say. How many hearts does the guy need, anyway? No *real* man needs more than one, and it should be used for manly stuff"—I pounded on my chest with my fist—"like pumping blood." There, that should do it. Neanderthal Cam could never be suspected of perpetrating a heart attack. Or writing sappy love letters, or making gift baskets...or opening a Pinterest account. I shuddered at that thought.

Nobody moved, so I patted Bebe's back. "Romeo has really outdone himself this time. I'd love to stay and admire the handiwork, but we have to get going."

"Uh huh, sure, whatever you say." Bebe was still in a daze, busy looking between the heart in her hand and the hearts in the yard. I could tell by the look on her face that this was starting to get real for her. She was finally understanding that whoever this guy was, his feelings were legit. Thank the heavens above, because I couldn't do this much longer. Not even girly Internet sites could sustain me forever. Topping this morning would be a challenge. But if I got more reactions like this, the effort would be well worth it.

BIANCA

I COULDN'T BELIEVE WHAT I WAS SEEING. THERE WERE COLorful paper hearts all over my front yard. Not just a few, either; there must have been four or five hundred of them. It would have taken him all night to put something like this together. Unless he had help. The letter was beautiful and the basket was sweet, but this was crazy. I definitely wasn't a big enough deal to deserve this kind of attention.

I held the note in my hands. It was a simple statement taped to my front door. *I just wanted you to know that you have my hearts.* Was this guy for real? I wasn't really *close* with any boys but Cam, so it's not like this guy knew me super well. How could he mean all of the things he'd been saying? Sure, I had a lot of guy friends. Some of them I've known for a really long time. But I couldn't imagine any of them doing something like this for me.

If my secret admirer was someone I didn't know well, I think I'd freak out a little. This morning's display was pretty hardcore. If he wasn't someone I at least talked to on a regular basis, then I'd be afraid I had a stalker. That would ruin how amazing this week had been. I didn't believe it at first, but now I'm pretty sure that somewhere out there, an actual boy, made of skin and bones, liked me. Me, not Beth. For the first time in my life, someone was picking me.

"Romeo has really outdone himself this time. I'd love to stay and admire the handiwork, but we have to get going."

I heard Cam talking to me, but it wasn't really registering; I was deep in thought. "Uh huh, sure, whatever you say." I folded my newest note neatly and stuck it in the pocket of my jacket. Then I went back into the house, grabbed my backpack, and headed to the car. The whole way to school, my mind raced. Who was this guy, and when would he finally tell me? I was going to be worthless today.

I went through my morning on autopilot, despite Cam's best efforts to pull me back into the land of the living. He tugged on my hair during first period and kept whispering to me when the teacher's back was turned. All he got in return were one-word responses and grunts. In government class, I'm pretty sure Beth and Cam had a whole conversation with me sitting between them, and I didn't catch a word of it. It wasn't until lunch that an epiphany brought me back to reality.

I was sitting at my usual spot, staring at Cam while he laughed and joked with the guys, when Brady came over and sat a few seats down. He saw me staring and inclined his head toward me. I waved in return. *Could* Brady be my secret admirer? I know Cam had dismissed the idea, but I had no other guesses. Brady was pretty confident, so it didn't make sense that he'd have to be so secretive. I mean, he'd already asked me out. We were going to the football game tonight, and then we'd probably grab some food or watch a movie. *Wait a second...* He'd suggested we watch a movie after the game. Did he mean go to a movie or watch one at his house? Or at my house. Perhaps a certain basketball movie that he knew I owned, because he'd purchased it for me. Had he been giving me a hint yesterday?

I racked my brain for any other hints he could have given me over the last couple of days. All of our conversations seemed pretty normal. He did ask me out, though, and that definitely wasn't normal. If Brady was the guy, then would he tell me tonight? Is that why he asked me out, so he could finally admit his feelings in person? *Oh my gosh, oh my gosh, oh my gosh. What do I do if he comes clean about all of this tonight? How do I respond?* I was getting frantic.

I was changing for PE, when I saw Beth and Angelica walk in. Beth would know what to do. She was always so grounded and way more experienced when it came to handling boys. Especially ones that lavished you with gifts and affection.

"Hey, Beth, can you come here for a minute?" I called out across the locker room. This conversation had to happen now, because once we set foot in the gym, she'd have Angelica stuck to her side like a leech. I didn't want to share the particulars of my love life with the queen of the gossip train.

"Sure, just give me a sec." Beth grabbed her gym clothes from her locker and walked over to me. Luckily, Angelica headed for the bathroom.

"I think it's Brady," I said. She looked at me, waiting for me to elaborate. "What if my secret admirer is Brady? What if he asked me out tonight so that he could tell me how he feels? What am I supposed to do?"

"First of all," Beth was smiling as she placed her hands on my shoulders, preparing for a lecture, "you need to take a deep breath and calm down. You're freaking out over something that hasn't happened yet. Second, the only way to answer that question depends on you and how you feel about Brady."

"How I feel about Brady is irrelevant. I need to know what to do if he confesses his undying love for me."

"You're wrong. How you feel about Brady is the most important part of your question. Do you want him to be your secret admirer?"

I thought for a second. Did I want Brady to be the one? No, I wanted it to be Cam. But I also knew that wasn't happening and that I had to be realistic. "I don't know," was all I could say.

"Well, then, let me ask you another question. Do you like Brady in a romantic way?"

"I'm not sure. He's funny and hot, and we get along so well, but…" I stopped mid comment. For a second, I forgot I was thinking out loud.

"But what?" Beth encouraged me.

"No way. You almost had me there, you sneaky little devil." I swatted Beth on the arm lightly, and she smiled in triumph. "I'm not saying another word. Who I do and do not like is a forbidden topic of conversation. Always has been, and always will be. Nice try, though. You're getting better. I'm going to have to start being more careful."

Beth sighed, shaking her head, and headed back to shut her locker. "Bea, you're completely hopeless, you know that?" She didn't look at me, but she was still shaking her head as she walked out of the locker room and into the gym.

Wow. That was a close one, Bianca. You almost screwed up royally. Better keep your big fat mouth shut, or the next amazingly romantic display of affection will have Beth's name on it instead of yours. I was mentally chastising myself for my carelessness. I'd have to ask Cam his opinion during chemistry. I was way less likely to spill my guts to him.

In sixth hour, Mr. Gardner finished his lecture about ten minutes before the dismissal bell, and he gave us free time to work on our homework. This rarely happened, so I should have been taking advantage of it, but instead I used the time to grill Cam.

"I have a question to ask you, and you can't tease me about it. Ok?" I asked seriously.

"Hmmm. I don't know if that's a promise I can keep." Cam pretended to be deep in thought.

"Fine, you big jerk. The one time I ask you to take me seriously, and you can't even give me five minutes?"

Cam chuckled. "Calm down, Bebe; I promise not to laugh, or make fun of you." He put his finger to his chest and drew an *X* over his heart.

I hesitated for a second, and he waited patiently for me to start. "I think Brady might be my secret admirer, and I'm worried about what to do if he admits it tonight on our date."

"Well, Bebe, you've come to the right man. Cameron's my name, and love is my game." He was using his radio voice. I rolled my eyes.

"Cam, you said you'd be serious."

"I am being serious," he defended, but his regular voice was back. "First of all, I already told you, Brady's not your guy."

"But how can you be so certain?"

"Because I know how guys think and how they act. I *am* a guy, remember?"

"How could you let me forget, with all your 'Me Tarzan, you Jane' comments?"

"I just know, Bebe, trust me."

"That's all you got? *He's not the one, trust me?* Some help you are." I looked away from him as tears pricked my eyes. I was stressed out and starting to get emotional. I didn't break down often, but when I did, it was ugly. I didn't want to lose it at school where everyone could see me act like a big baby. Cam noticed my rapid change in mood, and his voice got softer.

"Bebe, look at me." He gently grabbed my chin and turned my face toward him. He leveled me with his gaze as his fingers left my chin and ran delicately up my jaw line to my hair. He took a piece and tucked it behind my ear and then dropped his hand to my lap where he grabbed my fingers. The moment was far too sweet to share with a room full of people.

"I really don't think he's the one. But I'll tell you what you *should* do when this guy admits who he is."

"What should I do?"

"You should kiss him." Cam said, matter-of-factly. I was stunned. This was not the answer I was expecting.

"I should kiss him? What if the guy is a stranger or super gross?"

"I have a feeling he won't be." Cam reassured me with a smile. "Whoever this guy is, he's clearly into you. He seems sincere, and for all his efforts, you owe it to yourself to see if there could be something there."

I stared at Cam as I contemplated his words. Normally he'd have acted like a jealous idiot or told me that the dude was a loser. But here he was, giving me advice to kiss a boy, one that wasn't him, and to give the guy a chance. My heart was breaking into the tiniest of pieces as I realized that Cam really never would think of me as more than a friend. I gave him a sad smile.

"I should kiss him, huh? He admits his feelings, and I shouldn't say anything? I should just grab his face and plant one on him?"

Cam's eyes grew bright. "Yep. That's it. That's how you'll know what to do. When you kiss him, either there'll be fireworks, or there won't. If there aren't, then you follow up the kiss with a thank-you and let it be. But if there *are* fireworks...you follow up your kiss with more kisses. Lots more." His grin was wicked and playful, and I couldn't help but laugh.

"That's your big plan, huh? Kiss him once, or kiss him lots. Believe it or not, that isn't the worst advice you've ever given me."

"Bebe," Cam gasped, "I have never given you bad advice." He plastered a shocked look on his face.

Good old Cam. I could always count on him to make light of a heavy mood. "I guess we'll see how good your advice is when I have to use it. I'll let you know how it all works out."

"You bet your sweet cheeks you will." He wrapped me in a giant hug, and for the rest of sixth period, the world was right.

CAMERON

It was a quarter after six. I'd been spying out my front window, when Brady came to pick Bebe up. I didn't expect any funny business so early in the evening, but I wanted to be sure. Kissing a girl at the beginning of a date is something I'd do, but I didn't think Brady was that smooth. The only info that Beth had gotten out of Bebe was that they were going straight to the game, and afterward they were going to dinner.

My dad agreed to let me borrow his car for the evening. Good thing, because my other option would have been to take the girls'. I don't care how awesome you are at tailing someone; they're bound to notice you following them if you're in their own car. I looked down at my clothes, the same black sweats combo I wore when vandalizing Bebe's yard, and decided it didn't matter if I looked good or not. This mission was about stealth. If I wore something nice, I'd have to beat the ladies off with a stick, and that would draw too much attention. I did trade in my ski mask for a dark gray beanie and a pair of binoculars.

I got in my ride, a nice generic-looking black SUV, and headed out. I hadn't bothered to follow them to the football game because I knew that's where they were going anyway, and I wouldn't have the added cover of darkness. When I arrived, I bought my ticket and went to the home team's bleachers. It was an away game, so it felt a little weird sitting with the home team, but I couldn't go to the visitors' side and risk being seen. I also didn't want to be bothered by anyone, so I found a big group of parents and scooted in next to them.

Beth knew I'd planned to sit with the home team, but she'd never find me in the sea of faces. We had to find a way to meet up without losing sight of Brady and Bebe. That part was going to be tricky. If they managed to lose us in the mass of people exiting the stadium, we'd be screwed. You can't tail someone you can't see.

I brought my binoculars up to my face and scanned the crowd across from me. I finally found them toward the center of the group. They were sitting by Mike and Caleb. *Perfect. No better way to kill the mood than two hours of sitting by Mike.* My own mood was improving, until fifteen minutes later when I realized that Brady and Bebe were doing a fine job of ignoring everyone around them. They were deeply engrossed in conversation. What was the point of coming to a football game if they weren't even going to watch it?

I sat through the entire game with binoculars glued to my face. I'm sure I looked like a creeper, but I didn't care. The game was a blowout, as usual. The home team fans were wild with excitement when they started exiting the bleachers. With everyone standing to leave, my view was obstructed, so I went to the front for a better look. By the time I got to the bottom of the stairs, the visitors side had cleared out enough for a good view of Bebe and Brady. It looked like they were headed down to say good-bye to Beth.

"What the hell?" I said out loud as a woman and her kids passed by. She glared at me, obviously offended by my language, but the outburst was totally warranted. Brady and Bebe were holding hands. Fingers freaking laced together and everything. And she was smiling. She looked happy. What had I gotten myself into? I was too emotionally invested to lose her now. They chatted with Beth for a second while she was gathering up her stuff. Bebe leaned over to give her a hug before they turned around and walked away.

I pulled my phone out of my pocket, dialed Beth's number, and watched as she fished it out of her bag.

"What's the plan, Stan?" Beth answered, skipping the hello.

"They're holding hands," I practically hissed into the phone.

"I noticed. Where are you?" She looked over at the home side bleachers, and I waved. "Make your way to the exit and I'll meet you there. Do you think you can keep an eye on them from far enough back to go unnoticed?"

"Of course I can. What do you think I am? An amateur? I brought binoculars."

"Binoculars? Really? That's subtle." I could see her sarcasm from across the field.

"*You* didn't notice me, did you?"

"No, but I wasn't looking for a big fat dork with binoculars." She laughed. "You better get going before you lose them. I'll see you in a second." Beth hung up the phone and started walking. I pulled my hood up over my head and stayed put until I saw them pass the entrance to the bleachers. Then I headed down the stairs with my face shadowed by my hood and my hands in my pockets. There were still people milling around, but the crowd had thinned significantly, so I wasn't well hidden. This was good and bad. The lack of people made it easier to track Bebe and Brady, but if they turned around, it would also be easier for them to notice me.

I felt someone walk up behind me, and I turned my head to see Beth a few feet away. I quickly turned it back so I wasn't looking at her, but spoke softly over my shoulder. "Don't talk to me or look at me; just keep walking past. They already know you're here, but if they turn around and see us together, it'll blow our cover."

Beth responded quietly as she caught up to me. "They know I'm here, but they also assume I'm taking the bus home. If they see me heading into the parking lot, they'll know something's off, whether they see you or not." She grabbed my arm and pulled me to a stop behind the concession stand.

"Why are we stopping? We're going to lose them," I complained.

"I thought that's what the binoculars were for, super spy." She smirked at me. "Just give me two seconds to change into something less obvious than my cheer outfit."

My eyes got big. "You're going to change right here?"

"You got a better idea? If I take time to go to the locker room, they'll be long gone before I get back." Beth was already pulling out clothes and unbuttoning her skirt. "Just turn around and keep your eyes glued to them."

"Maybe I should watch you change," I teased. "Bebe might get jealous if she knew I'd seen you in your underwear." Beth swatted me in the arm.

"Turn around, you perv, and make sure nobody's coming. We're wasting time."

Beth must have mastered the art of the quick change, because fifteen seconds later, she was done. Her cheer skirt and sweater were switched out with a pair of black yoga pants and a navy blue hoodie. "Do you still see them?" she asked as she pulled her blonde hair into a loose bun and tucked it under her own beanie.

"Yes, but they're getting pretty far away." I started walking again, and Beth shoved her discarded clothes into her duffel bag before she caught up to me. She examined me as she walked, and then looked down at her own outfit.

"Are you sure the dark clothes were a good idea? We might blend in better if we were dressed regularly. We look like a couple of dumb teenagers out for a night of mischief."

I grinned at her. "That's exactly what we are, so the

outfits are appropriate. Besides, we do blend in…with the shadows…" I whispered the last part, trying to sound mysterious.

Beth grunted. "Ok, 007. Wait a second while I turn on your theme music."

I ignored her jab and quickened my pace. I watched them reach Brady's car. He walked Bebe to the passenger side and opened the door, then waited until she was safely in before shutting it and walking to the driver's side. Who did he think he was? A gentleman, or something? The engine roared to life in his Charger. I had to give him credit for one thing: Brady had a pretty sweet ride. All I had was a bike. One point for Brady.

We continued toward my car, which was parked by the entrance on the opposite side of the parking lot from Brady and Bebe. I watched Brady back his car out, but instead of heading toward the gate he was closest to, he pointed his car in our direction.

"What's he doing?" I panicked.

Beth was scanning the parking lot, her face twisted in a frown. "Looks like the gate is closed in front of the other exit."

"Great. They're going to drive right past us."

"Calm down; just pull your hood down lower and walk slowly. They probably won't even notice us, much less recognize us."

There was no calming me down. I'd turned into a crazed lunatic. I watched as Brady turned his car down our aisle and reacted without thinking. I dove between the two closest cars, pulling Beth down with me. At least I had the fore-thought to pull her on top of me as we tumbled to the pavement so she wouldn't get hurt. Beth tried to get up, but I held her down as Brady's car passed. When I was certain the coast was clear, I released her from my grip and jumped to my feet, sprinting the last twenty yards to my car.

"What the crap was that?" Beth was yelling at me from behind.

"Hurry, they're pulling out. We're going to lose them."

I jumped in the driver's seat and turned on the car, slapping it reverse.

"Geez, let me get the door shut before you peel out like a mad man." I ignored her comment while Beth slammed her door and buckled her seat belt. She was fuming mad at me, but I didn't have time to respond. I exited the parking lot and punched on the gas. They'd already made it through the intersection I was approaching. The light turned yellow, but I didn't brake and sailed through right before it turned red.

Once I'd caught up to Brady's car, I pulled into the other lane and stayed back a few car lengths. I looked over at Beth, who was glaring at me, arms folded across her chest. Man, was she pissed.

"What?" I asked, shrugging my shoulders. I'm not a dummy, so I already knew what, but I figured it best to feign innocence.

"You know, it doesn't matter how many gifts you give her or how many hearts you stick in our yard. If you get me killed, you're never going to get the girl."

Beth was right. I was being pretty irrational, and almost running a red light wasn't exactly keeping her safe. "I'm sorry. I just freaked out for a bit...they were holding hands. At a football game. That's a public declaration."

"Cam, it's not that big of a deal. It's not like they were cuddling or kissing."

"Not yet, at least." I huffed under my breath.

The rest of the ride remained uneventful. I managed to keep a good distance without having to run any more lights that were pink around the edges. It was a Friday night, so the streets were busy. I don't think it was obvious that I was following Brady's car. We'd been on the road for a while, when we hit a busy strip mall and Brady turned into the parking lot. I looked up at the restaurant sign.

"Chili's? Really, Brady? You could have at least picked someplace classy," I said to myself. I actually really liked Chili's, and so did Bebe. I just needed something to complain about.

"Shut up." Beth laughed. "Chili's is like your favorite restaurant. You're just being a bad sport. Bebe probably even picked it. You know how much she loves fajitas."

I pulled into the parking lot on the other side and parked the car. We waited a few minutes before getting out and walking to the front door. Once inside, I scanned the dining room until I found Bebe and Brady sitting in a booth toward the rear. It was the middle table in a bank of five booths. All of them were back-to-back but separated by tall seats with frosted glass partitions on top. Each booth sided to a wall on one end and a walkway on the other.

Once we got to a table, I felt confident Beth and I could remain hidden; getting there unseen, however, was going to be a problem. We walked up to a perky hostess who looked about our age.

"Welcome to Chili's. How many in your party?"

"Just the two of us," Beth answered her.

I watched as the hostess looked down at her seating board and crossed off a table on the opposite side of the room from where we needed to be. "Actually," I cleared my voice, "can we sit over there?" I pointed to the booth behind Bebe and Brady. It seemed like the best option for concealing ourselves. The hostess turned to see where I was pointing and then looked at me with a slight frown. I knew my request would mess her up. Time to pull out the big guns.

I whipped out a wide smile so that the dimples could work their magic and slung my arm around Beth's shoulder. "Please?" I pleaded. "I know it might screw up your rotation, but my sister here has a really weak bladder, so she likes to sit close to the bathroom."

Beth elbowed me in the ribs, hard. "Gee, big brother"— her voice was filled with menace—"way to embarrass me."

I laughed as I answered. "Sure thing, sis. That's what brothers are for."

I'm not sure if it was the dimples or the fact that the hostess now thought I was here with my sister and not on a date, but she was suddenly very willing to accommodate.

"I think I can make that happen." She smiled at me, then winked. Beth gave me a look that said she was going to throw up. Hey, I couldn't help it if I was beautiful. And she shouldn't complain, because right now it was working to our advantage. I knew the hostess would take us in the most direct path, which would march us right past Brady and Bebe. I took off as she leaned over to grab the menus and walked along the wall side of the booths rather than the open side. That way we could approach our table from behind the half wall at the end. I slowed as we reached the corner and let the hostess pull in front of us. Just as I hoped, she positioned her body by the divider between our table and theirs, briefly blocking us from Bebe's view.

I quickly pushed Beth into the seat that backed to Brady, then slid onto the bench next to her. The hostess gave me a weird look as she handed us our menus. I guess choosing to sit right *next* to your sister instead of across from her was the wrong thing to do. I didn't have any siblings, so I hadn't thought about my choice looking awkward. I smiled up at the hostess and nodded my head at Beth. "She doesn't read very well. I always sit next to her at restaurants, to help her with the menu."

I heard Beth choke on her spit as the hostess rolled her eyes at me. "Sure you do. Your waitress will be Rebecca, and she'll be over in a minute." She walked away.

Beth picked up her menu and whacked me with it multiple times. "You stupid..." she started to yell at me, and I slapped my hand over her mouth.

"Shhhh. They'll hear us," I lowered my voice, hoping she'd take my cue.

She remembered where we were, then pulled my hand from her mouth and went back to yelling at me, in a whisper this time. "You stupid jerk! I'm your sister who can't read *and* wets her pants?" Her face was a very, very bright shade of red.

"At least you're cute. That totally makes up for the incontinence." That one earned me another slap on the shoulder. Beth buried her face in the menu, content to ignore me when Rebecca, our waitress, strolled up to the table. "Hey, you two. What can I get for you this evening?"

"I'll have a bacon cheeseburger with onion rings and a Coke," Beth whispered. She sounded ridiculous, but we were close enough that if we talked at a normal volume we ran the risk of being heard. Brady might not recognize our voices, but Bebe sure would.

I didn't realize how hungry I was until she ordered. "Mmmm, that sounds good. I'll have the same," I added, in a whisper as well. The waitress gave us a look that clearly said she was confused by the whispering. I grabbed my throat and smiled as I explained. "We both have laryngitis; this is the loudest we can talk."

Rebecca laughed at my obvious lie as she jotted our orders down and started to take our menus. I put my hand on her wrist, continuing to whisper. "Can we hang on to those for a bit? In case we want something else?"

"Sure thing, kid. I'll be right back with your drinks."

After Rebecca walked away from the table, Beth looked at me with wide eyes. "How much do you intend to eat? Now I look like the girl who can't read, wets her pants, and eats like a pig." She folded her arms across her chest and stuck out her bottom lip. Beth was a champion pouter.

"I'm not going to order more, silly girl. I thought it

would be helpful to have the menus in case Bebe or Brady gets up to use the bathroom. We'll need something to hide behind."

"Oh. Well, in that case, good thinking," Beth agreed. Rebecca returned with our sodas, and Beth took a big swig before continuing. "I hope you brought a lot of money, because you're paying for dinner. You owe me that much for dragging me out on this crazy escapade."

I chuckled quietly. "Fair enough. Now stop talking so we can eavesdrop."

We sat there in silence for a few minutes, listening to the two of them talk about the football game. Their conversation was coming in crystal clear. Looked like Beth and I would be whispering for the remainder of our meal. At least I could hear what they were saying. That *was* the whole point of the mission, after all.

Brady and Bebe talked, and talked, and talked. About anything and everything: basketball, chemistry class, their families and friends, hobbies, favorite movies, and music. On and on and on, until all of our dinners had been eaten and cleared away. I was getting bored; they hadn't said a single thing that was interesting. How could Bebe seriously be into this guy? He was about as exciting as a coat hanger. Beth must have agreed, because she was starting to squirm.

"How much longer do we have to sit here? I've had like twelve Cokes, and I really need to pee."

"Well, you can't go here. Going *in* to the bathroom won't be a problem, but when you come out, Bebe will have a clear shot of your face. I'll get the check, and then we can run across the parking lot to the gas station."

I was signing my name on the credit card slip, when suddenly the night got a whole lot more interesting. Our waitress came out with a large order of drinks for the big group across the aisle from us. She'd set the drink tray full of ice waters and soda on a stand in the aisle, right where our booth joined with Bebe's. At the same time, Brady and Bebe's conversation took a bad turn.

"So, Bianca, do you by any chance have a date to the homecoming dance?"

Beth whipped her head toward me, and her eyes got big. She'd obviously heard the change in conversation, too. Damn it. Brady was going to ask her to homecoming. This was not happening. I looked around, frantically wondering how I could stop it without being seen. Jumping up and shouting in protest probably wouldn't go over very well.

"Actually, I haven't been asked to the dance yet."

Man, asking girls out is so awkward. That's one of the reasons I never did it. He sounded like a dork, and she sounded uncomfortable. I wasn't sure I could stop the train wreck waiting to happen, but I came up with a plan anyway. Beth wasn't going to like it, either. Everything was happening so fast that I didn't have time for a better one.

I grabbed Beth by one hand and her purse in the other; we were going to have to make a run for it. I slid toward the open end of the booth and turned to face the aisle. As discreetly as I could, I kicked the base of the stand holding the giant tray of drinks. The stand tipped away from us, and the tray slid off. More than a dozen glasses came crashing down, spilling on the floor, the poor waitress, and most importantly, all over Brady.

Everyone was momentarily distracted by the chaos, so I stood and pulled Beth out of the booth. Heads down, we walked as fast as we could without drawing attention. Once we cleared the building, we sprinted to the car and left the parking lot. Beth looked out the back window for any sign that an angry mob was in pursuit. Remembering her urgent need for a bathroom, I stopped at the neighboring gas station and parked out front.

"Why are we stopping?" Beth asked.

"I thought you said you had to pee? I stopped so you could use the bathroom."

Beth unbuckled her seat belt. "You knocked that tray of drinks over, didn't you?"

I wasn't exactly feeling bad, so I found no reason to lie. "Guilty as charged." A wide smile spread across my face at the thought of Brady sitting in his booth, soaking wet and freezing cold.

"You promised you wouldn't ruin their date, that we were just going to observe."

"Don't be so dramatic, Beth. I didn't ruin their date. They'll have a good laugh about it later, I'm sure. I couldn't let him ask her to the dance, and I didn't know how to stop it without them seeing us. I panicked. Spilling the drinks was the first thing I could think of."

Beth sighed "Cam, you realize you didn't stop anything. You only delayed it. If he was going to ask her to the dance earlier, then he'll still do it, probably even tonight."

"Maybe," I replied thoughtfully, an impish grin forming on my mouth. "But *I'd* be a lot less likely to kiss a girl good-night if I was covered in soda."

Beth was trying to be mad, but she had a hard time concealing her smile as she got out of the car to find the bathroom. When she got back in, she looked tired. "Please tell me we're done for the night? I need to get home before Bea does. She'll probably head into my room first thing and tell me all about the disastrous dinner. I need time to practice my shocked face."

"Fine, we'll go home. I learned what I needed to, anyway."

"What?" Beth asked as I pulled onto the street and headed for home. "That he plans on asking her to homecoming?"

"No, that Brady is boring and safe. He could never make Bebe happy."

I turned up the radio, and we didn't speak again until we reached home. I parked my dad's car in the driveway and walked Beth across the street. "Thanks for coming."

"You're welcome. Go home and get some sleep." She smiled knowingly. "Spying on them from your front window won't stop a goodnight kiss."

"If you say so, Mom." I hugged her and walked back to my house. I *should* go to bed like Beth had instructed, but there was some masochistic part of me that wanted to wait until they got home. Would they even come home soon? They had to; it was almost eleven. Mr. Barnes never let Bebe stay out past eleven. I grabbed a blanket and sat backward on the couch, looking out the front window. Fifteen minutes later, Brady's Charger pulled up across the street. He got out and walked Bebe to the door. The front porch light was on, so I could see them clearly, though I couldn't hear a thing they were saying. *I wonder how hard it is to find bugging equipment?*

They stood on the porch talking, face-to-face, maybe a foot or two apart. She was holding her jacket across her stomach, and he had his hands in his pockets. Brady said something, and Bebe smiled really big while nodding her head yes. Then Brady got a big goofy grin on his face, too, and I knew she'd just accepted his invitation to the dance.

Brady stepped closer to Bebe, and I watched in horror as he leaned in for a kiss. She closed her eyes and waited while he pulled a hand from his pocket and placed it on her cheek. Everything was moving in slow motion, drawing out my agony. I felt like I was going barf; I couldn't watch this. Instead of shutting the blinds like a decent person would have done, I acted like a royal jackass for the second time that night.

I reached into the pocket of my hoodie, pulled out my keys, and pointed the fob out the window toward my dad's car. Then I hit the panic button. The alarm blared to life, beeping and buzzing and wailing. Lights flashed, illuminating my driveway through the darkness. Brady had been millimeters from Bebe's lips, so when she jolted in surprise, the top of her forehead whacked him in the nose. I doubted it hurt him, but it totally killed their moment, and I laughed out loud. Unfortunately, after a minute of examining my dad's car and determining the coast to be clear, they laughed, too. This was no fun. I hit the panic button again, and the car went silent.

I guess Brady decided not to tempt fate, because when they were done laughing, Bebe shook her head and Brady smiled. Then he leaned over, hugged her, and kissed her on the cheek. I blew out a breath of relief. Brady may have gotten himself a date to the dance, but at least he didn't defile Bebe's lips. Perfect lips that were meant for me.

I was running out of time, and if I didn't make my move soon, I was going to lose Bebe to someone else. If she wanted Brady, if Brady would make her happy, then I wouldn't stand in her way. I just hoped that once I made my intentions clear, Brady would be a nonissue.

BIANCA

The evening had been going really well. Brady and I had fun at the game. We didn't see much of it because we were too busy talking. That's what makes a football game an ideal first date. Something to do if the conversation is bad, but if it's good, you can ignore your surroundings without feeling guilty. We'd basically done just that. I couldn't even tell you the final score, only that it was another blowout, and not in our favor.

He'd taken me to dinner after the game, Chili's at my request. I love, love, love me some fajitas. We spent another hour and a half eating and talking while I waited expectantly for some sort of admission that he was my secret admirer. Only, it didn't come. I was so sure it was Brady. I mean, who else could it be? Nobody. It *had* to be him. But he didn't say a word about it or even hint at responsibility for the gifts. I was beginning to think nothing was going to happen, until the mood shifted toward the end of our dinner.

"So, Bianca, do you by any chance have a date to the homecoming dance?"

That caught me off guard. I hoped this was going to turn into an invite, because the dance was only a week away. At this point, I wasn't sure Mr. Mysterious was going to admit his identity, much less ask me to the dance. "Actually, I haven't been asked to the dance yet." I crossed my fingers under the table and held my breath.

"Well, in that case, I was wondering..." Brady didn't get a chance to finish his question, because at that exact moment, an entire tray of beverages tipped sideways and spilled all over the floor next to us, all over our table, and, unfortunately, all over Brady. He was completely soaked from his belly button to his knees. He tried to jump up so he could avoid the spill, but since we were in a booth, there was really no escaping. All he accomplished was banging his thighs on the underside of the table.

"Ouch!" he cried out, and quickly sat back down. But when he stood up, all the liquid that had spilled on the booth seat spread out, so when he sat back down it was in a large puddle of ice-cold water and soda. "Sh..." Brady started to say something vulgar but quickly put a lid on it and looked up at me with a sheepish grin. "Sorry. I try not to swear in front of the ladies. When I stand it's going to look like I didn't make it to the bathroom. Not to mention, my ass is freezing."

I tried my best to hold back the laughter, but after five seconds of biting the inside of my cheek, I bust out in a gut-grabbing howl. Brady was a good sport because looked slightly amused instead of angry. I'm sure *I* looked like a rabid hyena and deserved a scornful glare, but he was a gentleman. Tears were escaping down my cheeks, and I thought our poor waitress was going to cry for completely different reasons.

"I am *so* sorry," she gasped. "I don't know what happened. Let me get you some towels."

"Don't worry about it. I don't think at this point towels will help much." Brady smiled politely at her. His graciousness was making her feel more guilty.

"I'll at least get you a towel to take home so you can put it on the seat of your car before you sit down." Poor Rebecca was trying desperately to salvage her tip. She left the dining room and came back a few minutes later with a large hand towel and the check. It read zero dollars. Brady looked at it, then at her.

"This really isn't necessary," he protested. "Accidents happen."

"Yes, it is. I'm so embarrassed. There's no way I'm letting you pay for your dinner."

"Well, thank you, Rebecca. That's very kind of you."

"It's the least I could do. I really am sorry. I hope this won't keep you from coming back." She looked hopeful; she was waiting for confirmation that Brady wasn't going to march straight to her manager and complain.

"I'm sure we'll be back. The little lady here *loves* fajitas.

Not sure I could keep her away if I wanted to." Brady winked at me. The waitress apologized one more time as we got up and then left to attend to her other tables. Brady reached into his pocket, pulled out his soaking wet wallet, and grabbed a soggy ten-dollar bill. He threw it on the table and held out his hand toward the exit. "Ladies first."

Super brownie points for Brady. Ten bucks would have been a generous tip, even if our meal hadn't been interrupted by a beverage bath. Considering that she hadn't charged us for our meal, it was like a million percent gratuity. We walked to the car, and he still opened the door for me, with a smile. As if he didn't have ice in his underwear, which I'm sure was a very good possibility.

"That was super cool of you back there. I think a lot of guys wouldn't have left a tip if they'd just been embarrassed in front of a date."

"They're jeans." He shrugged. "It's not like she ruined them. Plus, I have seat warmers, so my bum will be toasty and dry before we get to your house." He reached over and pushed the button for his seat warmer, then pushed the one for mine. Within moments, my rear was feeling nice and cozy. *Our next car totally needed seat warmers.* "Not to mention the fact that she was more humiliated than I was. The meal was free; a tip was the least I could do." Brady's face turned thoughtful before he chuckled, "If I'd have known dinner would be free, I'd have taken you someplace nicer." He raised his eyebrows up and down playfully, and I laughed.

"Well, it definitely made for an interesting first date. Something to look back on and laugh about next time."

The words came out before I could think about what I was saying. I realized the implication a little too late and hoped he wouldn't pick up on it. That was way more bold than I'd intended it to be. We pulled up to my house and Brady parked the car, then came around to open my door and help me out. As we walked to the front porch, he called me out on my previous slip.

"Something to laugh about next time, huh? Does that mean there will be a second date?"

I assessed him for a moment before answering; I didn't want to seem too eager. "I think you've totally earned a second date, if you want one."

"Well, in that case… Would you like to go out next Saturday night, to homecoming? We can go to dinner first. I'll be prepared with rain ponchos so that your dress and my suit won't get ruined by stray drinks."

I laughed as I nodded my acceptance. "I'd love to go to homecoming with you. But I think you're the only one who needs a poncho. Just make sure you pick me up while wearing it. The photo op will be priceless." He laughed at my jab—a real laugh, not just to be polite—and I laughed because he was laughing. As our laughter died down, it got quiet very quickly, and I knew this was the moment I'd been dreading.

All night long, my mind had strayed to this scenario. It was a first date, if you didn't count the Slurpee run, which I didn't. I wasn't sure if I should expect a goodnight kiss, but this moment was feeling very much like a kissing moment. It's not that Brady wasn't kissable. With that gorgeous smile, he was most definitely *extremely* kissable. I wasn't sure I was ready to move on completely from Cam. Kissing Brady would be admitting to myself that I was giving up on the boy I really liked.

We were standing pretty close, close enough that he wouldn't have to move closer to kiss me, just lean in a little. Brady broke the silence first. "I had a really good time tonight." His voice was suddenly huskier and hesitant.

"I had a lot of fun, too," I replied. He looked nervous, and I decided that if he had the guts to kiss me after the whole dinner fiasco, that I had the guts to kiss him back. I looked into his eyes, and he started to lean in. *Oh my gosh. This is it. Brady Jones is going to kiss me...* I leaned forward to meet him and let my eyes flutter closed. He was so close now that his lips were brushing mine ever so slightly. Mine started to part in response, when the loudest sound imaginable pulled me away with a jerk and a scream. I jumped. Literally jumped, and in doing so, whacked Brady in the nose with my forehead.

"Crap, Brady, I'm so sorry. Are you ok?" I asked while he put a hand over his nose and nodded in confirmation. Then we both turned toward the noise that had nearly caused me to give him an unsolicited nose job. Cam's father's car was parked in the driveway, and the car alarm was going off, wailing at a deafening level. We stared at the car, trying to figure out what had caused the alarm to blare. I couldn't see anything suspicious. Must have been one of the random stray cats that roamed the neighborhood.

Brady looked back at me, shaking his head. I couldn't

believe how rotten his luck was. Poor guy. I couldn't help it. For the second time that night, I laughed at his misfortune. I was kind of a crappy date.

"Sure, laugh it up." Brady was smiling, so I knew he wasn't upset with my reaction. He sighed and looked at me, probably deciding whether the mood had been totally ruined. "I'd love to pick up where we left off, but I think I'd be pushing it. Soggy pants, battered nose, I'm not sure I want to know what strike three might deliver. Time to bow out gracefully." He grabbed me for a hug without pulling me close enough to get me wet, then pressed a gentle kiss to my cheek. "I'll see you Monday, Bea." With that, he turned and walked back to his car, pausing to flash me one last smile before he got in and drove away.

I sighed and headed inside, unsure whether I was disappointed that Brady hadn't kissed me or relieved that I'd been able to postpone cheating on Cam. I climbed the stairs and entered my room, desperately needing to sit down and process what had happened this evening. I was going to kiss Brady, and that felt really unfair, since deep down I was wishing it'd been Cam. Brady was such a decent guy. Pretty much perfect, by most girls' standards. But I wasn't most girls, and I wasn't sure I could ever feel the same way about him as I felt about Cam.

I hadn't even gotten my jacket and shoes off before Beth threw my door open without knocking. "Sure, just come on in. I'm not naked or anything." My sarcasm was very clear, but she totally ignored it.

"Two things. First, what in the heck was all the noise

about? And second, I need details, lots and lots of details. Explain the first thing quickly, so we can get to the second. That's more important." Beth's excitement was radiating, so I decided to let the intrusion slide.

"Well, the noise was Cam's dad's car alarm going off. I can't for the life of me figure out *why* it did, but it was absolutely horrible timing. Brady's lips were practically touching mine when it happened, so instead of getting a kiss, I almost broke his nose. I got startled and jumped; then I smacked into him."

Beth's eyes went wide, and she threw her hand over her mouth in shock. "No way. He was going to kiss you?" She gave a girly shriek and started bouncing on my bed.

"Focus here, Beth, focus." I snapped my fingers in front of her eyes. "I swear, sometimes it's like you're my pet Chihuahua instead of my sister. I was totally embarrassed. Needless to say, the kiss didn't end up happening. But it could have been worse." I snickered to myself. "I could have been Brady. I'm surprised he had the nerve to kiss me, after the catastrophe at dinner."

For a brief moment, something flashed across Beth's face, an emotion I couldn't place. If I didn't know better, I'd say it was guilt. Since that didn't make any sense and it only lasted a split second, I figured I was imagining it. Beth's mouth formed an *O*, and she pushed for me to expound. "This sounds juicy. Please tell me before I die, waiting in anticipation," she begged.

"Ok, drama queen." I hit her with my pillow as I sized her up. "Stop being so peppy. You're the walking personification of cheerleaders right now. There's a reason for the stereotype, you know." She ignored my insult and waited patiently for her juicy story. The girl was on a mission. "You're hopeless, too, you know. Guess it's hereditary." Beth nodded like a bobblehead Barbie doll, still bouncing up and down on my bed. I shook mine and laughed but moved on with the story.

"Well, we had a great time at the game, and then he took me to dinner at a restaurant of my choosing."

"Wait, wait, let me guess." Beth interrupted me as she put her fingers to her temples and squinted as if she were trying to read my mind. "You guys went to Chili's?" Her answer earned her yet another slap with my pillow. "Geez, Bea, you're so predictable."

"I fail to see how the restaurant choice is important," I defended myself. Beth snickered at my protest but didn't say anything else. "So anyway, we went to dinner, and before you say anything, yes, I did get fajitas. Don't bother making fun of me if you want to hear the rest of the story." This time Beth could barely contain her laughter, but she ran her fingers across her mouth, zipping her lips. I waited a second, just to be sure.

"Dinner was fun, too. There was never a lull in the conversation or anything. As a matter of fact, Brady is almost too perfect. It's like he was meant for you, or something."

"Now who needs to focus? Get to the catastrophe already."

Beth was getting impatient, and I was enjoying the torture. "Oh, all right. Calm down. So we got to the end of dinner and I thought he would ask for the check, but he totally changed direction and brought up homecoming. He asked if I was going with anyone, and I said I wasn't. Then, right when I thought he'd ask me, our waitress knocked over a tray of drinks. It spilled all over him."

"No way." Beth gasped. "Oh, how horrible. I bet your waitress felt awful."

"She did. So awful, in fact, that she didn't charge us for the dinner."

"Well, that's lucky. Was Brady super angry?" Beth's mood shifted. Instead of excited, she seemed really concerned about Brady all of a sudden. Weird.

"Not at all. He was way sweet about it. He threw down a nice tip for the poor lady, even though he was soaked to the bone and freezing his ass off." Beth gave me a dirty look, which I knew was over the swear, but I threw my hands up in defense. "Hey, his words, not mine."

"I guess, given the situation, I can forgive the potty mouth," Beth conceded.

"I'll say. It was like twelve of those giant restaurant glasses. Half were ice water, but the other half were soda. Not only was his ass cold, it was probably sticky, too." I made sure to throw in the extra swear that time, just for Beth's benefit. "So he walked out of the Chili's all calm and composed, opened my door for me, and drove me home. Did I mention that his car has heaters in the seats? Butt heaters are amazing, Beth. We really need those in our next car."

She gave me a look; I was straying from what was important again. I finished my story without giving her a chance to chastise me. "After he got me to the door, he asked me to homecoming, and of course I said yes. The mood was totally screaming *kiss me, kiss me.* He went in for the kiss, and right as our lips brushed, Cam's car alarm went off. That's just stupid, dumb luck right there. I mean, what are the chances that both his first homecoming proposal *and* his attempt to kiss me could have been interrupted so horribly?"

"Yes..." Beth mused, "What *are* the chances?"

"I swear, not even the universe itself could have planned it better. It's like a big, flashing neon sign that says *Don't go out with Brady. It's a bad idea.*" The words tumbled out of my mouth before I realized what I was saying. *Wait, was this really a sign?* Maybe I shouldn't go to homecoming with Brady. Maybe tonight was just a preview of things to come.

"Oh no, you don't." Beth was stern. "Don't even go there. You're not going to read into tonight's events. The drinks and the car alarm were just a coincidence. I can guarantee it wasn't because of you, or Brady. And the universe was definitely not behind it, either." She sounded so sure. I wished I could believe her. "You're just being a chicken, because you have no self-esteem. Though, for the life of me, I can't figure out why. A really cute, really nice guy likes you. You don't know how to handle it, so you're getting all superstitious. You'll ruin everything before it even starts."

"Why don't you tell me what you really think? Geez, Beth, could you be any harsher?"

"I'm sorry, Bianca, but it's time you accepted the truth. There is *nothing* average about you. You're pretty and smart and crazy athletic. I couldn't do half the things you do on the basketball court, and I know for a fact that guys think that's hot. I've heard them talking about it in PE."

My mouth fell open. What? Guys said I was hot? In PE, of all places?

Beth continued her rant. "You're fun to be around, and I don't for one second believe that horse crap about the universe sending all the boys you like to ask me out instead. I think the fact that there's a guy leaving you love notes, presents, and a yard full of hand-cut hearts proves it."

Wow, she was on a roll. I wanted to argue, but the second I opened my mouth, she shot me a look that screamed *Don't you dare.* "Whoever he is, he isn't sending *me* all of those romantic things. He's doing them for you. Since we're pretty much a package deal, I'm positive this guy knows who I am. But he's not choosing me, is he?"

Beth paused to take a breath. She must have seen the shock on my face and the horror in my eyes, because her voice softened. She reached out to grab my hands. "Bea, you're amazing in so many ways, and for some reason everyone can see that but you. I know your instinct is to deny it, but you have an extremely romantic secret admirer *and* a not-so-secret, very sweet, totally hot date to homecoming."

"They may be the same person, you know." It was all I could manage to get out.

"But maybe they aren't." She smiled. "That would make at least two boys who are crazy about you. If I did a little digging, I'm sure I could find at least a couple more."

I'd just received quite the tongue lashing, and I was feeling overwhelmed. I'd never really thought I had bad self-esteem. I just wasn't full of myself like a lot of other people I knew. Since when did not being arrogant translate into feeling horrible about myself? I wasn't the rock star that Beth was. I'm obviously not the Greek god that Cam is. But I liked myself well enough. I felt ok about who I was, recognized good things about me...sometimes. Horror struck me. Was I one of those people that everyone thought was self-deprecating in an effort to get compliments?

For the second time this week, I started crying. I looked at Beth. "Do you think I'm one of those girls who goes around complaining about themselves, just so people will say nice things about me? Is that what everyone else thinks?"

"Oh, good heavens, no." Beth put her arms around me. "I doubt that anyone besides me or Cam even notices your insecurities. You come across as very confident."

I breathed a sigh of relief. "I don't feel like I'm *not* confident. I've always thought of it as more like being self-aware. I know that I'm not a dork or anything. I can just recognize that I'm not quite as awesome as either of you." I smiled at my sister as I sniffled. I hoped that she could understand where I was coming from.

"I understand how you think, and I want you to know that you think wrong." Beth was so matter of fact, I actually wanted to believe her. "Now stop being stupid and stubborn so you can pay attention to the two super studs vying for your attention."

I laughed at her terminology. "Super studs, huh? My secret admirer could be a super geek, you know? Or a super freak, a super psycho, a super creep-o..." I trailed off.

"I have a feeling he isn't. My gut is telling me that he

might be the perfect man for you." Beth had a dreamy look in her eyes. "What if Brady and your secret admirer found out about each other? Maybe they'd fight over you."

"I don't think I'd like it if two guys got in a fist fight over me. That would make them both super Neanderthals. It'd do me no good in the boyfriend department."

"Whatever. I think it'd be romantic." Beth got up and headed for the door. "I also think you need to have some seriously sweet dreams tonight. About two dashingly handsome men battling for your hand. You're in a gown, they're on horses, maybe jousting or fighting with swords. Probably in tights, so you could see their cute butts." She winked at me.

"I can't believe we share DNA." I laughed at Beth's wistful expression. "You're such a girl. You're also forgetting that I don't have a face to go with suitor number two. That makes it awfully hard to dream about him jousting, or whatever your warped mind thinks he should be doing. And tights? Really? Not very masculine, if you ask me."

"To each their own." She waved me off. "Tights, basketball shorts, whatever works for you. As far as suitor number two is concerned, I'm sure you won't have a problem finding someone's face to fill in the blank with." She raised her eyebrows up and down suggestively.

"I have no idea what you're talking about." My denial was half-hearted.

"Whatever you say, Bea. Goodnight, sweet dreams." Beth left the room giggling and closed the door behind her.

Maybe Beth was right. Maybe I should be less hard on

myself. Someone out there obviously liked me, and Brady had just asked me on a second date. He almost kissed me, for goodness sake. If Brady isn't my secret admirer, then there may even be two somebodies that liked me. I didn't know who the second somebody was, but my sister was definitely right about one thing. I could totally come up with a handsome prince to fill in the blanks of my dreams. One with brown hair and blue eyes and adorable dimples…and killer abs. He would absolutely *not* be in tights, but he probably wouldn't be in a shirt, either, so I think Beth would approve. I lay down and closed my eyes, ready for a rendezvous with the man of my dreams.

CAMERON

IT WAS SATURDAY MORNING. I SHOULD HAVE BEEN SLEEPING in, but that would imply that I had slept last night. I hadn't, at all. I couldn't get the almost-kiss out of my head. Apparently, Brady was more of a man than I was. He was covered in soda, and he still had the balls to kiss her. I couldn't even buy her a gift and give it to her in person. I'd had to break into her locker. I was pretty sure Brady had asked Bebe to homecoming. I didn't want to assume, but I couldn't ask her about it, because I shouldn't know it happened at all.

We needed a friendly game of one-on-one. Bebe was always more willing to spill her guts when we were playing ball. Some of our more serious conversations happened then. I know it's a strange time for a heart-to-heart, but when we're playing, she's so competitive that her physical guard is up all the time. That leaves her mental and emotional guards compromised.

I waited until eleven before I knocked on the door. As much as I'd like to see her in her sleepwear again, I doubt that'd get her to open up to me. Bebe answered the door with a grin. She was in a pair of short running shorts and a thin T-shirt. Her hair was up in a messy bun. "I was wondering how long you'd wait to knock on the door."

"I wanted to make sure you were up and dressed first this week," I answered. She picked up her tennis shoes from the basket by the door, then chucked them at me.

"Laugh all you want now," she said. "Once we hit the Perkins's driveway, you won't be laughing anymore. You'll be crying like a baby, 'cause you got your butt whipped by a girl." She grabbed her basketball and started down the porch. "Bring my shoes, will you?" She smirked at me over her shoulder. She wasn't going to get away with that kind of talk before we even started.

"Nice shorts. Showing a little more leg than usual. What happened to the basketball monstrosities? Worried you might lose? Trying to distract me with your blindingly sexy legs?" I waggled my eyebrows suggestively. If only she knew the thoughts those gorgeous legs gave me. My taunt wouldn't ruffle her feathers. She was unflappable on the court, but I loved trying anyway.

We reached the driveway, and Bebe dribbled, took a shot, rebounded, and passed the ball to me. I did the same. We took turns shooting like this for about five minutes before she snatched the ball out of my hands. "Ok, quit stalling. That's enough warm-up for you." She walked back to the sidewalk and waited for me to catch up.

"If you're so confident, why don't you let me take first ball today?"

"No way. Rules are rules. Your height advantage gives me the handicap. I get first possession on principle, even if I *don't* need it."

"That's a whole lot of confidence coming from such a tiny person…"

"Oh, it's on now. You did *not* call me tiny." She chucked the ball at me. "Check."

I passed the ball back to her, and she didn't even bother easing onto the court. She shot straight past me for the layup. "One to zip. You gonna play or just stare at my blindingly sexy legs?" She threw back at me. I loved that she made me work for my wins. I almost always won, but she made me work for it.

We played hard for the next fifteen minutes. She was very physical on defense, which I loved because it gave me lots of excuses to touch her. Sometimes I'd even throw in a dirty move. Grab her wrist or yank on her shirt to gain an advantage. I didn't need the advantage, but I did need to touch her. She'd always have the advantage on me there. We stopped to grab some water. The score was 10-12, and I was in the lead.

It was unusually hot for September, probably close to ninety-five degrees. There wasn't a cloud in the sky. I was sweating like crazy, so I pulled my shirt over my head and wiped my face with it. When I looked up, I noticed Bebe staring at my stomach. My heart sped up. Finally, she was noticing. I'd worked extremely hard over the summer for my physique to look like it did. Partly to get cut for basketball, and partly to impress Bebe. Her face said that my plan had worked. She was impressed, *very* impressed. I couldn't help grinning.

"Like what you see?" I flexed my chest for her.

"Crap, Cam. When did you get so many muscles?" She was trying to play it cool, but I'd caught her looking, and she knew it. The redness in her face wasn't just from the sun.

"I spent a lot of time working out this summer. I knew I'd need a way to distract you on the court. Is it working?" I asked the question like I was teasing, but I wanted her to admit that she was attracted to me.

Bebe shook her head and took the ball out. "You're going to need a lot more than a hot body to distract me." She checked the ball and took off again, but this time I was faster. She thought my body was hot, huh? Let's see if she could handle the distraction when it was right up against her. I darted in front of her, and she slammed right into my solid block of muscles. When she tried to back away, I grabbed her around the waist and pulled her tight against me. She dropped the ball and I scooped it up, straight into the basket.

"Ok, because that wasn't a foul or anything." Bebe stopped and threw her hands on her hips, waiting for me to admit to my cheating.

"Hey, all's fair in love and basketball." I shrugged my shoulders with an innocent look.   "So that's how we're playing now?" She glared at me before her mouth drew into a wicked smile. "Fine. I can play that game. A shirt for a shirt."

Her words didn't register until she reached down and pulled the hem of her T-shirt up over her head. Shirt off, she mimicked me, wiping the sweat off her face with it, then throwing it to the grass. She had a sports bra on—a cute one that was pretty covering. I'd seen a lot of girls in a lot less when they wore swimming suits. But those girls weren't Bianca, and this was the most of her skin I'd ever seen.

Short shorts and a sports bra. I'd died and gone to heaven. Bebe had an amazing stomach. Flat and toned, like an athletic goddess. Not like one of those super skinny chicks. The kind you're scared to break if you hug them. Bebe had honest to gosh muscles. While much more feminine than mine, her six-pack was unmistakable. It was *so* incredibly hot.

"What's the matter, Cam? Like what you see?" Much more than she knew. I didn't even try to hide my staring. If I didn't snap out of it, I'd need to hose myself down. Bebe used my temporary brain dysfunction to her advantage and stole the ball, launching it at the basket. It was a perfect shot from the three-point line, but in one-on-one it was only worth two points.

"Twelve, twelve," she shouted. "Looks like my distraction worked. You going to play ball or peeping tom?"

I shook my head. I hadn't moved an inch since she'd taken off her shirt. "I vote peeping tom. You can't expect me to play while you're half naked."

"Why not? You expect *me* to play while *you're* half naked.

I'm just following your lead."

"It's not the same," I argued, even though I knew I wouldn't win. I didn't want to win. I definitely didn't want her to put her shirt back on.

She looked at me and pretended to think. "You know, someone wise once told me that all is fair in love and basketball."

"Fine, have it your way. But don't be mad at me when you can't handle the heat."

"I'm sure I'll manage."

The rest of the game was magical. I know I sound like a chick admitting that. I'm not entirely sure how a basketball game *can* be magical, but my head was in the clouds. I felt all giddy and gooey. We kept playing hard and aggressive. Only now, every time I found an excuse to bump into her or brush up against her, it was my bare torso against hers. My nerve endings were on fire, and I thought my brain might explode if this didn't end soon.

I finally won the game but only by one point. Her distraction proved more than successful. We stood there, panting and sweaty, smiling at each other from ear to ear.

"Good game, Barnes," I complimented, and I walked over to the hose in my side yard for a drink. "Even if it was dirty."

Bebe followed behind me and waited for her turn. "Hey, save some water for the rest of us," she complained. I finished drinking and then put the hose over my head. It was hot outside, and I was feeling hot in more ways than one. I definitely needed to cool off. I watched as the sweat dripped from Bebe's temple and made an executive decision. She needed to cool off, too.

I placed my thumb over the end of the hose for maximum distance, then flipped it to face her. She screamed as the cold water hit her and tried to run, but the grass was wet, so she slipped instead. Now that she was defenseless, I walked over and sprayed her. She curled up into a ball to protect her face. After a few seconds, I figured she'd gotten what she deserved, and I started toward the spigot. But she reached out and grabbed my foot when I stepped, and I ended up falling face-first. Without missing a beat, Bebe was on her knees, scrambling right over me for the hose that I'd dropped. I grabbed her by the waist and flipped her on her back, pinning her arms above her head.

"Oh, you're in trouble now," I warned.

"Me?" She shrieked through her laughter, "You're the one who started it."

"The real question is, will it be water torture or tickle torture? Perhaps we could revisit the ever-effective face lick?"

"Cameron Bates, don't do it. Don't you dare, you'll regret it. I promise." I had her pinned, but not very hard, and she wasn't really struggling to get up. She could have easily. That's the moment my world stopped. Time was standing still. I was staring at her and she was staring at me, our bodies pressed together. I thought in that moment that I detected heat in her eyes. Like she was feeling the same thing I was. That she finally wanted from me what I'd wanted from her since the moment we'd met. The fire that was burning me up was begging me to make my move. *Kiss her, Cam. Kiss her like crazy.*

I leaned in closer, so that our noses were only inches away, and then I turned my mouth and whispered in her ear. "Don't do what? Maybe this?" I very gently slid the tip of my tongue across her earlobe and down her jaw. I could feel the goose bumps on her arms as I reached her chin, then ran the tip of my nose back up her cheek until it was touching hers. Bebe closed her eyes as we lay there, nose to nose. This was it. I was going to do it.

"Bebe…" I whispered.

"Yes?" Her response was barely audible.

I paused a second too long. A car pulled into Bebe's driveway and honked the horn. Just enough of a distraction to pull me away from the moment. We both looked over to see Brady getting out and heading to the front door. *Damn. I hesitated, and now I've missed my chance.*

I let go of Bebe's arms and stood up, offering her my hand. "I'm guessing he's here for you." She grabbed my outstretched arm and used it to pull herself up off the grass.

"I'm guessing you're right." She smiled, but it didn't reach her eyes. They searched mine, waiting for something. I wasn't sure what she wanted, though. My perfect moment had passed.

"Must have been a pretty good date last night, if he's already back for more?" I tried to play it off like I didn't care. That I wasn't fishing for information.

"I'd say it went pretty good. He asked me to homecoming." Her comment came out like a question, but she didn't elaborate. Bebe stared at me, waiting for a specific response,

I'm sure, but I didn't know what to give her. So, I took the coward's way out.

"That's great. Now you can come with Beth and me. It'll be much more fun with you there." On the outside, I gave the acting performance of my life, but on the inside my heart was screaming at me to stop being such a pansy. Bebe's face fell, almost imperceptibly before putting on a big smile.

"It will be fun, won't it?" She turned and called out to Brady, who at this point hadn't noticed us over here. "Hey, Brady. Looking for me?"

He jogged across the street to us. "As a matter of fact, I was." He smiled that damn sparkly grin as he turned to me and held out his fist. "Hey, Cam, what's up, man?"

I bumped his fist with mine and tried to be nice. "Not much. Just playing some ball with Bebe here. Showing her how it's done."

"Yeah, I think you're a little confused on who was showing who." She smirked at me, back to her regular old smartass self. As if the intense moment we shared barely a minute ago had never happened. She turned to address Brady. "So what's going on?"

"Well, I was on my way home from work and wondered if you wanted to grab a Slurpee with me?"

"Yes. I need a Slurpee. It's so stinking hot out today. You must have been reading my mind." She looked at me. "You want to come?"

As if I'd be the third wheel right now. I had no desire to see them flirt all afternoon. I may have crashed a date in secret, but I have enough dignity not to tag along on one openly. "That's ok. You two kids have fun. I'm going to hit the shower."

Bebe's eyes looked sad. Or, at least, I thought they did. I was probably just delusional. It looked like she *actually* wanted me to go with her and Brady on their mini-date. Now I was losing my mind. I turned around and walked inside. Bebe said good-bye, but I only waved over my shoulder, without looking back. I couldn't watch Brady steal her away from me.

I stood in the shower, eyes closed, lukewarm water running over my head and down my face. I thought about how Brady must have felt last night. He'd been so close to kissing Bebe when I interrupted him. I almost felt bad about the car alarm...*almost*. My final effort had to be big. So big that Bebe couldn't deny how I felt about her. I might not be able to keep her and Brady from going to the dance together, but the next guy who got their lips that close to hers would be me.

BIANCA

I went to 7-Eleven with Brady and got a Slurpee, and that's about all I remember from my Saturday afternoon. I'm pretty sure I showered. My room looks a bit cleaner, so I must have tried to tidy it up. I didn't wake up hungry on Sunday morning, so I probably ate some dinner. My laundry had been cleaned, folded, and put away. I'm almost certain I wouldn't have done that voluntarily, which means that the magical laundry elves paid me a visit and I missed the entire thing. My mind was blurry.

After Brady dropped me off, I'd practically become catatonic. I couldn't process what'd happened in Cam's yard. One minute we were playing basketball. The next we were flirting. That turned into stripping and ended with Cam's shirtless chest pressed up against me. When he licked my ear, it felt entirely different than the time he licked my cheek. That was playful. This was… I don't know what it was. Other than completely, mind-numbingly sexy. Oh. My. Gosh. How can someone be so embarrassed and so thrilled at the same time? Those two emotions can't coexist, can they?

I'd gotten crazy goose bumps when his breath hit my neck and he ran his nose up my cheek. I knew he'd noticed. I'd been an idiot and taken off my shirt so my skin was completely exposed, betraying my reaction. When he said my name, he sounded unsure. I've never heard Cameron Bates sound anything but confident and cocky. But the way Cam had looked at me, his emotions seemed raw. He'd looked vulnerable. It was awesome and scary all at the same time.

I was sure for a second that he was going to kiss me. I've been kissed enough times to know what *the look* looks like. Cam had *the look* written all over his face. I'd been ready for it, too. Even though I was nervous, I'd felt at peace. The moment was right. Being kissed by Cam would have felt amazing. Even *almost* kissing him felt amazing.

This brings me to my current state of confusion. It was Monday morning, and I still had no clue why Cam had been about to kiss me. He'd never shown interest before. My best guess was that being half naked and soaking wet was enough to give his hormonal teenage brain a momentary lapse in judgment. I should have asked Beth what she thought about the whole situation, but I knew she'd read into it. I was confused enough. I didn't need false hope.

"So, Bebe. Do you anticipate getting any flowers today?" Cam was talking to me, but I hadn't been paying attention.

There were about ten minutes left in first hour.

"Huh? What? Oh. Flowers. I don't know. Maybe, I guess." I looked up and saw three student office aides walk in the room, each carrying a few bundles of carnations. It was Homecoming Spirit Week, and as part of the festivities, the student council was selling things that you could buy for someone and have delivered during first hour. Today's item was flowers. Ms. Cutter hated this tradition because it took ten minutes from her class each day. Her students loved it, though, because it took ten minutes from her class each day. She was very vocal in expressing her opinion on the matter.

Ms. Cutter put on her grumpy face as she made an announcement. "All right, everyone, settle down and listen up. When you hear your name called, raise your hand so we can get this done quickly." She looked expectantly at the first student aide and the girl jumped into action, calling out names.

"Bianca Barnes?" I raised my hand, and she came over with a pink carnation. I responded with a thanks and looked down at the note attached.

Hey, Bea. I just wanted you to know I was thinking about you. Have a great day.
- Brady

"Oh, how sweet," Cam crooned over my shoulder.

The first aide had finished passing her flowers out, and the second one started calling out names. "Cameron Bates?"

"Over here, bro." Cam's hand shot up, and the guy brought him his flower. As the aide was walking over, Cam leaned into me. "Bebe, you shouldn't have…"

"I didn't." I snickered.

"Bianca Barnes?" I heard my name called again. What the heck? Maybe my secret admirer had sent me one, too? I raised my hand, and the guy who'd just delivered Cam's flower came back with another one for me. I looked at the tag this time, and it read:

I'm giving out three flowers today, for my three best girls. I'm sure it goes without saying, but you're my number one.
Love, Cam

I sent Cam's sappy remark right back to him, batting my eyelashes. "Oh, how sweet. Thanks, Cam." He smiled and looked down at his flower's tag.

"Hey." He was incredulous. "You really didn't send it to me."

I laughed loudly. "I told you I didn't. Who's it from, anyway?"

"Angelica." he grumbled, then glared at me. "I guess I know who really loves me."

"Cam, you're *my* number one. I thought it went without saying." I made a kissy face.

He pouted. "Yeah, well, it couldn't hurt to send a guy flowers every now and then to remind him of that." His fake disappointment was adorable.

"I'll be sure to remember that next time."

"Or you could be sure to remember it tomorrow when they're selling candy..."

"I'll keep that in mind." I chuckled.

The third office aide was working on her flowers when she called out, "Ms. Cutter?" The class snickered, and our teacher's cheeks turned bright pink. She held out her hand to accept the carnation.

I turned to Cam, eyes wide as Ms. Cutter silently read the note attached to the flower. "You didn't? You're such a suck-up."

"Hey, someone's got to make the lady happy. I'm doing my part to keep us out of detention." Cam was a smooth one.

Ms. Cutter smiled, and her eyes twinkled when she looked back at us. "Thank you, Cameron. That was very kind."

"Anything for my best teacher." He grinned, releasing the dimples. The class snickered again.

"Bianca Barnes?" I looked up. My name had been called a third time? What the hell was going on? If Beth sent me a flower, I'd be in trouble, because I hadn't even thought about sending her one. I raised my hand, even though it was unnecessary. The aide was already headed over to me. But she didn't have just a single carnation. She had a whole bouquet. It had pink carnations and baby's breath sprinkled around a dozen red roses, all situated beautifully in a glass vase. There was a chorus of *oohs* and *aahs* from the class.

I looked at the delivery girl. "You can buy all this for a

dollar? You guys must have a sweet hookup on flowers."

She laughed as she responded. "Nope, I wish. Someone dropped it off in the office before school and asked us to deliver it when we did the rest of the flowers."

"Do you know who it was?"

"No, I wasn't here when it came in. I think they left it with the secretary or something. There should be a note, though."

"Oh, ok. Thanks," I said, then looked down to read the note.

Bianca,
I figured you'd get at least a couple flowers today, but I knew that just a couple of flowers wouldn't do you justice. You deserve so much more.
Yours - ?

"Great, now my single flower looks pathetic." Cam was reading the card over my shoulder. "How am I supposed to impress you with this guy hanging around? He needs to come clean so I can send him packing." I knew Cam was joking, but the idea of him being jealous had me dancing internally.

The bell rang, and I put on my backpack, then picked up the gigantic vase of flowers. I'd have to take them to second period because I didn't have time to go to my locker. As I walked down the hall I got a few questioning looks and a lot more *oohs* and *aahs*. A girl I passed was holding a single flower. When she saw mine, she hit her boyfriend in the arm and said something to the extent of *That's how a real man sends flowers.* I was making quite the spectacle.

I sat the flowers on the ground during my second class, careful not to kick them over. It seemed a shame to put something so beautiful on the floor, but if I put them on my desk I'd have had no room to work. I got to my locker before government class and was met by a squealing cheerleader. Beth was squealing an awful lot lately.

"Bea, they're so beautiful," she breathed. Cam walked up behind me, and she looked at him. "Almost as beautiful as mine is." Beth smiled and then gave Cam a hug and a kiss on the cheek. "Thank you, Cam."

"Well, I couldn't let my favorite twins go without a flower today," he said. "But it looks like neither of you needed *me* to make sure you got flowers." Cam nodded his head toward my vase and then to the three additional flowers in Beth's hand.

"Yes, but I like your flower better." Beth sighed. "These are from Josh Sutton. I think Bea was right. Maybe I let him down a little too gently…"

I laughed. "I've told you a million times, Beth. You've *got* to stop being so nice to all the random guys that ask you out. A little rejection is good for a man. Puts hair on their chest," I insisted. Cam nodded in agreement.

"You're one to talk, Cam," Beth accused. "Mr. *I have no interest in Angelica Valdez, but I'll flirt with her all day long and make her think she has a chance.*" Beth must have seen something in Angelica that I didn't, because she was always sticking up for her. Cam's eyes dropped to the floor as the warning bell for third period rang. He must have felt bad.

The rest of the school day went by quickly. I left my flowers in the locker room on top of my locker during PE, chemistry, and basketball conditioning. I knew that was a gamble because anyone could have taken them, but I didn't want to flaunt the flowers in front of Brady. I hadn't mentioned my secret admirer to him at first, because I thought it might be him. Now I wasn't so sure it was Brady, but I still didn't want him to know. If it wasn't him, I was worried that he'd give up on me because he thought he had serious competition. But I didn't know if he had serious competition yet, since I didn't know who the guy was.

Did that make me horrible? I kept feeling guilty about keeping Brady on the hook. I was honestly into him, at least a little bit. And it's not like we were getting serious. Two dates and an almost-kiss were far from serious. That's what dating is about, right? Figuring out how you feel about someone? Seeing if you have a connection? I hoped my guilt was unfounded. I went to bed that night staring at the beautiful flowers on my desk and wondering what tomorrow might bring.

I'D STOPPED BY THE OFFICE BEFORE CONDITIONING ON MON-day to buy Cam a candy gram. I knew after yesterday's comment that I'd be in trouble if I didn't. But I didn't want to play into his ego, so I'd picked my favorite candy instead of his. We sat in English class Tuesday morning, anxiously awaiting the last ten minutes, Cam making obnoxious remarks. "Man, I'm starving. I think some candy would really hit the spot. You know, I didn't get any flowers from an important person yesterday. My hopes are extra high this morning that she loves me enough to buy me a box of candy..."

I ignored him. The door opened, and the same three student aides from yesterday filed in. The first two were carrying movie-theater style candy boxes, but the last one was carrying a giant teddy bear that was holding a basket filled with *multiple* candy boxes. My eyes got wide, and a thought crossed my mind. *Holy crap on a stick. That better not be for me.* Ms. Cutter grumbled something under her breath and clapped her hands to shush us. The room was buzzing with excitement.

The delivery crew followed the same protocol as yesterday. Cam had received his box of Junior Mints. I hadn't bothered to attach a note. I was pretty sure he didn't need one to know they came from me.

"Aww, shucks, Bebe." Cam was acting goofy. "I didn't know you cared. Since Junior Mints are *your* favorite, I'm assuming you sent me these with the intention of cuddling up at lunch and sharing them?" He was puckering his lips, and I was barely containing my laughter.

I held out my hand. "Or you could just give them to me now."

He jerked the precious candy away from me, then opened the box, pouring the minty goodness into his mouth.

He grinned and chewed. "No cuddling, no candy."

Right then, I heard my name called. "Bianca Barnes?" I turned to the front and saw that the only delivery which hadn't been made yet was the giant basket-wielding teddy bear. I raised my hand, and the girl who presented the bouquet yesterday handed me the extravagant gift.

"Looks like you have a fan," she said, then headed out of the room, not giving me time to ask if she knew who the sender was. I looked at the accompanying card.

Bianca,
I wasn't sure what your favorite kind of candy was, so I figured I better send one of each.
Yours - ?

"Oh my gosh, this is getting out of control," I said, reading the note aloud to Cam.

"What's wrong? Not enough Junior Mints in there?"

"What's wrong?" I mimicked, "are you jealous of my candy bear?"

"Nope. Not a bit. There's enough candy in there for both of us. There must be at least ten boxes. You don't even like Milk Duds. Hand them over." Cam held his hand out expectantly.

"I can't," I protested, looking around the room. "What if the guy is in here? His feelings might be hurt if I give some of my gift away." I didn't believe my gift giver was in the room, but I wasn't going to hand over the candy so easily.

"I'm sure your man isn't in here. And if he is, I bet he wouldn't care about you sharing some candy with your poor, starving best friend." Cam was pouting.

"Oh fine, you big goon. But just the Milk Duds."

Cam snatched the box from the basket and shoved it in his bag. "Thanks. Now I have something to look forward to at lunch." The bell rang and he stood up, swinging his bag over his back. "You're the best." He said as he scooped me up into a giant hug, my feet dangling over the floor. He planted me back on the ground then walked out the door. I shook my head and sighed. Time for another day of *gawking at Bianca and her lavish gifts*.

I was a little embarrassed by all the staring, but that emotion was subdued by my curiosity. It'd been a whole week since my secret admirer had stared showering me with gifts, and I still had no clue who he was. I'd originally figured that this was just an elaborate buildup to a homecoming invitation. But I suppose it was unlikely at this point, since the dance was only a few days away. I was going to feel super bad if he did end up asking me, because I already had a date. What would I say then?

I thought back to Saturday and my intense heart-stopping moment with Cam. For a minute, I imagined that all this attention was coming from him. That eventually he would proclaim his undying love for me. *Oh, Bianca, you really are hopeless, aren't you?* Maybe it was Brady, and he'd come clean the night of the dance? That thought made me nervous, because I'm pretty sure I wasn't ready for a declaration of undying love from him.

By the time Wednesday morning rolled around, I wasn't sure what to expect. I'd received something in first hour the last two days, so I figured there was a good chance I'd get something this morning as well. I knew the student council was selling discounted school swag today. Not exactly as cute or romantic as Monday or Tuesday and definitely not anything I needed. As a member of the basketball team, I had plenty of items with Franklin High School Hawks printed on them: T-shirts, sweatshirts, key chains, foam fingers. I was totally curious if the boy would try to use spirit week items today or skip them altogether.

As the deliveries were being made at the end of first period, my foot was bouncing up and down anxiously. I didn't want to admit it, but I'd be pretty disappointed if nothing came for me today. As stressed as it made me, a part of me enjoyed being showered with presents and made the center of attention. Maybe that made me a snot, but at this point I didn't really care.

"Bianca." The friendly office aide approached my desk and handed me a Franklin Hawks water bottle. I stared at it, mouth open. He'd gotten me a water bottle. How could he possibly know that I needed a water bottle? Of all the Franklin High paraphernalia, this was the one item I actually needed. I'd broken the top of mine at conditioning on Monday afternoon and hadn't had a chance to replace it yet. Cam snatched the note from the bottle as usual, and read it out loud for the people sitting around us. They were looking at the water bottle, obviously unimpressed with the gesture.

"Bianca." Cam cleared his throat, then switched to the sexy radio voice.

I was informed that your last water bottle met an unfortunate end this week. That same little birdie also told me water isn't your drink of choice. Check inside.
Yours - ?

I shook the bottle, and sure enough, something was flopping around inside. I opened the lid and dumped out the contents. In my hand I held a twenty-five-dollar gift card to 7-Eleven. I stared at the card in shock, then held it up for all to see.

"I knew it wouldn't be just a water bottle," the girl to my left said. "It wasn't a big enough statement." Her eyes were excited. Seems a few of my classmates were living vicariously through me. I, however, narrowed my eyes at Cam and held the card in his face.

"Sweet," he said. "Twenty-five dollars might get you a month's worth of Slurpees. Unless you do the right thing and spring for mine, too. Then it'll only last a couple weeks." He was grinning and rubbing his hands together, but I was getting angry. Either my secret admirer was Brady and the gift card was intended to give me a clue, or Cam had info and he was holding out on me.

"You," I accused, angrily pointing my finger into Cam's chest. *Too bad I'm so upset. I can't even take a moment to enjoy his yummy pecs under my finger.* "You better start talking." I gave him a serious stare. "This guy wouldn't know I'd broken my water bottle and that I loved Slurpees unless someone told him. I think that someone is you." I waited a second for my implied threat to register with Cam. I expected him to look shocked or scared, or at least guilty. But none of it happened. He only laughed at me.

"I swear, I didn't tell anyone anything." He was shaking his head. "This guy could have found out about your water bottle from a number of people. Are you forgetting that you made a huge scene over it when the damn thing broke? In front of everyone in the gym. That would include all the girls *and* boys basketball players, *plus* a number of cheerleaders and at least a handful of passersby." Cam paused. "And let's get real here for a second. You stop at 7-Eleven multiple times a week and get the same Coke Slurpee. Every. Single. Time. Maybe the guy's seen you there? Maybe he works there?"

I listened to Cam defend himself. Unfortunately, both of his points were true. It wasn't a secret that I loved frozen beverages and frequented the convenience store. And, while I wouldn't have called it a *huge scene*, I might have been overly dramatic at the loss of my favorite water bottle earlier this week. I sighed in defeat, hating that Cam was right. I was back to square one.

On Thursday the student council was selling little stuffed animals for five dollars. There were a variety of cute ones to choose from. Since I'd gotten a gigantic teddy bear Tuesday, I wondered if such a small stuffed animal would be enough for my secret admirer. You couldn't get much more grand than the one I'd already received.

I didn't hear a word of what Ms. Cutter said in English that morning. I sat in my seat, staring at the clock, waiting to see what my secret admirer would send. The door to the classroom opened and our delivery team filed in, arms filled with little stuffed animals. I waited to see if a fourth person came in carting a cage with a white tiger or something else ridiculous. But it was just the three of them, only carrying items the student council was selling. I breathed a sigh of relief. I wouldn't have to make a spectacle of myself today.

"Cameron," the first office aide called out, bringing him a cute little monkey.

"Angelica's pulling out the big guns this week," I teased. He looked at the card and then smiled.

"Nope." He was obviously excited, so it must not have been from Angelica. Now my curiosity was piqued.

"Well, well, well. Which other bubbleheaded babe is it this morning?"

Cam grinned at me. "Be nice, or I'll tell Beth you called her a bubblehead." I was surprised, and I could tell he was satisfied by my reaction. I snatched the monkey out of his hand and read the note.

Cam,
I thought you could use an accomplice while you "monkey" around. LOL.
Love, Beth

I laughed as I read her words. "She's sure got that one right, doesn't she?"

Cam grabbed his stuffed animal back from me and cradled it protectively. "I think I'll call him Mr. Monkey Pants. He can stay in my locker and help me plan all my shenanigans."

"Bianca." I looked up to find the same girl headed toward me, this time shaking her head. "Man, this guy must really like you. If things don't work out with him, you should give him my phone number."

I laughed at her as I accepted the stuffed animal. "Thanks. I'll do that." I set my newest gift on my desk. It was an extremely cute little white unicorn with a rainbow mane and sparkly gold horn. Looks like my mystery guy was running out of money. Thank heavens.

"Wow, he's really outdone himself today." Cam whistled long and low.

"What are you talking about? This is the most reasonable thing he's done so far."

"Guess our definitions are a little different, then, because I don't know if I'd call jewelry reasonable..."

"Jewelry? What the heck are you talking about?" I looked back down at my little unicorn, and that's when I saw it. There was a small gold band around its sparkly gold horn. I hadn't noticed, because it kind of blended in. And let's be honest, I really wasn't expecting jewelry. I pulled the ring off to examine it. The band was thin and simple, with a small jewel set in the top, a light-green sparkling gem. A peridot, my birthstone. It was beautiful, but I started freaking out anyway.

"Oh. My. Gosh. He bought me jewelry? I can't keep this. This is way too much."

"Why don't you read the card before you have a panic attack?" Cam had already looked at the note and handed it to me.

Bianca,

I thought you deserved a gift as beautiful as you are. One last thing before I take a chance and tell you who I am tomorrow. Hopefully you aren't disappointed.

Yours - ?

P.S. Don't freak out; it wasn't as expensive as you think. ;-)

I sat there, mouth agape. I didn't know what to say. After a minute, Cam broke the silence. "What's the big deal? The guy told you it wasn't that expensive."

"It's not about how much money it cost. Ok, well, it is a little, but it's more about what it means. Think about it. Jewelry is something you get a girlfriend. Someone you're committed to. Someone you have a relationship with. It's not something you give a stranger."

"He isn't a stranger. He obviously knows you pretty well. I mean, the guy knows where you live, he knows your locker combination and your class schedule, he knows you frequent 7-Eleven, he even knows your birthday… That is your birthstone, right?"

"Yes." I looked down at the ring, the panic welling up

inside of me. I faced Cam with fear in my eyes. "I can't believe it. I have a stalker." I shook my head. There were no words to describe how I was feeling right now. "The guy is an obsessive lunatic. What on earth could I have possibly done to make him like me enough to buy me jewelry?"

"Stop being so dramatic."

"I'm serious, Cam. This guy could be a deranged maniac. My life could be in danger. What do I do with it? I can't wear it; he'll think I'm agreeing to marriage or something. But if I don't wear it and he sees my empty finger, it might make him upset. He'll probably sneak into my room one night and try to kill me. Remember? The guy knows where I live."

Cam laughed...and laughed...and laughed. "You need to chill out. He isn't a stalker. What happened to thinking it was Brady? He could have done this, you know."

"Nope." I shook my head emphatically. "It's not him. This isn't his style. He sent me a flower on Monday, and he signed his name. Why would he do the rest secretly? We're already going to homecoming together, for crap's sake. What'd be the point in keeping up the act?"

"I sent you a flower, too. Maybe I'm your secret admirer?"

"Stop messing with me, Cam. I'm really freaking out here."

The bell rang, and Cam sighed as he stood up. "I wouldn't worry, Bebe." I jumped out of my seat and I leapt into his arms, squeezing him tight.

"Hey, now." He tried to comfort me. "I really don't think you have anything to worry about." Cam patted my back reassuringly and rested his chin on the top of my head.

"But just in case, I'll bring my pepper spray tomorrow."

I snorted into his chest. "You carry pepper spray?"

"No." He chuckled, and I relaxed a little. "I don't need pepper spray, silly. I carry the guns with me at all times." He flexed his biceps around me, and I laughed. "If the guy is a creeper, I'll protect you."

I looked up at Cam, blowing out a breath. "One more day, then I guess we'll know for sure. I'm never going to sleep tonight."

He let go of me and headed toward the door. "Just fall asleep thinking about my guns. You should have no problem, then." A wink and a smile, then he was gone, leaving me to stress on my own. I looked down at the beautiful ring and slipped it in my pocket before I walked out.

CAMERON

I LAY ON MY BED, STARING AT MY CEILING. I WASN'T GOING TO sleep any better than Bebe was. I'd meant for the ring to be sweet and meaningful. I guess I didn't think about how Bebe would react. I knew who was stalking her, but she didn't. I really hoped she wasn't freaking out right now. That might make what I had planned for tomorrow go less smoothly than I was hoping. I was getting nervous about revealing myself.

After Saturday afternoon, I'd had a burst of confidence.

She'd come home from her Slurpee run less than forty-five minutes from the time she'd left, which had me hoping that she hadn't really wanted to go in the first place. Not to mention the fact that I felt her body tense up and cover with goose bumps when I ran my nose up her cheek. I'd been ready to kiss her, and for the briefest moment, I'd felt like she wanted me to. It was the first good sign I'd ever had that she might return my feelings for her.

I knew that waiting until Friday to tell her would kill me. Maybe if I'd told her sooner, I could've convinced her to stand Brady up and go with *me* to homecoming. I'd spent the weekend coming up with a plan. The only problem was that it would involve other people. Unfortunately, it would take time to execute, and Friday was the soonest I could make it happen. So, I'd spent all week sending her gifts during first period. Her reactions had been very encouraging, until today. Maybe the ring had been a mistake. I pulled out my phone.

C: Do you think the ring was overkill?

B: Yes and no.

C: What does that mean?

B: Well, yes, because a ring is something that would imply a certain level of seriousness. And since she doesn't know you're the one that gave it to her, she's been really stressed out all night.

B: But no, because once she realizes it's from you, I think she'll love both the ring itself and what it represents.

C: I hope you're right.

B: Trust me. So what do you have planned for the big reveal tomorrow?

C: Not telling, but it IS big, and I'm going to need your help.

B: Intriguing… What do you need from me?

C: I need you to sit with her at lunch tomorrow. Make her sit at the table by the lunchroom door. The one where nobody ever sits. And save a seat for me.

B: If we suddenly switch up our lunch seats, won't she be suspicious?

C: Probably, but it doesn't matter. After lunch tomorrow, she'll definitely know I'm the one and I want to be sitting right next to her when she realizes it. I hope she doesn't slap me or run away crying or something.

B: She won't. Stop stressing. You're just as bad as Bea.

C: Is she stressing right now?

B: I already told you she was. Wouldn't you be? She's finding out who's secretly in love with her tomorrow.

C: Yeah, I guess I'd be stressed. Maybe I should call her?

B: I think that would be a good idea ;-)

C: So, can I count on you getting her to the right table tomorrow at lunch?

B: Are you kidding? I want a front row seat to the show. Of course I'll do it.

C: Thanks, Beth. You're the best.

B: I know. ;-) BTW, Cam, I'm proud of you. I didn't know you had all this in you. I think that Bea is one

lucky girl.

C: Night, Beth <3
B: Goodnight, Romeo.

I dialed Bebe's number, and she answered on the second ring. "Hey, what's up?" she asked.

"Nothing; just wanted to see how you were doing? Beth said you're still stressed."

Bebe sighed heavily. "I'm trying not to be. But I don't know how I'm supposed to react tomorrow. This guy has put in a ton of effort, not to mention he's spent a lot of money. I feel like I'm obligated to give him a chance even if I don't want to. Like I owe it to him to be super excited, regardless of who it is."

"Listen to me. You don't owe this guy anything. He had to have known he was taking a risk by putting himself out there. That's probably why he's done everything in secret. I'm sure he's just nervous about how you'll react. He can't blame you if he tells you who he is and you aren't interested. You haven't done anything to lead him on. How could you have?"

"I don't know. I'm already sure I won't be into him. And he's been super sweet. Probably the nicest that any boy has ever been to me. I feel guilty, and I haven't even had to turn him down yet."

"How can you already know you won't like him?" This was not sounding good. Did she have a suspicion that it was me? Was she trying to tell me something? "Is it because of Brady?"

"What do you mean?" Bebe asked.

"I mean, you said this morning that you don't think your secret admirer is Brady. Are you disappointed that it might not be him?" I'd been wanting to ask this question, but couldn't find the right way to bring it up. I waited for her response. She took forever before answering.

"No, that's another problem I have. I like Brady, but I'm not sure I like him enough to date him seriously. He's really great, but I just can't seem to feel for him the way I feel for..." Bebe paused for a second. "Well, the way I think I should feel. Does that make sense?"

The way she felt for who? She changed her words at the last second, but I caught it. I was a fool to hope that she was thinking about me, but I'd been awfully foolish lately, so I might as well hope. "It makes sense. If you aren't feeling it with Brady, then you aren't feeling it. You have to follow your heart."

"Wow. That was way deep. Have you been binge watching *Dr. Phil* or something?"

"Nope, *The Bachelor*. I can't get enough of that show."

Bebe laughed; the mood had been successfully lightened. "I actually hope that my secret admirer isn't Brady. If it's some random guy I don't really know, it would be easier to turn him down. But if it *is* Brady and I'm not ready to be more serious with him, it'll make Saturday night super awkward. I just want to go to homecoming and have fun. Not spend the night stressing about expectations."

"I know it's cheesy, Bebe, but I meant what I said. You

have to follow your heart. If you find out who this guy is and you aren't feeling it, then be honest with him. He'll move on. Maybe as a shell of a man, but he'll move on."

"Gee, thanks. Like I could feel any guiltier. If you were here, I'd slug you right now."

I laughed. "I'm sure you would. Why do you think we're having this conversation on the phone?"

"Because there's no way my dad would let you up in my room at this time of night."

"Ok, that too." I was smiling now. I wished I was there, so badly. "Promise me one thing."

"What's that?"

"Give the poor guy a chance. I don't mean go out with him even if you don't want to or anything. I mean, consider him. Take a minute to really decide if you could make something work, before you break his heart. I think he deserves at least that much."

Bebe sighed again. "I suppose that's fair."

I needed to get off the phone before I told her how I felt, right now. That would ruin my big slam-bang finish. "You should get some sleep. You have a big day tomorrow," I teased.

"You're right. Maybe I'll lie down and start thinking about your big guns. You promised they'd help me have sweet dreams. If they don't, I'm holding you personally responsible for my poor night's sleep."

I was already responsible for her poor night's sleep. Hopefully I wouldn't be the cause of her sleepless night tomorrow, too. With any luck, she'd go to bed tomorrow night dreaming about a lot more than my muscles. "Goodnight, Bebe."

"Goodnight, Cam."

BIANCA

I FELL ASLEEP EVENTUALLY, BUT I WASN'T THINKING ABOUT Cam's guns when it happened. Well, I suppose I was, but they weren't protecting me from a creepy stalker. They were holding me as he whispered in my ear and trailed kisses along my neck. Ironic that last night I didn't want to go to sleep, but this morning, I'd give anything to stay that way.

I decided to make extra effort with my appearance today. I woke up an hour early so that I could flat iron my hair. All of my wavy, tangled locks needed at least that long to get under control. I also put on more makeup than normal. Not enough to look cheap and plastic, but enough that it was evident I'd put the stuff on. I wasn't known for dressing up, but it wasn't unheard of, and I did own plenty of girly clothes. This morning I chose a jean skirt that hit me mid thigh, a pink racer back tank top with a cream-colored lace overlay and a pair of brown flip-flops with a wedge heel. I appraised myself in the mirror before heading downstairs. *This is as good as it gets. He can take it or leave it.*

"Wow. You clean up nice." Beth smiled, taking me in from head to toe. "Busting out the fancy flip-flops, I see."

"Technically, I don't think they're considered a flip-flop if they have a heel. At least, they shouldn't be. I get extra points for wearing the ones with the heel, don't I?" I heard the side door open and shut. Cam walked in to the kitchen.

"I don't know about that," she questioned as she turned to Cam. "Let's get his opinion. Do Bea's shoes still fall under the flip-flop category since they have a heel on them? She says they don't, but I say they do because the strap still runs between the toes."

Cam looked me up and down, just like Beth had, but his gaze was much slower and deliberate. Especially when examining my legs. Finally, when he'd stared at me long enough to make me think there was something wrong, he spoke up. "I don't think it matters if they're flip-flops or not. They make her toes look cute and her legs look sexy. Good enough for me." He walked over and gave me a hug. "What's up with the dressy clothes? I'm not complaining, but I figured you'd want to look extra sloppy today, to deter any potential stalkers. You know, baggy sweats, skip the shower, et cetera."

"I thought *you* told me that I should at least consider the guy?" I argued. "What if he's super hot? Maybe you're right, and I should give him a chance. If you were him and you admitted your feelings to me today, wouldn't you rather

I look good when you did it?"

Cam was grinning at me now. "You make an excellent point. And yes, if I was going to confess my secret feelings for you today, I'd want you to look good when I did it. In fact, I'd want you to be wearing that exact outfit."

He winked at me, then stole the bagel from my hand and walked out to the car. Good thing I was getting used to this whole breakfast-stealing routine. I'd actually just finished my own bagel and had made that one for him. He didn't need to know that, though. I reveled in my small victory as I grabbed my bag and headed out the door to the car.

I sat in English class, wondering if my secret admirer's declaration would come during first period like all of his other gifts this week. I knew the student council was selling cards for a dollar, but that seemed anti-climactic compared to the jewelry I'd received the day before. I honestly didn't know what to expect.

At ten minutes before the end of class, the office aides entered the room. A few of the kids who sat around me looked at the cards that were being held by the messengers and then back at me. This kid in the front row named Dustin spoke loudly to no one in particular. "Looks like Bianca's boyfriend is running out of ways to one-up himself." The class snickered.

"Don't be so sure," the girl who'd delivered my previous presents said to Dustin. She walked over to me, not bothering to call my name. She handed me an envelope before continuing. "She hasn't opened the card yet. Maybe there's two first class tickets to Paris in there, or the deed to a quaint love nest on the beach?" She smiled at me and walked away. *Oh my gosh. There better not be plane tickets to Paris inside.*

I stared at the sealed envelope and took a deep breath. The aides continued passing out cards, but the majority of eyes in the classroom were trained on me. Even Ms. Cutter was looking in my direction. Seems everyone wanted to know what was inside as badly as I did.

"Just open it already," someone called from the front. It was a guy, but I had no idea who.

I broke open the seal on the envelope and slid out a generic greeting card that had flowers on the front and the words *Thinking of You*. I held my breath as I opened the card.

Not yet. But definitely before the end of the day. I promise.
:-)

I blew out the breath I'd been holding, partially relieved and partially frustrated that I'd have to wait longer to get answers. The card delivery girl spoke the words that everyone was dying to ask. "So, what's inside?"

"Sorry to disappoint you guys, but it's just a card. And a cryptic one at that."

I held it up for the class to see as I shrugged my shoulders. I heard whispers from different places in the room. "Well, that's disappointing." And, "Pretty lame, if you ask me." I stared at the note for a minute, trying to decipher if there was any deeper message hidden between the lines.

"Guess you'll just have to wait a little longer." Cam

leaned over my shoulder and spoke close to my ear. "I hope I'm there when it happens."

The bell rang, and I gathered my belongings. I had a feeling this was going to be a long day. I spent the rest of the morning on edge, waiting for some kind of surprise around every corner. Fourth period was particularly agonizing. What if he did something big and embarrassing in the cafeteria, right in front of everyone? There's no way I could turn the guy down in front of half the school.

I left the classroom and went to my locker. I was stalling, and I knew it, but the idea of being surprised in the lunchroom was starting to make me panic. I took a deep breath and headed toward the cafeteria. If I skipped lunch altogether and he had something planned, I'd feel bad. Maybe he'd chicken out and I'd never find out who'd done all these awesome things for me.

I got into the lunch line, alone and agitated. I felt someone cut in line behind me and tensed up, refusing to turn around and see who it was. Was this it? Was the guy of my dreams standing right behind me? Or was it the guy of my nightmares? I couldn't look.

"Boo." Someone leaned in and whispered in my ear. I jumped and I heard Beth's light laughter ringing behind me. "What the heck, Bea?" she said. "What are you so worked up about?" Beth grinned. She knew exactly what I was worked up about.

"Not funny." I glared at her, trying to regain my composure. "Why are you so late to lunch?"

"Oh, no reason," she sang, letting me know she *did* have

a reason. "I was just thinking that maybe we could have lunch together today? You know, in case something were to happen and you needed moral support." There was a mischievous glint in her eye. One that I wouldn't bat an eyelash at coming from Cam, but on Beth it was weird.

"What do you know, Beth?" I insisted.

"If I did know something, I couldn't tell you. Trust me on this, and join me for lunch." Beth was grinning like a fool.

"Fine," I agreed hesitantly. I paid the cashier and picked up my tray, then stopped and surveyed the cafeteria. "You don't expect me to sit with the cheer squad, do you?" I asked.

"Don't be silly." Beth gently slapped my arm. "What kind of a jerk do you think I am? I know you're stressed already. No reason to make it worse. I think sitting by Angelica for a whole thirty minutes might send you over the cliff." Beth snickered. I released the breath that I hadn't realized I'd been holding. At least I dodged *one* bullet today.

Beth started walking and I followed, but our trip was short. She plopped down at the table next to the lunch room door. It was right by all the trash cans, and I wrinkled my nose. "Can't we move a little closer to the side of the room? Sitting next to the trash cans isn't exactly my idea of an appealing lunchtime atmosphere." I was being snarky. It didn't really bother me to sit next to the trash cans. They were empty still, so they didn't stink. The real problem was that this was a high traffic area. I didn't want to be where everyone could see me if something happened.

"Nope," she replied. "It has to be this table." Beth didn't

elaborate, and an overwhelming sense of doom crept into me.

"Hello, lovely ladies." I looked up, and Cam was smiling down at me. His dimples were showing, and he looked happy. "Do you mind if I join you today?" he asked.

"Not at all," Beth replied. Their lips weren't moving, but it was obvious that their eyes were speaking to each other.

"Ok, what's going on here?" I asked, about to lose it.

"Nothing's going on." Cam smiled assuredly, sitting down next to me.

"You two are so full of crap that you're turning brown. We haven't eaten lunch together even once this year. So why today of all days? Something's going to happen, isn't it? I know you know, and I want one of you to tell me right now." I looked at Cam, and he was still grinning at me, a twinkle in his eye. He obviously wasn't going to say anything, so I turned to Beth. She was facing me, but her head was hung and she was biting her bottom lip, avoiding eye contact.

"Look, you guys, if one of you doesn't tell me what's going on in the next ten seconds, I'm getting up and leaving." Frustration was seeping through my tone. Both Beth and Cam sat there, looking at me with their mouths pressed in tight smiles. I moved to pick up my tray and stand, when someone tapped me on the shoulder. I turned my head to find multiple people behind me. In fact, it looked like it was the whole JV basketball team. What the heck?

A tall, skinny sophomore—I think his name was Jason—stood in the center of the group and spoke to me. "Are you Bianca Barnes?"

"Yes?" My response came out as a question.

"Well, Bianca, we've been recently informed that you've lost that lovin' feeling." Jason watched me, waiting for a response.

All I managed was a fumbled "Huh?"

He reiterated his original statement. "It's been brought to our attention that you've lost that lovin' feeling." This time he didn't wait for a response before he turned to the rest of the team with a command. "Ok, boys, you know what to do."

All at once, ten members of the boys junior varsity basketball team pulled their hands from behind their backs and put on a pair of dark aviator sunglasses. Then Jason did something that stunned me, keeping me glued to my seat. He started singing. Seconds later, I was being serenaded, *very loudly*, by the entire team.

They proceeded to reenact the entire bar scene from *Top Gun*, one of my favorite non-basketball movies of all time. I instantly recalled a memory from not that long ago. I'd told Cam once after watching it together, that if a guy was ever going to pick up on me, singing "You've Lost That Lovin' Feeling" was a surefire way to get a yes.

Cam had laughed and told me that a *real* man wouldn't have to resort to such cheesy tactics. I argued that Tom Cruise was as real of a man as they get. I don't think I'd ever told anyone else that. Cam, Beth, and my dad were the only people I'd ever watched the movie with. Who'd know to sing *that* song? And maybe I was hearing them wrong, but it sounded like they were singing *Bebe* every time the word should have been *baby*. There was only one person who ever called me Bebe.

The blood drained from my face as I was flooded with understanding. I turned to Cam while the team finished their serenade. He was watching me carefully, the hint of a smile overshadowed by a look of worry, his eyes waiting for me to make the connection. *Oh. My. Gosh. Was Cam my secret admirer?* There was *no way* this was happening. No possible way this was real. No way that Cam was sitting there, silently confessing that he had feelings for me. Feelings that said he wanted to be more than friends.

The guys were done singing, staring at me, waiting for me to say something. But my mouth wouldn't open. I looked at Beth, who had a huge grin across her face. She'd known all along. I looked around the room as hundreds of watchful eyes were waiting for me to react. Brady was sitting with Mike at the boys' normal lunch table, the two of them whispering in confusion. I guess Brady hadn't known.

I couldn't breathe. The cafeteria was starting to spin as I was gasping for air. Everyone kept looking at me, waiting, but I didn't know what to say or do. I was freaking out. I should have leaned over right then and thrown myself at Cam. I should have put my arms around him and thanked him for all the wonderful things he'd given me this week. I should have planted my lips on his and told him how long I'd been waiting for this moment.

But I was overwhelmed and embarrassed at being put on the spot in front of all of these people. And I was angry that I'd been deceived for the last few weeks, by the two people who'd promised not to lie to me. So, I didn't do any of the things I *should* have done. Tears filled my eyes, threatening to spill over, and my face heated up. I stood. *Don't make a big scene of it, Bianca. Show some dignity.*

I thanked the JV team for the concert and gave the best smile I could muster before suggesting that none of them quit their day job. Then, without looking at Beth or Cam, I simply walked out of the cafeteria and into the hall.

"Bebe, wait." I heard Cam call out loudly as the door closed behind me. I knew I didn't have much time before he followed me into the hall, but I didn't have it in me to talk about this right now. The tears I'd worked so hard to hold back in front of everyone were starting to spill down my cheeks, and my eyes were getting blurry. I took off in a run just as I heard Cam bust through the lunchroom doors.

"Bebe!" he yelled desperately, running down the hall after me. "Just hold up for a second so we can talk."

It broke my heart to hear him so upset. But I was really embarrassed and angry and overwhelmed. I couldn't do this, not today. I ran into the girls bathroom, the one place I hoped he wouldn't follow me. I headed straight to the sink and splashed cold water on my face, then dried it with a paper towel, staring at myself in the mirror. I was a mess. There was no way I could stay here at school.

I couldn't sit through sixth hour next to Cam. But I couldn't go home because Beth had driven me to school, and I was equally pissed at her. Unless I could convince someone else to ditch class and take me, I was stuck. Brady probably would, but I'd feel selfish for asking. It wasn't fair to string him along when I knew how I felt about Cam. Especially now that I knew how Cam felt about me. I was desperate, though, so I pulled out my phone anyway.

Me: I'm guessing you just saw the lunchtime entertainment?

B: Who didn't? What's going on?

Me: Long story. I need a favor. Would you be willing to drive me home?

B: Right now?

Me: Yes. I know it would make you tardy for fifth period, so if you can't, I understand.

B: No, that's fine. I have study hall during fifth. I'll barely be missed. Meet you at my car.

I breathed a sigh of relief, until I heard a knock on the door.

CAMERON

I watched as Bebe stood and left the cafeteria. I'd called after her, but she didn't stop. I couldn't believe this was happening. I knew I was taking a risk by making my final declaration so public, but I also thought *Go big or go home.* Right? I needed her to know, without a doubt, that I was the one behind all this nonsense. *And* that I wasn't ashamed for the whole world to know how I felt. My plan had backfired. The worst part is, that at this moment, I wasn't sure if she was just upset about being embarrassed or if she was disappointed that her secret admirer was me.

"Damn it," I cursed, burying my face in my hands. I would have been content to wallow for a while, but Beth punched me in the arm. "I know, I know. I'm going," I snapped at her before I jumped from my seat and followed Bebe out the door. She was halfway down the hall by now, and I could tell she was crying.

"Bebe!" I yelled out. "Just hold up for a second so we can talk."

She ignored my request without even looking back and ducked into the girls bathroom. The cafeteria doors opened behind me, and Beth walked out.

"Where'd she go?" Beth asked.

"Where do you think?" I snapped for the second time. "The one place I can't follow her."

"Hey. Don't jump up my butt over this. I didn't do anything wrong. You didn't even tell me what you were planning to do," Beth scolded. I hadn't meant to be rude; she didn't deserve to be on the receiving end of my frustration. I looked at her, afraid I might actually cry.

"I'm sorry, Beth. It's not your fault. I know that. I shouldn't have snapped."

She put her arms around me, and I returned the hug. Right now I needed someone to tell me that it was going to be all right. "Cam, she's probably just embarrassed. It'll blow over like it always does. Do you want me to go talk to her?"

I took a deep breath and released Beth from the embrace. "No. I'll do it. She deserves an explanation. The cat's out of the bag now, and I can't take it back. Might as well tell her how I feel. If she doesn't feel the same, at least it won't be hanging over me anymore."

Beth bit her lip and nodded her head just once. "Good luck" was all she said before walking back into the cafeteria.

I watched her leave, then made the longest walk of my life. I had about one hundred feet between me and the girls bathroom, but I swear it took me hours to get there. I had no clue what to say to Bebe, but I hoped the right words would come out.

I knocked on the door to the ladies room. "Bebe, will you please come out and talk to me?" Nothing, absolute silence. "I know you're in there. I watched you go in and my eyes haven't left the door, so I know you haven't come out." I waited again but still no answer. "I have all day. I'm not leaving this spot until you talk to me."

"Go away, Cam," Bebe yelled through the door. Not exactly the response I was hoping for, but ten seconds ago she wasn't speaking at all, so I considered this a win.

"I'm *not* going away until we talk. And I'd prefer not to do this through the bathroom door, but I will if I have to." A few girls I recognized walked past as I was talking loudly through the door. They looked like they wanted to head in, but I didn't need that kind of distraction. This was hard enough without an audience.

I faced them, flashing a heart-stopping smile. "Hello, ladies. I know I look like a nut job out here, but the love of my life is in there, and I've pissed her off pretty good. Would you mind watching the door for a few minutes? Give us some privacy while I grovel?" My smile had the desired effect. The shorter of the two girls looked at me with glossy eyes and nodded her head vigorously. The taller girl squinted her eyes at me before nodding in agreement.

"I saw what went down in the lunchroom, buddy. You might need more than a minute or two." She snickered.

"I'll be quick, I promise," I assured her. Then I cracked open the door to the bathroom and spoke loudly again. "Bebe, I'm going to count down from five. If you're not out here by the time I get to zero, I'm coming in after you. Five, four, three, two, one..." Man, I'd hoped that would work, but today just wasn't my lucky day. I opened the door a little wider before speaking again.

"If there are any girls in this bathroom, other than Bianca Barnes, I'd like to respectfully request that you vacate the premises as soon as possible. I'm coming in, and I don't want to get slapped." I heard someone snort inside and waited a few more seconds, but nobody emerged so I opened the door all the way and walked in.

I'm not sure what I expected. The girls room looked much like the boys room. It had more stalls and no urinals. But the tile, mirrors, and sinks were all the same. The biggest difference was that it was like twenty times cleaner and didn't smell anywhere near as awful as the men's bathroom. I won't even describe what that smelled like most of the time, but the ladies room smelled like bathroom air freshener.

All the stalls were open except the handicap one at the end. I could see Bebe's flip-flops sticking out underneath the door. "Aren't you at least going to come out so I can say this to your face?" I pleaded, standing outside her stall door.

"I told you to go away." Bebe sniffled. She'd definitely been crying.

"You understand why I can't do that, right?" I asked. She waited a moment before responding to me.

"I don't want to talk right now, Cam." More sniffles. "Please, just leave."

"Fine, Bebe. If you don't want to talk, I won't ask you to. But I came in here because I have something to say, and I'm not leaving until I do. I never thought I'd be telling you this for the first time in a ladies bathroom…" I trailed off, and she huffed loudly. "However, you've left me no choice."

I took a deep breath. *Just do it, Cam. Be a man.* "Bianca Olivia Barnes, I love you."

I waited, even though I was pretty sure she wouldn't respond. Part of me still clung to the hope that she'd throw open the door and smother me with kisses. Of course, that didn't happen. I'd just confessed my love while she was standing next to a toilet. Not the most romantic setting. Instead of getting a heated post-fight make-out session, I continued my speech.

"I'm sorry I didn't tell you sooner. I was scared that you wouldn't return my feelings, and I didn't want to ruin our friendship. But I got to a point where being friends wasn't enough anymore. I want to hold your hand and kiss you and tell the whole world that you're mine. Then I want to kiss you some more. Lots more. And after we're done kissing, I'm going to march up to Brady and tell him to take a hike… Then I'm going to kiss you again." Bebe released another loud huff, but this time I could tell that a smile accompanied it.

"I started all the secret admirer stuff because I thought it would help prove to you that my feelings were real. I didn't mean for it to go on so long. I know I had to lie to do it, but I assumed it was the acceptable kind of lie..." I paused; still no answer.

"You looked so happy every time I left something, and that made *me* happy. I loved being able to show you how I felt. And I loved that you actually accepted the gifts as a real gesture of affection. For once you seemed to believe that, to someone out there, you were every bit as worthy as Beth. Bianca, you've never been second to your sister. Or anyone else. Not for me, at least. For me, it's always been you."

I finished speaking, proud and relieved that I'd finally been able to say everything I felt. A giant weight had been lifted from my shoulders, but my chest still felt heavy. Bebe wasn't talking. In fact, I could hear more sniffles; she was crying again. I sighed and headed toward the door. My couple of minutes were up, and I didn't want a teacher to catch me in here. The last thing I needed was to finish one of the crappiest days of my high school career in detention.

I grabbed the handle but spoke one more time before pulling the door open. "I'm leaving now. I promise I won't bother you again. You know where to find me when you're ready to talk. I hope that no matter how you feel, you'll at least give me the courtesy of telling me the truth. I'm so sorry if I hurt you."

With that, I left the bathroom. Lunch had ended, and

263

the hallway was starting to buzz with people and gossip. It appears I'd made quite the commotion. True to their word, the two sophomore girls had kept the bathroom clear for me. There was already a line starting to form, and all the girls who'd been unaware of the drama going down inside were getting frustrated. I looked at the duo still dutifully guarding the bathroom door and winked.

"Thank you, girls. If I can ever return the favor, just let me know," I said, flashing a smile. The tall girl raised one eyebrow, silently saying *Yeah, right*. The shorter girl got really giggly. The rest of the female population looked confused or stunned to see me exiting the women's restroom. One girl was disgusted, like maybe I'd been doing something naughty inside.

Let them think what they wanted. I didn't care anymore. I'd done what I needed to do. I'd told Bebe that I was her secret admirer and that I loved her. The ball was in her court now. I could only hope that her next move wasn't a game ender.

19

BIANCA

I waited for Cam to leave the bathroom before I blew my nose. My face was streaked with tears, and snot was running everywhere. I didn't want to be seen like this, but now that lunch was over, the halls would be crowded. I heard the door open, and for a second I was worried that Cam had come back.

A bunch of girls entered, whispering about the hot boy who'd just left the women's restroom, and I breathed a sigh of relief. Then I realized that if they'd seen Cam leave, they'd know that I'd been in here with him. Great, now the whole world was going to think I was hooking up in the bathroom at lunch. Maybe I *should* let everyone see me looking so pathetic. No boy would make out with a face like this. Or maybe I should confirm their suspicions. I mean, who else besides me would be stupid enough *not* to kiss Cam just now?

I wanted to wash off my face again, but when I emerged from the stall, half a dozen girls stared at me. I went with option number two. "He was such a good kisser, it brought me to tears," I bragged, faking confidence as I held my head high and strutted to the door. After leaving the bathroom, I walked as quickly as I could to the parking lot where Brady was waiting by his car. When he saw my face, a look of concern passed over him.

"Are you ok, Bea?" He paused, then shook his head. "Sorry. Stupid question; of course you're not ok."

I gave him a weak smile, and he opened my door for me. "Sorry it took me so long to get out here. Thanks for waiting," I apologized.

"No problem," he replied. He closed my door and hopped into the driver's seat.

We'd made it most of the way home before Brady spoke again. "You look like you could use a Slurpee." He turned into the 7-Eleven parking lot as he made the offer.

I smiled sadly. "That'd be great. I probably need a really big one today."

We each grabbed the largest cup possible and filled them to the top, Brady with cherry and me with Coke. Then we walked to the counter. I pulled some cash out of my pocket, but he stopped me. "This one is my treat." I didn't have the energy to protest, so I just nodded my head in thanks and put my cash back in my pocket.

We got back in the car and drove the rest of the way to

my house in silence again, each sucking thoughtfully on our frozen drinks. Brady turned the corner onto my street and pulled to a stop in front of my house. He unbuckled his seat belt and turned to me. "So, you want to tell me what that whole scene was about in the lunchroom?"

"Do I have to?"

"No, but having a Slurpee in hand always makes it easier to talk. Especially if you're upset about something. And most definitely if that something you're upset about is being the recipient of an unexpected serenade."

I laughed quietly. "A Slurpee helps with that specifically, huh?"

"Yep," Brady insisted. "It says so in fine print, right here on the bottom of the cup." He pointed to the small white lettering around the lower rim.

I laughed again, this time a little louder. I didn't want to tell Brady what was going on. He was the last person I wanted to talk to about this. But the reality was that I loved Cameron Bates, and if he truly felt the same way, I'd need to have this conversation with Brady at some point. No reason to wait until I was done being pissed at Cam.

I looked up at Brady and sighed. "You really want to know? The truth might not be what you want to hear."

"Lay it on me, Bea; I can handle it."

I took a deep breath, then gave Brady the abbreviated story. "Well, the past week or so I've been receiving all kinds of gifts from a secret admirer. He was giving me presents and telling me how much he liked me in romantic notes. I didn't have any clue who that person was until today when the

JV basketball team gave their little performance. Turns out that my mystery man is none other than Cameron Bates." I waited for Brady to respond, but he was quiet for a minute before he finally did.

"And how do you feel about Cam?"

Wow, this conversation was getting awkward really fast. *Just tell him the truth, Bianca. Don't mislead him. It's not fair to Brady.*

"Honestly?" I looked at Brady apologetically, and his answering smile told me that he knew what was coming next.

"Honesty is always good."

I took another deep breath, held it to the count of five, then blew it out slowly. "The truth is that I've been crazy about Cam since the day we met. I just never thought that he'd return those feelings. He's never indicated that he liked me until now, and I always felt like he was way out of my league. You know?"

Brady looked at me with an intensity that I hadn't seen in him before. "Well, I can't say that I'm happy to hear that. I'm actually pretty disappointed." He paused, thinking before he continued. He seemed to be choosing his words carefully. "But you need to be clear on something, Bianca. Cameron Bates is *not* out of your league. If anything, it's the other way around. It's important that you understand that."

Brady watched me, waiting for acknowledgment of his statement, so I nodded once, eyes downcast. He kept going. "Also, it sounds like he really likes you, and if you like him back, then I don't want to stand in the way of that." He turned his beautiful smile on me. "And, as much as I like you, I don't think I'm ready to bust out in song for you. Not quite yet, at least." He was teasing me, and I was super glad that this conversation wasn't getting any more uncomfortable.

"I'm so sorry. I wasn't intending to lead you on. I didn't know how he felt, and I really like hanging out with you. Plus, you're easy on the eyes, so that helps a ton." If he could tease and I could tease, then maybe something would go right for me today.

Brady laughed. "Well, *at least* there's that. I guess I don't have to leave your house today feeling *completely* rejected." He slapped his heart dramatically.

"Oh, please don't feel rejected," I insisted. "Promise me you won't." I stuck out my pinkie so he'd know how serious I was.

He grabbed my pinkie finger with his. "I promise."

"Thank you. You have no idea what a relief that is right now."

"I can imagine," he answered, then paused. He had something else on his mind, and I was waiting for him to drop the bomb. "So, about homecoming. I would totally understand, given the current situation, if you wanted to cancel our date so that you could go with Cam."

"No way!" I exclaimed as I reached for his hand. "I'm still kind of pissed at him and Beth. If Cam had wanted me to go to the dance with him, he should have asked first. I'm not going to ditch you at the last minute. Unless, of course, you don't want to go with me now." I looked at Brady, my eyes begging, hoping that he wouldn't back out on me. "I'd still like to go to the dance with you. We are friends, after all, and it'd be lots of fun."

"Well, in that case, I'd still love to be your date. I'll just shove my dreams of a goodnight kiss back in my hope chest." I laughed loudly and sincerely this time, grateful that Brady was being so cool about all this.

"Perfect. I've got an amazing dress. It would have been a pity not to wear it tomorrow."

"I guess our plans remain in place. I'll pick you up at six o'clock, and we'll have an awesome dinner before tearing up the dance floor. Cam can drool over you from the sidelines, wishing he'd been able to man up sooner, and we can make him incredibly jealous."

I leaned over and wrapped him in a huge hug. "In case you didn't know this already, you are absolutely, positively the best guy on the planet."

He hugged me back. "Well, if that's so, then you can do me a favor and tell all the eligible ladies you know how wonderful I am."

"You can count on it."

CAMERON

BETH WAS WAITING FOR ME OUTSIDE MY CLASSROOM AFTER sixth period. She looked crushed. This wasn't good. If always-happy Beth was so down, things must be really bad. Bebe hadn't shown up to sixth hour, which meant she probably wouldn't be at basketball, either. I wasn't too surprised. I'm guessing she went home, but I wasn't sure how she got there. It was pretty far to walk.

"I screwed up, didn't I?" I asked Beth.

"I'm afraid we both did. I think she's just as mad at me right now."

"I knew this would happen. I knew she didn't like me that way. This is why I didn't want to tell her in the first place. What am I going to do, Beth? I can't let this ruin our friendship." I was pacing the hallway like a caged dog, alternating between wringing my hands and running them through my hair. "She's probably skipping basketball, for heaven's sake. Coach Lambert will be pissed. She wouldn't risk the wrath of the beast unless she really hated me."

"I told you, she doesn't hate you. She's angry at you. There's a difference. If every fight ended up in the loss of a relationship, Bea would have divorced me a long time ago." Beth smiled. She was trying to make me feel better, but it wasn't working. "I think she just needs some time. I can almost guarantee she's mad about being lied to again. She probably won't talk to either of us right now, but she won't stay mad forever. She didn't even make it twenty-four hours last time." Beth linked her elbow with mine. I hoped she was right.

"Fine." I threw my free hand up in frustration. "I'll give her space. I told her I would. But she better not think I'll leave her alone forever. This is *not* how things are supposed to end. We're supposed to get our happily-ever-freaking-after."

Beth released my elbow and placed both of her hands on my shoulders in an attempt to calm me down. "I'm sure she'll be easier to approach tomorrow, after she's blown off some steam. I know how she feels about you. She can't really hide it, no matter how hard she tries. Bea won't stay mad forever. But we better let her decide when she's ready. The more you push, the harder she'll fight."

Beth was right. The last thing I wanted to do was push Bebe farther away than I already had. I blew out the breath, shoulders slumping in defeat. "I've waited this long; I guess I can wait a little longer. She only gets one day to be pissed, though. I'm not going to let everyone's homecoming plans be ruined over this."

"Um, Cam, I don't think that we'll all be going to homecoming together now. Do you?"

Crap. I hadn't even thought about that. Beth and I were supposed to go to the dance with Bebe and Brady. There's no way she'd want to go with Beth and me now. And even if she did decide to come with us, I wasn't sure I could spend all night watching Bebe and Brady together, while I felt like a first-rate loser.

I looked at Beth. "Maybe we should cancel our plans for homecoming. I bet there's someone you could find to go with at the last minute. I've already bought tickets. You and your new date can have them."

"No way, Cam. You are *not* going to bail on me right now, unless it's to take Bea instead. I'm sure that we can think of some way to make this right." Her words sounded confident, but her expression was betraying her true emotions. I knew she wasn't any more sure of her claim than I was. We headed toward the locker room in silence. Right before we got there, a light bulb went off in my head. I knew what we could do. I only hoped we could pull it off.

"Beth, I think I have an idea how to salvage homecoming. Unfortunately, the plan will depend on cooperation from Brady. I feel like a jerk asking him to help me out, but it's the only way I can think of."

Beth pulled out her phone and looked at the time. "I'm going to be late if I don't get to practice right now. Just tell me what you want me to do."

"Meet me here after practice, and try not to be late." I instructed. "We need to catch Brady before he leaves today."

BETH MET ME AT THE LOCKER ROOM AFTER PRACTICE AS planned. "So what's your big idea?" she asked. I started to tell her, but right then, Brady walked out of the locker room with Mike.

"You'll find out right now. Just go along with it," I said, then jogged to catch up with Brady and Mike.

"Yo, Brady. Can we talk to you for a second?" They both turned to look at me. I gave Mike a glance, then added, "Alone?"

Brady raised one eyebrow in a look that said my request sounded questionable. He spoke to Mike in a low voice that I couldn't hear, then Mike headed down the hall and

Brady crossed toward us. "Hey, Beth." He smiled at her, then looked at me. "What's up, Cam?"

"Well," I started, "Beth and I need to talk to you. About Bianca."

"Oh yeah? This should be interesting." He dropped his backpack and basketball duffel on the ground at his side, then leaned back against the wall, arms folded across his chest. "Go ahead. I'm all ears." An amused smile played across his lips.

I looked at Beth, and she nodded at me once in encouragement, before I turned to Brady and spilled my guts. I told him how I felt about Bebe. I told him how I'd come up with a plan to woo her as a secret admirer. I even told him that Beth and I had sabotaged his date and that I was responsible for spilling the tray of drinks on him. He looked really annoyed at that piece of info, so I tried to make my apology as sincere as possible. I didn't admit that I'd triggered the car alarm that kept him from kissing her that night, though. If I came clean, I'd have felt obligated to say sorry for that, too. But I wasn't sorry, so I figured that little secret could stay with me for now.

When I was done, Beth stood by my side, staring at her feet in shame. I looked at Brady, waiting for him to punch me in the face. He didn't punch me, though; instead, he shook his head as he addressed Beth. "You should be ashamed of yourself, Beth." Her head snapped up, surprised that he'd called her out first. "You're her sister; you should have her back. Always." Beth's eyes welled up with tears, and her bottom lip trembled. Brady's hard expression softened as he continued. "But, I understand that you were doing what you thought would help Bea, even though you went about it in the stupidest way possible." He smiled when he delivered the blow, which took some of the sting from the bite.

He was less gracious as he spoke to me. "And you"— He stepped forward and pointed his finger into my chest— "should lose your damn man card. Not for doing a bunch of nice crap for Bianca, but for not being man enough to tell her how you felt." I cringed at the insult but didn't defend myself, because he was right. "All of that being said," he went on, "I really like Bianca. And since I'm not a complete a-hole, I'm going to help you out."

My eyes widened in surprise, and Beth spoke aloud for the first time. "*How* are you going to help us?"

"Bea and I had a long chat when I took her home today. Turns out that she's nuts about Captain Dic... Um, I mean Captain Butthead over here." Brady nodded in my direction, though he was talking to Beth. He'd caught himself before letting a curse word fly in front of her, but I knew what he was going to call me, and I deserved it. "Though, for the life of me, I can't figure out why she likes him so much." He shook his head as if he were truly mystified, but he was smiling and there was no malice in his tone. "Bianca's friendship means a lot to me. I'm sure Cam has a big plan, or he wouldn't have approached me. Am I right?"

I nodded my head slowly.

"Ok, then, lover boy. What's the big plan?" Brady and Beth waited.

It's now or never, Cam. It may be a stupid idea, but it's

the only one you have. I opened my mouth, and my words came out like vomit. Faster than I could process them. "Let's switch dates to the dance…"

Beth stared at me, mouth open, but a wide grin spread across Brady's face. "I like where this is headed; keep talking."

"Bebe's stubborn, and she's not talking to Beth or me. I assume you two are still planning on going to the dance together tomorrow night?"

"Indeed, we are." Brady scratched his chin. Wheels turning in his head.

"Well," I continued, "let's not give her a choice. If we switch dates and you leave her stranded with me, she'll *have* to hear me out if she wants to go to the dance. And if she doesn't want to go with me, I'm happy to stay home and try to persuade her to stop hating me in other ways."

Brady looked at Beth. "What about you? Are you ok with this plan? You know it has the potential to seriously backfire. And neither of you are in a good position to accept another strike."

"I know, but I'm not sure what else to do," Beth answered him. "If Bea really told you that she likes Cam, then the only thing standing in her way now is her own stupid pride. I think if Cam can just get her alone for two minutes, she'll give in. She can never stay mad at him for very long."

Brady appraised us thoroughly before speaking again. "If our little scheme makes her even angrier, I'll claim innocence. I won't admit to *willingly* helping with this plan. I'll tell her you tried to blackmail me or held me at gunpoint or something. You two understand?"

We both nodded our heads. I felt like I was being scolded by my mother. Nobody besides my mom or Bethany (my other mom) ever spoke to me like this. Freaking Brady Jones.

"Ok, then. Beth, would you do me the honor of escorting me to the homecoming dance?" Brady flashed his pearly whites.

"I'd love to, Brady." Beth answered. I'm not sure Brady noticed, but she was blushing a pretty pink. Guess he had that effect on all the ladies. Maybe when this was over, I could learn some of his secrets. Except if everything went my way, I'd never need to flirt again. I'd already have the only girl I wanted.

We spent the next fifteen minutes hashing out the details, until we had a solid plan. Then we said good-bye to Brady, and Beth drove me home. I lay in bed that night, once again thinking about Bebe. This time, I wasn't sad. I was excited for what tomorrow might bring. At this time tomorrow night, Bebe might finally be mine. And maybe, for once, I could go to bed thinking about the kiss we'd actually shared instead of dreaming about the one I was always hoping for.

BIANCA

I spent Friday afternoon in my bedroom. I felt bad about skipping the last part of school. I never skipped because I hated doing make-up work. The regular homework load was plenty without heaping more onto my plate. But I couldn't face Beth or Cam, and it was impossible to avoid them completely at school. When my dad got home, I told him I wasn't feeling well and that I'd come home early. Better for him to find out from me than the unavoidable call from the attendance office.

Normally when I'm down, I put on *Love & Basketball*. But today I wanted to wallow in my misery. So I rented *Top Gun. Geez, Bianca, you're such a glutton for punishment.* I rewound the bar scene at least half a dozen times. Cam's gesture today had been really sweet. I wonder how he got the whole JV team to go along with it? I chuckled at the thought.

Wait. No laughing. You're supposed to be upset with Cam. Not giggling about how sweet he is. I wanted to be angry, but by the time the movie had ended, there wasn't much fight left in me. All I could think about was how Cam had done so many amazing things for me this past week. How he told me he loved me—in the girls bathroom, of all places. I felt bad about that one. I doubted he'd wanted to say it in such a horrible setting. I suppose I didn't give him much of a choice.

I walked over to my dresser and fished the ring he'd given me out of my jewelry box. I sighed as I slid it on my left ring finger and examined it carefully. It would never pass as an engagement ring, but I was a lovesick girl and I could pretend, just for today.

I spent the rest of the evening practicing what I was going to say to Beth and Cam. I wanted them to know how upset I was before I gave in and forgave them. *You guys are idiots. That was a really stupid plan. Did you think I wouldn't find out? I can't believe you lied to me…again. Way to embarrass me in front of the whole school.* All the standard lines reeled through my head. I practiced my best angry faces in the mirror, too. I suck at angry faces. Guess that's why it was a good idea to stay in my room tonight.

I'd waited by my window for Cam and Beth to get home from school. I wanted to see them when they got here. See if they looked as upset as I wanted them to be. Beth pulled in the driveway and Cam got out of the car, then headed across the street to his house. My heart fell a little. *Well, what did you expect, stupid? That he'd come rushing up the stairs and throw himself at your feet? He said he loved you, and you told him to go away.*

It was bedtime now, and I hadn't spoken to either of them. Maybe I was being irrational. Maybe I needed to reexamine the reasons I was mad. Maybe I should give in and talk to my sister. The second the thought passed through my head, there was a knock at my door. "Bea? Are you in there? Can we talk, please?" Sometimes I really believed we had a super twin sense. Well, at least Beth did, anyway.

"Fine, come in." I lay back on my bed. Beth opened the door and stepped inside. One look at her apologetic face, and I knew I'd practiced my angry speech for nothing.

"Bea, I'm really sorry." She paused, then shrugged her shoulders. "I don't know what else to say."

"How about starting with *why you didn't tell me what was going on?*"

"It wasn't my secret to share. Cam was scared to tell you how he felt. Honestly, I don't blame him."

"I don't understand why he was so scared. Cam's not scared of anything."

"He was afraid you wouldn't return his feelings and he'd ruin your friendship. Don't you think his worry might have been justified?" Beth asked, frowning. "He made a grand display of affection today, and you ran away. He probably thinks you hate him."

"I guess I could have reacted better, huh?" My admission didn't mean I wasn't still upset. "But you both promised after the stupid note fiasco last week that you wouldn't lie to me again. Then you turned right around and did it anyway. Not to mention the fact that you embarrassed me in front of half the school." I wasn't yelling. More like arguing for argument's sake.

Beth held up her hands in surrender. "I didn't know what he was planning at lunch. I swear. He just asked me to make sure you sat at that table and that I saved him a seat. Honest." She paused. "You do understand why we lied, though, right?"

"Well, I do now. But that doesn't make it ok," I grumbled, folding my arms across my chest. I don't know why I couldn't just drop it.

"No, it doesn't." Beth admitted in frustration. Then her voice softened, probably to keep me calm before her next question. "But haven't you been lying to both Cam and me? After all this, are you *still* not willing to admit that you like him back? Not even to me? He's obviously not going to call me up for a date."

"He doesn't have to call." I huffed, biting my cheek to suppress a smile. "He's already got a date with you tomorrow." Even though it was a crappy situation, some sick part of me still enjoyed feeling like I was right.

Beth waved me off. "That's just an unfortunate technicality. You know for *sure* now that Cam is totally into you. He's written you love notes, showered you with gifts, had you serenaded in front of a cafeteria full of people." Beth smiled on that point.

I looked down at my bed before whispering, "He told me he loved me. Today at lunch."

Beth gasped. "He did?" she asked. Her eyes went wide. I bit my lip and nodded in shame. I really should have responded differently to that admission.

After her shock wore off, she broke into a grin. "Now you *have* to admit you like him; you don't have any reason not to."

I winced as I bit my lip and shook my head no. I just couldn't do it. Beth sighed. I could tell she was trying really hard not to be frustrated with me.

"So, let me get this straight," Beth reasoned. "Cam opened up and told you he loved you. But, you won't admit you love him back because, somewhere deep down, you're still doubting how he feels about you?" I nodded yes in silence. It's scary how well she knew me.

Beth put her hands on her hips and cocked her head to the side. "I'll tell you what I think. I think you know this is the real deal, and you're just too chicken to act on it." She paused for a second to let her words sink in. "If you don't pull your head out of your butt and swallow your stubborn pride, you're going to lose him." Her voice softened. "Is that what you want?"

I looked out my window toward Cam's house. I'd been acting stupid and prideful. I knew it, Beth knew it. "I'm sorry," I said. "I don't know why, but I still have a hard time believing that a guy as perfect as Cam could be into someone like me."

Beth rolled her eyes. "Someone like you? You mean a cute, funny, smart, athletic girl that he has loads in common with? Yeah, super hard to believe." She was laying the sarcasm on pretty thick.

I laughed at her. "Well, when you say it like that, you make me sound like a moron."

"Hey, if the shoe fits…"

I picked up my pillow and threw it at her, then focused on my hands in my lap. "What do I do now?" I asked, not wanting to meet her eyes and admit that I was scared. After a second, I decided to be real. "I'm completely petrified of confronting Cam."

"Bianca, you have no reason to be scared. The guy already told you he loved you; now all you have to do is say it back."

"I don't know if I can do it." I winced.

"How about you practice?" Beth smiled. "Tell *me* how you feel about Cam. Tell the *universe* how you feel about Cam." Beth waved her arm around the room, then waited, foot tapping. I couldn't speak. My stomach was all jumbled up.

"I can wait all night," Beth warned. "Just do it. Take a deep breath and say it. Out loud."

I needed to do this. I *could* do it. *Just do it already, Bianca.* I took a deep, long breath, then slowly let it out. "I love Cam," I whispered.

Beth smirked. "What was that?" She put her hand to her ear. "I couldn't quite hear you."

I took another breath. "I love Cam," I said a little louder.

Beth's natural cheerleader broke free. "I'm still not convinced. Neither is fate. *Come on*, Bea, show the universe who's boss. How do you feel?"

Adrenaline shot through my veins and from somewhere deep inside, courage bubbled up and took control of my vocal cords. "I love Cameron Bates!" I yelled at the top of my lungs. Then I slapped my hand over my mouth in shock. Beth was grinning, and I took a few more deep breaths, this time in an effort to keep myself from having a panic attack. I can't believe I'd just said that. Not only out loud, but to Beth, Cam's freaking homecoming date.

I sat quietly, watching and waiting. I'm not sure what I thought would happen. Maybe that Cam would come running through the door and sweep my sister into a kiss. But after a minute, nothing happened and I realized that I'd already known it wouldn't. I pulled my hand from my mouth, revealing a smile that I couldn't hold in any longer.

"Feels good, doesn't it?" Beth asked. My smile widened in response. "Now, the only thing left to do is go claim your man." She grabbed my hand and started to pull me up from the bed. "And you should do it right now, because he's a huge mess. I've never seen him so worked up about anything."

"What do I say to him? I feel so stupid and embarrassed. He's going to be mad at *me* for being mad at *him*. Considering all he's done for me in the last week, I deserve his anger. I've acted like a really big jerk in the last twelve hours."

"Start with an apology," Beth suggested. "Or, even better, how about you don't *say* anything. Skip the talking and just *show* him how you feel." Beth waggled her eyebrows suggestively.

"That sounds like an awesome plan." I sighed. "But I see one small problem still."

"What's that?" Beth asked.

"I can't just march over to Cam's house, plant one on him, tell him I love him, and then go to homecoming with a different boy."

"Hmmm." Beth was thinking out loud. "That is a problem, isn't it? Maybe if you just explained to Brady..." she trailed off.

"Nope. I'm not going to do that to him." I paused for a minute, debating how much info to share with her. Finally I gave in. "I told Brady that I liked Cam today."

"Wow," she breathed, though she didn't sound as surprised as I expected her to be. "How'd he take that?"

"Really well, actually. He was very cool about it and extremely mature. I felt horrible, because if Cam wasn't the one for me, I could probably really like Brady. He offered to back out on our homecoming plans so that I could go with Cam. But I wasn't going to tell him I wasn't into him, then top it off by leaving him without a date. Or any time to find a new one. I'm not that horrible. Brady and I agreed to go to the dance together, as friends, and I have to stick to that agreement."

Beth frowned at me. "Well, I guess you're right, then. If you aren't going to the dance with Cam, maybe you shouldn't tell him how you feel yet."

"I'll tell him after the dance tomorrow. I promise. I won't even wait until Sunday morning."

"You know," Beth said, "Cam seeing you with another guy all night and not knowing how you really feel about him is going to be just as bad as if he did know."

"Probably," I answered, grumbling. "But if he wanted to avoid all the drama, he should have asked me first." I still placed a little blame on Cam for this mess. I *could* be going to homecoming with him tomorrow. *Dancing, in his arms, kissing, making out...* I know, I know, I'm a selfish twit.

"Touché," Beth agreed.

"I promise I'll tell Cam how I feel after we get home from the dance, but you have to promise not to say anything to him until I do. I don't want to ruin Brady's night, and I think it's better for Cam to hear how I feel from me than from you." I warned her with my eyes. I knew she was tempted to walk out of my room and text Cam with the news right now.

"Ok, I promise." She sighed. I knew keeping info like this to herself for a whole twenty-four hours was going to push her limits. "But you have to promise me that as soon we get home, you'll march straight over to Cam's house and declare your love. And make it awesome. You know, to make up for the torture you'll be putting him through during the dance."

Cam was lucky to have a girl like Beth on his side. I smiled at the thought of kissing Cam repeatedly as I saluted my sister. "Yes, Mother. I won't let you down."

It's a good thing Beth and I made up yesterday, because it would have sucked to get ready for the dance without her.

My dad had to work today, and he felt really awful that he wouldn't be there to take pictures and see us off. He did let us know, however, that he'd be done before we got home, reminding us that there'd be no *late-night monkey business*. The dance went from eight to eleven, and he figured we'd want to get dessert after, so he graciously extended our standard eleven o'clock curfew to midnight.

To make up for missing our evening, he handed us three hundred dollars and told us to go out to lunch, get our nails done, our hair done, and then get Cam's mom to take some pictures of his beautiful daughters. He really is the best dad a girl could ask for.

We got home from the salon around five, and I have to admit that my hair looked fabulous. I always got really hot when I danced, and I didn't want my neck to get covered in sweat. You know, in case Cam would be kissing it later tonight. So I went with the full updo. Every single one of my unruly waves was pinned neatly into place on the top of my head and covered with a pound of hairspray. My hair wasn't going anywhere this evening.

Of course, this might be a problem when it came time to take it down, but I'd worry about that later. Beth's hair was equally fabulous. The top half was piled on her head much the way mine was, but the bottom half was pinned to the back of her head so that some of it cascaded down her neck and shoulders. She and Cam were going to be the most beautiful couple at the dance.

"Now it's time for makeup." Beth clapped her hands giddily. I frowned at her. Makeup was definitely not my forte.

I was good with mascara and lip gloss. Maybe even a little blush and some concealer to cover the black bags under my eyes. But giving myself an evening look was not something I knew how to do. Beth patted the seat of the toilet in the bathroom we shared. "Your throne awaits you." She waited for me to take a seat.

"You don't have to do my makeup. You won't have time to get yours finished, if you work on my face first," I argued with her.

"Oh, pish posh. I'll have plenty of time. Besides, no offense, but you wouldn't know how to apply evening makeup even if you had a magic wand to do most of the work. Now take off your shirt and sit down before we run out of time. The clock's ticking."

"Why do I have to take off my shirt?" I questioned.

"Because your shirt has a high collar, and I want to make sure that your foundation blends into your neck. You don't want a big fat makeup line, do you?"

I sighed as I unbuttoned my shirt and threw it over the edge of the tub. I didn't want foundation at all, but there's no way I was getting out of this, so I complied. Beth looked down at my bra and frowned. "Is that what you plan on wearing under your dress?"

"What's wrong with my bra?" I asked. "It's not like anyone is going to see it."

"I know that." Beth was irritated by my lack of knowledge on formal underwear. "But if you wear a plain bra, you'll feel plain. If you wear a sexy bra, you'll feel sexy."

"I don't own any sexy bras. They aren't practical. You're

lucky I'm not in a sports bra."

"I have a cute one that you can borrow. It's pink and lacy, so it'll go perfect with your dress. Plus, it's a pushup." She'd started on my face, and my eyes were closed, but I could imagine the excitement on hers at the thought of getting me into girly underwear.

"I don't need it to match my dress. Remember, nobody will see it. Besides, I don't think I could fit in one of your bras."

"It's not necessarily about matching your outfit," Beth corrected. "But you can't wear the wrong color. A black bra might show through under your pink dress. Plus, your dress has a really wide neckline so your current straps would totally stick out. My bra can be strapless. It's also a few years old. Back when I bought it, the ladies weren't so big yet. It'll be fine on you."

At least her newest argument made sense. I didn't have a problem with my plain old practical bra, but I really didn't want it hanging out of my dress, either. "Fine," I conceded. "I'll wear your stupid bra."

"And the matching thong?" The words were phrased as a question, but they were delivered as a command.

"No way, Beth. I draw the line at a thong. I don't want to be picking my underwear out of my butt all night."

"Do you want a massive underwear line cupping your cute little bum in that tight dress of yours? You know Cam and Brady will both be checking it out. They are guys, after all."

"Ok, ok." I sighed. "I'll wear the thong. But let the

record show that I am totally uncomfortable with wearing your old underwear, even if it is clean and hasn't been worn in years."

"Oh, the bra hasn't been worn in years, but I'm wearing the thong right now." Beth laughed at her joke as I reached out with my eyes closed to hit her, though I'm not sure what I got. "Stop, Bea. Don't move!" she shrieked at me. "Do you want eyeliner over your whole lid?"

Half an hour later, Beth put her instruments of torture down and stood back to appraise me. "Wow, Bea, that boy is going to go crazy when he sees you," she breathed.

"Which one?" I asked, frightened to see what she'd done to my face.

"Both." She laughed and waited as I sat, unmoving, on the toilet lid. "Well, turn around and look already."

I did as she instructed, and when I caught my first glimpse in the mirror, I barely recognized myself. I looked like me, but just…more. I didn't look like Angelica with my makeup painted on, but all of my features were very enhanced. Especially my eyes. Beth had given them this light and smoky look. It was amazing. I didn't know how she did this stuff.

"Thank you, Beth. It looks beautiful." I smiled at her.

"No, you look beautiful," she corrected. "Now go get your dress on, so I can see the finished masterpiece. I still have to put on my face." She turned me around and shooed me out the bathroom door.

My dress was really pretty, and I was actually excited to

wear it. The dress was pink and lace covered the entire thing. It was form-fitting and had a wide, shallow scoop neck. It wasn't super low cut in the front; it barely showed my collarbone. The neckline dipped with a *V* in the back. Not enough to need a backless bra but enough to provide ventilation for when I got hot dancing. It hit me above the knee and the sleeves were tight, coming down to just above my elbow.

I loved the dress because it was unique. Not too many girls wore dresses with sleeves nowadays. The best part is that the base material had some sort of spandex-like stuff in it. It was stretchy, which meant I could move in it without the dress riding up to my butt every time I raised my arms.

Beth walked into my room with the dreaded bra and thong combo, threw it on my bed, then walked back into the bathroom. I stared at the itty-bitty undies for a moment before giving in and putting them on. Then I slid my dress on quickly and zipped up the back. I opened my closet to grab the matching pink shoes Beth made me buy. I'd wanted brown ones because I knew I'd never wear pink shoes again, but she insisted that they had to match the dress.

At least I won in the heel department. Beth had picked out a pair of strappy stilettos. I'd shot her down right away. I'd break my ankle wearing that crap. But Brady was a lot taller than me, and I knew I needed a pretty major height boost. So after looking all day, we found a pair of strappy pink shoes with a four-inch wedge heel, and Beth was satisfied.

I put on my shoes and walked to Beth's room since she

had a full-length mirror. I opened her closet door to check out my final appearance. Beth walked in behind me. "Bianca Barnes, you look smoking hot." She whistled a catcall.

"I look like a piece of bubble gum," I retorted. I actually thought I looked pretty good, for me, but I wasn't going to give her the satisfaction of admitting it.

"Good thing Cam has a major sweet tooth," she said. I shook my head and laughed as I walked out her door and down to the kitchen. I was getting hungry, and it was going to be at least another hour before we ate dinner. I needed a snack. I was opening the fridge, when I heard Beth holler from upstairs. "Bianca, don't you even think about eating right now! You'll ruin your lipstick!" Forget twin sense; she had eyes in the back of her head. *Just like a mom.* I smiled at the thought but shut the refrigerator door.

The doorbell rang. Beth was still getting dressed, and Dad wasn't here, so I walked over to answer it. I paused for a moment, nervous that it might be Cam. We hadn't spoken since yesterday in the bathroom. I opened the door and tried to hide my sag of relief when it was Brady standing on the porch.

"Hi, Bianca." Brady gave me the once-over. "You look stunning." He smiled, then glanced at the stairs, where Beth was making her grand entrance. She had on a blue floor-length dress with capped sleeves and a skirt that was full but not fluffy. She was walking down delicately, one hand on the rail and one holding up her skirt, so as not to trip on it. She looked like a princess. This scene belonged in a teenybopper movie about prom night.

"Thanks, Brady. Come on in." I opened the door wide for him as Beth approached us. "Are we waiting for Cam?" I looked at Beth, not sure what the plan was.

Brady cleared his throat and reached for Beth's hand. "Actually, Bea," he started, a nervous look on his face. I was confused at the action. Why was he holding Beth's hand? "Beth and I have decided to go to the dance together. I'm sorry to ditch you. You look so beautiful. But I thought maybe it'd be better if you and I didn't go as dates."

Brady led Beth through the front door, and she grinned over her shoulder. Then she blew me a kiss and shut the door behind her. What the hell just happened? Did I really get stood up by the nicest boy in the world, right before the homecoming dance? This could *not* be happening. Even the universe, which hated me so much, wouldn't be this cruel to me. Would it? I was on the verge of tears, and crying would ruin the amazing makeup job that Beth had done. I guess it didn't matter since I wasn't going to the dance anyway. I was about to hyperventilate when the doorbell rang again. I reached to open it, yelling angrily as I did. "Beth, if this is your idea of a funny joke, you can shove it up…"

The door flew open, and my heart stopped beating. My entire body froze up. Cam was standing in front of me, looking like a model from a men's magazine. He stared at me, in all his godlike glory, wearing a dark blue suit with a pink tie. One that almost exactly matched the shade of my dress. His hair was messy, in that perfectly styled

I-want-you-to-think-I-don't-give-a-crap kind of way. His blue eyes were sparkling and his smile was wide, his adorable dimples quickly melting my frozen body into a puddle of mush.

"Hello, Bebe. I was wondering if I could get you to join me at homecoming?"

CAMERON

B~~EBE OPENED THE DOOR, AND ALL RATIONAL THOUGHT LEFT~~
BEBE OPENED THE DOOR, AND ALL RATIONAL THOUGHT LEFT my brain. She was cute every day, but tonight she looked beautiful. Radiant. Sexy as hell. Her dress hugged her curves in all the right places and showed off her amazing legs. Tight as it was, the dress still managed to scream classy, not slutty. Beth had obviously done her makeup, and Bebe's eyes looked so vibrant, I could have stared at them forever. If it weren't for her lips. Man, those lips. They were covered in a pinky-orange color and had a layer of something shiny over the top. I wanted nothing more than to pull her into a kiss and see if they tasted as good as they looked.

Common sense returned. I smiled at her and managed to speak. "Hello, Bebe. I was wondering if I could get you to join me at homecoming?" She stared at me; it seemed like forever. Her eyes were shiny, as if she'd been about to cry before I rang the bell. Brady showing up at the door and stealing Beth away was all part of the plan. I'd been standing on the porch outside when it happened. We didn't want to wait too long before I rang the doorbell. Specifically, to avoid the meltdown that was apparently on the verge when she'd opened the door.

I stepped over the threshold and shut the front door behind me. She still hadn't uttered a word. "Please, Bebe, say something. Anything." My voice was soft and pleading. I was so nervous that she still hated me for deceiving her. Bebe pursed her lips together, then shook her head no. She reached up and pressed a finger to her eye, keeping a tear from spilling onto her face. I waited for the gentle letdown, but she surprised me.

Bebe stepped close enough for our chests to touch. She lifted her arms and slowly ran them through the short part of my hair before grabbing the back of my head and bending it forward. She paused, just for a moment, as our noses touched, and looked me in the eyes. Then she closed hers and smashed our lips together.

I was completely taken aback. I'd walked over there expecting to grovel for forgiveness, and instead I was experiencing something that I had waited two very long years for. I quickly regained my senses and returned her kiss, with all the pent-up emotion that I'd been carrying around for so long. I wrapped one arm around her waist and the other firmly across her back, pulling her tight against me. Her body felt like a glove that fit perfectly.

She parted her lips to run her tongue across mine, and a small groan escaped my throat. Her lip gloss absolutely tasted as good as it looked. The kiss was intense and passionate, and I never wanted it to end.

Eventually, she pulled away from me with a glint in her eye. Her cheeks turned red when I smiled at her, and she looked down, embarrassed by being so forward. I kept one arm around her waist and used the other to tip her chin up. "What was that for? I expected to get my butt chewed out, not get my lips chewed up."

She giggled bashfully, and she shook her head slightly. "A wise boy once told me that when I figured out who my secret admirer was, I should skip the talking and go straight to kissing him. Then, if there were fireworks, I was supposed to kiss him a lot more."

"Sounds like a very, very, wise boy," I agreed. I spun Bebe around and pressed her back against the door, trapping her in place. "And were there fireworks?"

"It was like the Fourth of July." She grinned. "I guess that means I'm supposed to kiss you again."

"Sounds good. Except I was supposed to kiss you first. You kind of stole my thunder."

"Well, I don't mind if you show me your thunder now..." she teased.

I threw my head back in laughter, and she snickered as she followed up her previous comment. "I suppose that did sound a little dirty, didn't it?"

I leaned in close, until our lips were grazing, and spoke softly. "How about I skip showing you my thunder, and we just kiss some more?"

Her body shivered and her breath hitched as I closed the last millimeter between us, sealing our mouths together. Much more gently this time. Her lips parted, and I lost myself in the moment. This was better than I ever could have imagined it. And trust me, I'd imagined this moment many different times. Finally, after who knows how long, I broke our kiss. "We better get going. Brady and Beth are waiting across the street at my house. Beth said something about needing my mom to take pictures or you guys would be toast?"

Bebe laughed and nodded her head. "They decided to wait for us, huh? What happened? Why didn't you guys just tell me you were going to switch dates?"

"When Beth and I proposed our plan to Brady yesterday, you still weren't talking to either of us. Believe me when I say that I showed up tonight not sure if you'd slam the door in my face. It was a risk I was willing to take." I pulled her in to a hug and placed a kiss on her forehead, and she leaned her head against my shoulder.

"I'm so glad you did." Bebe let go of a deep breath before continuing. "I'm sorry I was so stubborn, Cam. I shouldn't have gotten mad at you and run away yesterday. I should have thrown myself into your arms. Right when the JV team finished their song. Props on that, by the way. I expect a full report later on how you managed to pull that one off."

"I have mad magic skills, Bebe, and a magician never reveals his secrets," I said, giving an evil laugh. She wasn't buying my explanation, so I told her the less exciting truth.

298

"Or, maybe I threatened each of them that they'd stay on the JV team an extra year if they didn't participate."

"I suppose that'd be enough to motivate me." Bebe playfully hit me on the chest, but I grabbed her hand so she couldn't pull it away.

"I'm the one who needs to apologize to you, Bebe. I've been in love with you since the day we met. You hit me in the head with your basketball, on purpose, and I knew from that moment on that there would never be another girl for me. You were it. I tried so many times to show you how I felt, but you were completely oblivious, no matter what I did. I wasn't sure how else to get through to you. I should have been man enough to just come out and say it."

Bebe shook her head. "Cam, it's not your fault I'm dense. I'm equally to blame. I should have picked up on the signals, or at least been a little more honest about *my* feelings."

I looked at her a minute longer. I *could* have kept looking at her forever. But if we didn't leave, then I'd never get to show off my amazing new girlfriend to the whole world. And the way she looked right now, she definitely needed to be shown off. Not to mention the fact that I was looking forward to dancing with her all night. Screw the fast songs. We'd be slow dancing to each and every song this evening.

I reached up and ran my finger across her lips. "You'd better fix your lipstick. Beth will be pissed at me if I've ruined all her hard work before we've even taken pictures. Plus, if you don't fix it, I can't mess it up again."

"You're very right. Only I don't think *pissed* is a strong enough word. She'd go full *crazy cheerleader* on you." Bebe pulled some lipstick and a tube of gloss out of her purse and walked over to the mirror above the foyer table to reapply. While she was doing so, I reached into my pocket and pulled out the ring that I'd bought her. Beth had grabbed it off Bebe's dresser and handed it to me after she walked onto the porch.

Bebe finished fixing her makeup. "Ready?" she asked with a smile.

"One last thing." I held up the ring, and her eyes narrowed on me.

"How'd you get that?" she asked in surprise.

"I had Beth bring it down. She handed it to me when she left." I grabbed her right hand and poised the ring in front of her finger, then looked up at her before I asked, "Will you wear my ring, Bebe? So that everyone can know you're my girl?"

"I've already been wearing it. All night, in fact, and on the other hand." She winked at me, and I laughed at the implication. I'd been laughing like a dork all night, but damn, she made me so happy. She watched as I slipped the ring on her finger, then grabbed her hand. I was ready to start what would probably be the best night of my life, up until now. As I began walking across the street, she tugged on my hand, pulling me to a stop. I turned to face her.

"Just for the record, Cameron Bates, I love you, too."

BIANCA

Two Months Later

"Hey, guys." Brady was waving at Cam and me as he walked over to us in front of the bonfire. Cam's chest was pressed to my back, arms wrapped around my waist. The fire was keeping me warm in the front, and his body was doing the same behind me. I was wearing his basketball sweatshirt, but the night was chilly and it wasn't quite enough.

"Hey, Brady," I called back as I waved him over.

"What's up, man?" Cam asked, holding out his fist for Brady to hit.

"I just dropped Beth off at the locker room. The cheer squad is meeting there first. They have some sort of big entrance planned." Brady rolled his eyes, but I knew he thought Beth was adorable when she was cheering.

It'd been two months since Cam and I had gotten together. Beth and Brady had been dating almost a month, though they only made it official and exclusive two weeks ago. I'm so glad that Brady and I never kissed, because if we had, Beth would've never gone out with him. There are some lines you don't cross. Kissing the same boy as your sister was one of them. Brady and Beth were the perfect couple, and if I wasn't so happy in my own relationship, I might have been disgusted by how cute they were together.

Tonight's bonfire pep rally was in honor of the season opening basketball games tomorrow. Both the boys and girls teams were expected to do well this year, and the excitement was buzzing through the air. When I'd learned that there'd be a bonfire tonight, I'd planned a little ceremony for myself. I reached into the pocket of Cam's hoodie and firmly grasped the letter I'd written earlier.

I'd been such an idiot for the last two years. Cam and I were as happy as two kids in *high school love* could be. I could have been enjoying my new relationship a lot longer if my superstition and self-deprecation hadn't gotten in the way. It was time to show fate that I was the boss of my own destiny. Cam and Brady were engrossed in a conversation about tomorrow's game, so I pulled out the note and read it one last time.

Dear Universe,
I regret to inform you that I will no longer be able to subject

myself to your harsh realities or your unfortunate turns of events. I've decided that I'm in control of my life and relationships. You don't get a say anymore. The power you once held over me has all but vanished, thanks to my best friend and my best man. I'm locking up my superstitions, insecurities, and MOST of my pride (hey, I'm holding on to this honesty thing) and throwing away the key. In their place, I have decided to practice a little humility and self-confidence. I hope this letter finds you very discouraged and displeased, because frankly, you can kiss my butt.

Sincerely,

Bianca Barnes

I'll admit that the letter was a little childish. It wasn't so much the letter itself that was important, as what it symbolized: the new and improved Bianca, complete with attitude adjustment. I folded the paper back up and stepped toward the fire, then kissed the note and threw it in the flames. I watched as it crumbled into ash, then floated away across the cool evening breeze. Never again would superstition keep me from going after what I wanted, because I was a good person and I deserved to be happy. Standing here in Cameron's arms was all the proof I needed.

ACKNOWLEDGEMENTS

I couldn't have done this without a lot of help. Thanks to my husband, Alan, and my beautiful children for your patience throughout this process. A big thanks to my editor Jen for being awesome and taking on my project even though she was already super busy. Thank you to Mom, Callie, Lenore, Karie, LauraLyn, Amanda and Colleen for reading the beta draft and giving such positive comments. It gave me the confidence to actually publish the dang thing. An extra special thank you to Josh for the cover design and formatting, everything looks amazing.

And finally, thanks to my baby sister Kelly Oram. This book wouldn't have happened without your feedback, instruction and general help. Trying to walk in your shoes has given me a greater appreciation for your talent and hard work. (Even though I was already your biggest fan.) You've been so gracious about *me* attempting to do *your* thing. Twenty years ago, if the roles had been reversed, I'd have thrown a temper tantrum. But you've been incredibly cool and supportive. You're an awesome sister and friend. I don't deserve you!

Made in the USA
Coppell, TX
27 September 2024

37743061R00184